DAUGHTER
OF NO ONE

By the Author

Rocks and Stars

Daughter of No One

DAUGHTER
OF NO ONE

by
Sam Ledel

2019

ISBN 13: 978-1-63555-427-4

This Trade Paperback Original Is Published By
Bold Strokes Books, Inc.
P.O. Box 249
Valley Falls, NY 12185

First Edition: June 2019

CREDITS
EDITOR: Barbara Ann Wright
PRODUCTION DESIGN: Stacia Seaman
MAP BY Sam Ledel, Stacia Seaman, and Therese Szymanski
COVER DESIGN BY Tammy Seidick

Acknowledgments

Thank you to Bold Strokes Books and to my wonderful editor, Barbara Ann Wright.

I would be remiss if I did not mention the night on which *Daughter of No One* started. My middle sister, Paula, has always been an honest wall off which I can bounce my ideas. A few years ago, she and I were watching a musical, laughing and overanalyzing everything like we were big-shot critics. I shared with her my ideas for this story, which led to an evening of rapid-fire brainstorming that lasted long after the credits from the musical rolled. Without that night, this book would not be what it is now.

Thank you also to my youngest sister, Sara, for her encouraging words on early drafts. Your taking the time to read those means the world to me.

And, Alyssa, thank you for your endless love and support.

Prior to the Fae-Diarmaid Treaty—established by the honorable King Grannus and Queen Dechtire—the Kingdom of Venostes was governed by three laws. While time has softened their implementation, all those who reside within the kingdom are expected to abide by these laws without question. They are as follows:

1. No tolerance will be given to the mingling of human and fae. Any parties suspected to be in a relationship that is anything other than platonic will be subject to inquiry and if found guilty, imprisoned.
2. Any woman of the kingdom who bears a child before she is committed to a husband will be shunned, for she has borne an Odium Child—the bringer of any kingdom's demise.
3. The Odium Child will also be shunned, as they are not a fit member of the kingdom.

    May the gods help them meet a swift end.

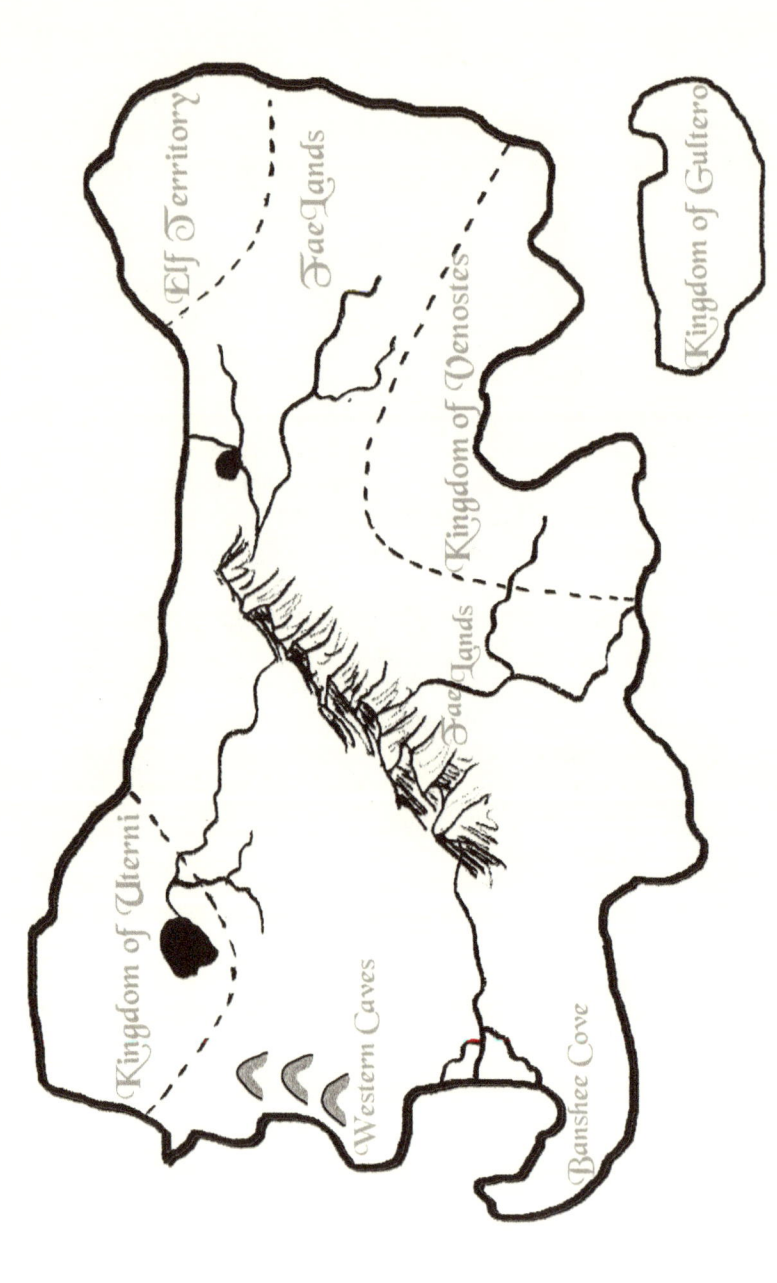

PROLOGUE

Jastyn Cipher walked under the dim light of the crescent moon. Normally, she did not tread through the Wood unless the moon was full or almost. But tonight, she had to escape. Today was her mother's wedding day to Elisedd of Marcra, the royal kingdom's horse master. She was happy for her mother, yet she could not find it within herself to feel the same joy. So, once the final candle was extinguished within their thatch-roofed home nestled in the outskirts of the kingdom, Jastyn slipped out and walked.

She had been wandering these woods since she was seven, exploring everything they had to offer. She even strolled them with her mother on occasion, when they would take in the warm midday sun. Other times, she walked with her friend Coran, the castle's stable boy. Tonight, though, she went alone.

The trees towered over her, and she craned her neck to peer up into the thick branches. She took comfort in the presence of the trees, and her eyes were drawn to bunches of leaves glowing gently with fairies' nests tucked deep within them. A hare rustled the moss near the base of a tree, seeking its burrow for the night. Whistling wind danced over her, spinning itself in her braid. Moonlight that reached the Wood floor she used as a guide, along with her saol, the small blue companion flame bouncing two feet ahead of her. With each step she took, it moved forward in turn. If she halted, so did her saol. It created a small circle of comforting light, though even without it she knew she would not be lost. Her saol was simply a minor conjuring she allowed herself after such a trying day.

As she thought back to the quick matrimonial ceremony, the

moving of furniture, the hearth burning brighter with new logs, her steps carried her deeper into the woods. Now was when she needed somebody to talk to. A reunion with Eegit might calm her anxious mind. The hedgewitch had found Jastyn hunting tree-dwellers for dinner when she was nine, only a year ago, and had taken to the feisty girl with dirt on her cheek. Eegit seemed as ancient as time itself, yet was always filled with lively vigor. Jastyn passed many days in Eegit's meadow, bringing her berries and small trinkets from the market. In turn, the hedgewitch taught her simple magic: mostly showy spells to amuse Jastyn on a long day.

Now, Jastyn passed a thin, trickling creek—where she spent summer days splashing about. This led to a larger river where the fisherman caught their fish for the royal market. The river widened behind her and eventually led to the sea at the edge of the kingdom.

Jastyn continued, the saol gliding along as she trod over thick grass and clusters of nuts left untouched by tree-dwellers. Mounds poked up from the earth around her, and she was careful not to disturb them and the gnomes living below.

An unfamiliar noise made Jastyn turn. It was too late for the deer to be out and not late enough for the wolves to begin their hunt. She froze, her saol doing the same and dimming itself at her uncertainty, the circle of light closing tighter around her.

She scanned the surrounding trees, now columns of pitch against an empty canvas on all sides. The saol grew smaller, then disappeared completely when there was another rustle, and a figure emerged from the dark.

Instinctively, she crouched low, grimacing for all the time she spent acquiring silly show magic instead of concentrating on her defensive skills. Yet, as the figure drew nearer, she thought less of defending herself as curiosity took over. Through the trees, a horse cantered out into a small clearing just ahead. Jastyn knew the clearing well: two petrified trees had fallen three years before on that spot. The village gossip claimed that rival fairy clans sought this part of the Wood for future dwellings. No compromise was reached, so the druids that lived in the yew trees petrified themselves and the surrounding land, leaving a graveyard of spoiled soil and scorched earth that no fairy or gnome could call home.

The horse was as black as the darkness it had come from. Astride it sat a man. His dark cloak billowed out on either side of broad shoulders. Jastyn could not make out his tribe. He did not wear the colors of the kingdom, yet she felt as if she knew him.

When the horse reared, she remembered. Her breath caught in her throat as the creature's red eyes grew wide, and its hooves beat against the air, the rider's gloved hands gripping tight to the reins. When its legs thundered back against the earth, she couldn't hold back her gasp.

At the sound, the rider turned his head. The hood of his cloak fell over him, casting shadow over every inch of the space where his face should be. She dared not conjure her saol to get a better look. She began to recall the tales her mother had told her when she was seven summers old: tales of a fae who rode the wild lands of this country on a horse said to have sprung from the blackest rock, its eyes burning with the flames that light the gate to the Otherworld and its hooves trumpeting the arrival of Death's chariot. This fae had never been witnessed so far from the Mountains of Ionad across the moors. And as the stranger walked his horse closer, Jastyn slowly stood. She tried to remember the rider's name when he spoke.

"You walk these woods when many would not dare to." His voice was low and hollow, but she sensed intrigue.

Jastyn pulled her shoulders back and willed her knees to quell their shivering. She swallowed, then said, "I know these woods well. I have walked them many times in day and at night with the company of the moon. I am not afraid."

She wasn't sure if she said that last part in defiance or more to encourage herself against the dark stranger before her. At her words, his horse snorted and shook its mane. The man tilted his head as if considering what the horse was saying.

"What is your name, girl?"

"I am Jastyn," she replied, her voice steady.

"Your full name."

The horse neighed, and Jastyn stepped back as its front legs reared. Her voice was smaller this time. "My name is Jastyn. Jastyn Cipher."

The man was quiet for a moment. "You are an Odium Child."

Jastyn flushed, but her eyes stayed on the man. "We do not use that term." She repeated her mother's words hotly, her voice rising. After a moment, she swallowed and forced her voice to be steady. "My mother chooses to walk in the light despite our situation, and we do not speak like that in our home." Jastyn tilted her head up, reminding herself to be brave.

She was not sure if she heard the distant cackle of a magpie or if the mysterious rider was laughing at her remarks. She pulled herself up more, glancing behind her to chart her path back to the village. When she looked back at the man, he spoke again. "Luck walks with you, girl. To not know one's own name at such a chance meeting as this. The gods must be up to something this eve."

Confused, Jastyn replied, "I told you my name."

At this, he moved the horse forward, its breath coming in white bursts that seemed to glow with red. "Brave, little one," he said with another tilt of his head. "But no, you did not tell me your name. Not your true name. How could you, when you are *gan 'athair*?" He paused, and the horse took another step forward. "You must be quite foolish, young Odium, to wander these woods alone at night."

Jastyn started to move backward, thankful she knew which trees to step between as the horse pressed closer. The man atop it sat straight and tall. "I've heard of you," Jastyn said, speaking carefully. "You are not welcome in the Wood," she told him, willing her courage to return to her so that she might use some small spell to ensure her safe journey home. As she spoke, the man pulled the horse to his left, which brought them both into a gap in the overhead branches where the moonlight could fall between them.

Jastyn's eyes went wide as the moonlight landed for a moment on the man's hooded face. No, not a face. Where it should be was... Jastyn's mind seemed to freeze and run acres at a time all at once. She gasped and stumbled on a gnome hill. As she tumbled backward, the horse neighed and reared back, its front legs kicking into the night. Jastyn didn't wait for it to land before she turned and sprinted through the woods. She didn't look back at the beast or the clearing or the strange fae who lingered in the black woods.

CHAPTER ONE

Jastyn lay in a soft patch of grass in the expansive meadow she passed many afternoons in, her gaze dancing over the full clouds drifting lazily through a rare azure sky. The blue wool tunic she wore pinched at her elbow where she had it crooked in order to place one of her hands behind her head. She breathed deeply, enjoying the smell of the hawthorn trees and bright bilberry flowers lining the edge of the meadow. The late spring breeze made the dandelions sway around her. She smiled at this brief feeling of contentedness until her reverie was broken by a withered hand thrusting itself into her vision, fervently shaking a dead hare over her face.

"You call *this* a fair trade? It's not worth a gnome's nose in meat or fur!"

With a sigh, Jastyn sat up, leaning onto one arm. She brushed strands of hair from her face, the rest of it cascading down her back in a braid. She blinked at the hedgewitch who stood with one hand on her bony hip. Her animal-hide tunic hung loosely on her slim frame. Torn and mismatched leggings sewn together from wool and cloth scraps adorned her legs, and leather shoes Jastyn had gifted her three winters ago barely clung to her feet.

"Eegit, I told you the market vendors are on to me. It's hard enough to get my own family's share of food and supplies. Besides, I told you to let me hunt tree-dwellers for you. They're just as good as ones found in the market."

Eegit ignored her, shaking the scrawny rabbit closer to Jastyn's face. "How am I supposed to cook up a Circling spell with offerings as measly as this?" As she spoke, her silver hair shook out in a wild mane on all sides of her wide and sallow face. Despite her age, which Jastyn still did not know for certain, Eegit's dark eyes were bright with life. And even though she was several inches shorter than Jastyn thanks to a hunch, she was as spry as half the woodland creatures scampering nearby.

"Come on, Eegit." Jastyn groaned, standing. She brushed off the pants she wore under a tunic, which fell to her thighs. A pleated belt, patterned with the yellow and blue of her village, looped around her waist, and the tail of it hung low off her left hip. She swiped grass off the hunting blade tucked in the straps of her right leather boot. "Don't be angry at me." Then she grinned as Eegit threw up her hands and walked over to a circle of round stones—arranged haphazardly in front of a one room hut built from fallen tree limbs—where a purple flame burned brightly. Eegit mumbled to herself as she grabbed the rabbit in both hands and, with strength that always surprised Jastyn, twisted off the creature's head, which she tossed over her shoulder before dropping the body into the flame. It sputtered and glowed brighter for a few moments as Jastyn walked over next to her friend.

"I know you tried, child," Eegit said as they stood watching the flame together. Jastyn turned to her, crossing her arms.

"Eegit, how many times do I have to tell you I am no longer a child? I reached my twenty-second-year last winter solstice. You remember."

Eegit frowned, glancing up at Jastyn. Several holly leaves were tucked amongst her mane of silver, and clusters of berries sat at the end of a branch popping out from behind her ear. Eegit squinted, then grabbed Jastyn's chin, pulling her closer. Her eyes roved over Jastyn's face, seeming to count the freckles that lightly dotted her forehead and temples. They followed wisps of Jastyn's strawberry-blond hair. After another minute, she said, "You look the same to me, child."

Jastyn laughed and threw up her arms as Eegit bent and grabbed an antler from a pile of bones sitting outside the circle of stones. Shaking her head, Jastyn reached into her back pocket, pulling out a small, brown drawstring pouch.

"Well, would a *child* be able to take this from the apothecary's stand when he wasn't looking?"

She held the pouch up proudly. Eegit turned back to her, eyes wide. Then she hopped gleefully over to Jastyn, eager hands rubbing together.

"Crushed serpentine stone?" Eegit asked as she gingerly took the pouch from Jastyn, who couldn't hide her smirk.

"It's what you'd been looking for."

Eegit giggled and skipped over to her hut behind the stone circle. "Finally!" she hollered over her shoulder. "The merchants are so stingy with their minerals these days." She disappeared into the hut, then re-emerged with a charred pot and a case Jastyn recognized as the one containing several dry herbs. As she crouched and opened up the case to browse its contents, Jastyn placed one hand on her hip.

"You still want to go after that spell, don't you?" Jastyn shook her head. "They say it's against the elements to try and bottle luck."

"Nonsense," Eegit replied, holding up several dried leaves in front of her face. She set the pot next to the stone circle. "That's ancient superstition."

"Besides," added Jastyn, "I thought we were going to begin with more complex magic. You know, now that I'm of age."

"Hush, child," Eegit replied, dropping a few of the herbs into the pot, then tossing a bony rabbit foot into the purple flame, this time prompting a flicker of red before returning to its original state. "All in good time."

"Speaking of time," Jastyn said, glancing toward the sky. The sun had begun its descent, casting shadows around the edges of the meadow. "I had better return home." She knew her stepfather Elisedd would be returning from the royal stables at sundown, and he didn't like it when she wasn't at home helping her mother over the fire. She didn't want to risk another argument.

"Go on then," Eegit called, mashing several dried leaves into her pot as she sat cross-legged.

Jastyn grabbed a small white sack with cornmeal and a few vegetables—her purchased market items for the day. "See you later, Eegit," she called, starting her way back toward a well-trod path she took to her village.

"And find me a better catch next time, girl!" Eegit shouted as Jastyn strolled back through the trees, grinning.

❖

Aurelia Diarmaid's entire body shook, and her breath came quickly as she hid behind a tan, high-backed chair, one of many in the vast, high-ceilinged rooms inside the castle. She closed her eyes, gathering herself.

"I know you're back there."

Aurelia held out her palm next to her waist where she conjured a small, deep red flame above her open hand.

"Come out, come out."

Aurelia leapt from behind the chair, her green dress spinning around her as she did. Just as a fair blue light zoomed toward her, she pushed her saol out to meet it. As the two forces met in midair above the black bearskin rug, a white light flashed, and Aurelia covered her face. Once the light faded and a dull smell of smoke filled the room, a slow clap began opposite her.

"Well done, sister."

Aurelia looked across the room at her brother Brennus, then straightened her shoulders and dusted off the arms of her dress, all while hiding a grin. "I told you that I was beginning to master that defensive spell."

Brennus swept a hand through his dark hair, tucking some of it behind his ear. He brushed off his hands and walked over to a long wooden table they had pushed closer to the wide fireplace on the left wall of the sitting room, which now seemed even warmer to Aurelia after all their running around. She helped him push one of the heavy wooden chairs back to its original position near the fire when her brother spoke. "I have to admit, you have improved. You're really not bad, for a princess." He winked, and she stuck out her chin at him. Even now that she was twenty years of age and he twenty-two, she and her brother still managed to tease one another as if they were children.

Brennus gathered his belt and sword from one end of the table and replaced it on his waist. His bright blue tunic puffed at the sleeves, and he worked to buckle the elaborate belt before replacing a smaller knife into one of the straps around his high leather boots. Meanwhile, Aurelia rearranged a few of the strands that had escaped the pins that pulled back the top half of her dark brown hair, the same color as her brother's. If it weren't for their different eye color, many would think the siblings twins. They both had fair skin, and the faintest blush always sat in their high cheeks. She'd been told that they even wore the same furrowed brow while reading. But while Brennus sported the more common dark hazel eyes seen throughout the kingdom, Aurelia had inherited her mother's rare sky-blue ones. Her father always teased her, claiming she should be able to see into the Otherworld with such a clear gaze.

"I think after one more lesson, I'll have that spell down," Aurelia said after a moment.

"We'll see about that." Brennus tucked his sword firmly in its sheath. "Maybe one day, I'll even let you try me in combat." He grinned, and Aurelia was about to reply when the heavy oak doors opened into the room, and in strode the queen.

"Mother," both Aurelia and Brennus said with bows of their heads as she walked across the room. Queen Dechtire's long red dress flowed out behind her, the silk edges of it barely touching the dark wood floor. Carrying herself as she did, she always seemed tall to Aurelia, though she was only slightly taller. Her light hair, the color of honey, was pinned up in a majestic bun, showing off the same fair complexion. Her light blue eyes were kind, and curiosity sparked in them when she glanced from Aurelia to her brother.

"I see the Asiatic studies are being neglected again," her mother said with a sigh, her eyes wandering toward a pile of unopened books that had fallen to the floor earlier.

"We were going to go over the language and history lesson," Aurelia started, rushing to gather the books. "But then…"

"Aurelia *insisted* I show her another defensive spell. You know how tenacious she can be, Mother, when she wants something."

"How do you think I acquired so much of our dear mother's healing knowledge?" Aurelia quipped as she scooped up a final book.

Their mother raised an eyebrow at Brennus, who smiled as Aurelia shot him a look from across the room.

"Whatever will I do with you two," her mother muttered as Aurelia, arms full of books, shoved them into Brennus's chest as the king's messenger walked through the open doorway.

"Queen Dechtire," he said. "The king requests your presence in the state room."

Their mother turned, and when she did, Brennus elbowed Aurelia's side, making her laugh. Their mother glanced back, warranting innocent looks from them both. "Tell him I am on my way."

"Yes m'lady. The king also requested that Prince Brennus join you."

All three of them looked at the page. "Oh?" her mother said, pausing a few feet from where Aurelia and her brother stood. "Whatever for?"

"His Majesty simply requested the young prince be present at this meeting. I do not know anything further."

Brennus, smiling, shoved the books back into Aurelia's arms and smoothed his pants and tunic. "See you later, sis."

Aurelia glared at him as he followed their mother from the room. She always disliked how her brother got to be in on everything happening in the kingdom. Of course, she understood he was to be king one day, but she was a part of this family, too. With a sigh, she supposed she'd just have to beg him to tell her about the meeting later, as per usual.

When Brennus and her mother reached the doorway, her mother turned back. "I'll send for the tutor," she told Aurelia. "There's another hour until dinner. Maybe you can get something other than magic accomplished in the meantime, darling."

Aurelia set the books down on the table and groaned. "But, Mother!"

The queen only smiled and carefully closed the doors behind her.

CHAPTER TWO

Aurelia rolled onto her stomach and stretched out on the sheepskin rug in one of the rooms down the hall from where she had been practicing magic with Brennus earlier that evening. This room was smaller but decorated elaborately, similar to all the others in the grand castle she called home. Most of the rooms and chambers housed portraits of her grandparents and their parents before them, along with fur rugs settled beneath tables carved from the finest wood in all of the Kingdom of Venostes. However, in this room there hung no portraits— only piles upon piles of books which her mother and father used to prepare lessons for Aurelia and her brother throughout the years. Many were old, having been written decades earlier by their ancestors or brought to their kingdom from visiting royals. The room itself smelled of the musky pages and stained ink, a smell Aurelia adored. Most of the time.

Now, however, she was restless. Aurelia lay near the fireplace where embers burned gently, yet her mind could not settle on the book lying before her. She glanced toward a rectangular window on an opposite wall. It faced the front of the castle gates, overlooking a narrow creek and the uneven dirt streets that led down into the market that sat between the castle and the villages tucked between endless, rolling green hills.

She sighed and thumbed through her book: a lecture on ancient dynasties in the lands of Asia. She usually found herself completely engaged when it came to learning about other kingdoms and faraway lands. Since their kingdom was on an island, Aurelia often dreamt of traveling to a new place full of different people who spoke unfamiliar languages and wore peculiar clothing. She spent many nights imagining how it might be once her brother was king and how she might sail away on his behalf, exploring uncharted worlds to make him proud. Perhaps then he would see her as a true equal and not just as his little sister.

With a huff, Aurelia closed her book and rolled onto her side.

"M'lady Aurelia, is something the matter?"

She looked across the room at Roisin, her handmaiden. Roisin sat in a wooden chair near the window across the room. She had fair skin like Aurelia, but unlike the princess, it gained color in the summertime. Her hair was bright red-orange, like the rowan berries found in the Wood. When Aurelia was nine, Roisin had moved from the eastern shores into the kingdom with her family, and her father had been hired as a cook in the castle. Her mother worked in the market selling bread, and Roisin had been chosen to assist Aurelia with her daily activities. She was a few years older than Aurelia, but the two got along well. The princess imagined their relationship to be one like sisters must experience, and she thought of her as a dear friend.

"Oh, Roisin," Aurelia said, propping her cheek on her open palm. "I simply cannot concentrate tonight."

Roisin finished pulling the thread on her embroidery. As she set the cloth down in her lap, she asked, "Why ever not?"

"It's these meetings," Aurelia said. "For the last six months, Brennus has been included on almost every issue or village complaint that's come to my father. And I know he's to be king one day, but *I* am the princess." She sighed again and rolled onto her back. "Shouldn't I also be informed as to what is going on within the kingdom?"

Roisin pressed out a wrinkle in her navy dress. "Perhaps it's a matter of official business. Or there is a new trade partner proposal from some interested kingdom."

"But why can I not know about it, too?" Aurelia's eyes roved the high ceiling as if the answer might be written there. She turned her head toward the glowing coals in the fireplace. She reached out toward them and closed her eyes. A soft red light began to glow between the tips of her fingers. Once it had grown to a ball the size of a tomato, Aurelia gently blew the red saol from her hand and watched it glide easily to the coals. Within seconds, her saol settled, and a new blaze burned steadily in the hearth.

"Your magic looks to be growin' stronger, m'lady," Roisin said, back at her embroidery.

"Seems that way," replied Aurelia, watching the deep red flames dance. "Brennus has taught me a lot." She faced Roisin. "Don't misunderstand me; I value everything my mother has shown me in regard to healing. Her skills are unmatched, and she is very knowledgeable."

Roisin nodded. "She brewed the potion that helped my father when he fell ill two winters ago. It saved his life."

Aurelia smiled. "Exactly. And I am proud to know my mother's trade, and I love that she helped your family. It's just..." Aurelia sat up, tucking her legs behind her so that her dress spread out across the rug. "Brennus is teaching me things I can eventually use out in the world."

Roisin raised an eyebrow. "Out in the world, m'lady?"

"Yes," Aurelia said, unable to contain the excitement in her voice. "Roisin, wouldn't it be wonderful to be outside this kingdom's walls? To go to the mountains! Or even to the western sea! Oh, just imagine."

Roisin shook her head. "M'lady, with all respect, I'm not sure I understand."

Aurelia tilted her head, then stood and crossed the room. She bent down next to Roisin, one hand on the arm of the chair. "Roisin, I'm saying that one day I will be able to leave this castle. Once Brennus is king, I know he will give me freedom to explore parts of our land that my forefathers never discovered. For so long now, I've been reading about these places that sound like dreams. Magical, beautiful places—some that are right outside these walls! And I want to be a part of them."

Roisin looked at her kindly, then patted Aurelia's hand and returned to her embroidery. "Maybe one day, m'lady. It sounds awfully exciting. And a bit tiresome, if I'm being honest."

Aurelia laughed and stood. "Oh Roisin, you've become too accustomed to castle life." Roisin smiled shyly.

Aurelia walked to the window. The moon was bright, half full and sitting high in the night sky. She relished the cool evening air. Lights from the village were dim. Her gaze roved toward the left tower of the castle and climbed the tall gray stones until they found the window glowing bright from the room where her family currently resided.

"Roisin, I must know what they're talking about."

Her maiden looked up. "But, m'lady, won't the prince tell you everything at a later time?"

Aurelia blushed. Roisin was at her side almost every moment of the day; so yes, of course she knew how liberal her brother was with information. He seemed to be on a different page regarding her right to know things compared to their father and mother.

"I cannot wait," Aurelia said, starting across the room toward the door. "I'm too anxious tonight. I must know. I have a right to know." She strode over to the door. Before pushing it open, Aurelia glanced back. "Aren't you coming?"

Roisin bowed her head. "With all respect, m'lady, just last week the queen chastised the pair of us for sneaking pastries from the kitchen after your father's birthday feast. I do not wish to hear such words again anytime soon."

Aurelia grinned. "You're scared, Roisin?"

"Of sneaking across the castle with you? No. Of your mother? Yes." Roisin shook her head. "Good luck, m'lady."

"Luck has nothing to do with it," Aurelia replied, pushing open the door and starting into the hallway on her own.

❖

Jastyn slowed as she walked the worn path that led toward her home at the base of a hill. The path now resembled a dry riverbed cutting through the grassy slopes outside of the castle's walls. She walked with the white satchel over one shoulder, stepping lightly along as the sunlight faded behind her. Every fifty paces or so, she passed houses that resembled her own: single story, thatch-roofed homes built by their village neighbors. Many utilized the great boulders found scattered throughout the Wood for walls, and each possessed a wooden door—usually slightly off-center—placed at the front. Jastyn waved to her mother's friend Kyra Feirmeoir, who sold eggs in the market.

"Evenin', Jastyn," Kyra said, brushing away her curly red hair as she poured out a bucket of water around the side of her house. The splash made a cluster of chickens squawk and flap their wings.

"Hi, Kyra. Is Coran back yet?"

Coran had been Jastyn's best friend since they were little. Jastyn and her mother had been low on rations one year when she was barely seven. Jastyn had also realized her petite stature and unsuspecting nature aided minor thievery in the market. She took to stealing bread and old meat off the back of carts in order to get herself and her mother—who believed the food to be donations from kind neighbors—through the winter. But one day, as she reached for a sweetbread, a man behind the cart grabbed her wrist. As he berated her, Jastyn looked frantically around and wiggled to break free. As the man raised a knife over her head, a boy of nine with the brightest red hair appeared.

"Sir, wait!"

Jastyn, whose eyes had been closed in fear of the worst, looked wildly from the man to the source of the squeaky voice beside her.

"Don't hurt my sister! Please."

"Sister?" the man growled, glancing between him and the light-haired girl trembling in his grip.

"She forgets that you need money at the market, sir. Here." He dug into a pouch sewed into his tunic and handed the man a bronze coin. "For the sweetbread."

After another look-over, the man released his grip on Jastyn. She shoved past the boy, who called after her. She pushed through crowds of people and dashed behind a dirty southern wall where she fought back tears and nursed her injured pride. After a few minutes, the boy found her and held out the sweetbread.

"Take it."

"You didn't have to help me," Jastyn had said between sniffs.

"He was goin' to hurt you."

Jastyn looked down and shrugged. "I was stealing."

"Well, sometimes my dad takes an extra fish from the boat when he gets done workin'. He says it's 'earned,' and we need it." He pushed the bread closer. "Like this."

With another sniffle, she grabbed the bread, tucking it close against her. "Thank you. And I would have said we were cousins."

The boy smiled.

"I'm Coran."

Jastyn wiped a smudge of dirt from her cheek, then shook his hand.

Now, Coran's mother stood shaking the bright red hair she gave her only son. "He's not back from the stables yet," she said, wiping her brow. "But any minute, he should be comin'; I saw Elisedd walkin' by just moments ago, so surely Coran must be returnin' soon."

Panic set in as Jastyn nodded and excused herself, hurrying along the path and up toward the last hill. She cursed under her breath for meandering in the Wood—again. She'd lost track of how many times she had been late returning home. And it wasn't even that she didn't like being home. It was just—

"Elisedd." Jastyn froze twenty yards from her open doorway. Her stepfather stood outside.

He wasn't a cruel man. Elisedd brought food to the table and wood for the hearth, and it seemed as if he made her mother happy. But as she stood there watching him kick dirt and horse manure from his boots against the door frame, Jastyn couldn't recall feeling at ease since he came into their lives. She could never pinpoint what it was exactly. He doted on her mother and deeply loved the daughter he had with her but seemed to tolerate Jastyn and her presence. She never understood his lack of compassion. But with time, as with most things, she grew used to his behavior and found joy in the most beautiful gift he ever gave her and her mother: her half sister Alanna, who stepped out of the house now, holding up a hand to the setting sunlight. When she saw Jastyn, she waved and called out.

"Jastyn's home!"

Elisedd turned as his daughter sprinted to Jastyn. His dark gaze fell on hers before Alanna crashed into Jastyn, nearly tackling her to the ground.

"Alanna! How are you?" Jastyn hugged Alanna tightly but continued to eye her stepfather over her shoulder. He watched her like a hawk, as if he was afraid Jastyn might hug Alanna too tightly if he wasn't there to supervise. When she released her sister, Jastyn stepped back and met Alanna's gaze.

"You were in the Wood again, weren't you?" Alanna asked under her breath, ignoring Jastyn's question. Her dark, nearly coal black eyes were alight with intrigue, and she practically bounced on her toes while her pale hands rubbed together.

Jastyn put her hands on her hips. "Whatever gave you that idea?"

Alanna, who was almost as tall as Jastyn despite having just turned thirteen, squirmed with knowing anticipation. She crossed her arms the way Jastyn had seen their mother do countless times. "You have mulberry leaves stuck to your boots, and you smell of tree bark."

Jastyn grinned and poked her sister's ribs. "Is there anything you don't notice?"

Alanna giggled, making Jastyn smile even wider. But almost as quickly as her laughter began, Alanna's smile faded, and the joyful noise turned into a fit of coughs. She covered her mouth as the cough wracked her whole body, quickly making her double over. There was a rasping in Alanna's chest which Jastyn hadn't heard before.

"I thought you were going to stay in the house, sweetheart." Elisedd strode to their side, reaching to hold Alanna's arm as her coughs continued. She took a couple of haggard breaths. Jastyn couldn't help but notice the cracks in her dry lips as she gave them a smile.

"Father, I am hardly out of the house. It's a stone's throw away."

Her cough subsided into occasional sputters, and she promised them she could walk back inside on her own. As she started for the house, Jastyn bent down to grab the sack of goods she had dropped when Alanna greeted her.

"Are those the week's rations?"

Jastyn turned to face Elisedd. She scanned his dark eyes and the blond hair that ran into sideburns down his face and collected into an angular beard. It still surprised Jastyn how quickly he could change from doting father to unwilling guardian in a moment's time.

"Yes," she replied, hiking the bag over her shoulder.

"You had better get inside and help your mother with dinner."

Jastyn nodded, not breaking eye contact until she stepped past him.

"And, Jastyn," he called, making her turn. "If you encourage Alanna to leave the house again, there will be no more trips to the Wood. Understood?"

With her chin raised, Jastyn clenched her jaw. The hand resting at her side balled into a fist. But she forced herself to take a deep breath. Then she nodded before turning to go inside.

CHAPTER THREE

Aurelia crept along a corridor in the left wing of the castle. After scurrying past the servants sweeping up the remnants of dinner in the main hall, scampering behind her mother's ladies of the court drinking wine in the common room, and climbing more stairs than she cared to, Aurelia finally reached the level of the castle where her family currently met. She paused against the stone wall at the top of the landing to gather herself and slow her breathing. Then she looked around the corner. At the end of the long, torch-lit hallway, she located the floor-to-ceiling pine wood doors, their dark iron rivets protruding like watchful eyes. Framing the doorway were two guards, each in the traditional deep blue and gold kilts held at the waist by a pleated belt. Their navy tunics lay under leather breastplates that matched their ankle-high boots. The men had shoulder-length blond hair that wrapped behind their ears in braids. Their stern faces looked straight ahead. Aurelia watched their grips loosen and re-tighten on the spears in their right hands.

This seemed like an awful lot of security for a standard meeting of her father's. Leaning her head back against the wall, Aurelia's mind raced with the things her parents and brother might be discussing behind such tightly guarded doors. But she quickly grew impatient—a trait her mother always claimed came from her father—and tried to keep her feet from tapping in anticipation. She needed a plan to lose the guards if she was going to hear anything inside that room.

Biting her bottom lip, she mulled over the spells she knew, most of which were medicinal and hardly useful in terms of creating a distraction. While she thought, her fingers played against her side, and her saol emerged between them. She loved the familiar warmth, though she knew her mother discouraged "idle magic," as she often called it. But Aurelia never saw the harm in a little mindless conjuring.

Right as she was considering a spell that compelled drowsiness, a low voice interrupted her thoughts.

"Princess?"

Aurelia jumped and threw her saol in the direction of the voice. It flew down a couple of steps until it was blocked and consumed by a larger yellow flame protecting the hand of her brother's best friend.

"Drest!" she cried, trying to keep her voice quiet. She glanced around the corner again. The guards were peering down the hall in her direction but had yet to move. She whipped back around, tugging Drest up the final step and next to her behind the wall. "What are you doing here?"

"I could ask you the same thing, Princess," he replied, matching her hurried whisper. He straightened his green tunic where she had grabbed it before running a hand through his thick blond hair that always fell over his hazel eyes. "Don't you and Brennus usually have studies at this hour?"

Aurelia gestured toward the other end of the hallway. "Typically, you would be correct. But Brennus has been summoned for a meeting with my father."

Drest raised an eyebrow. "He's been called to attend another meeting?"

"I know!" Aurelia cried. She cleared her throat before continuing. "Well, I feel it is right for me to be informed. As the princess, of course."

Drest eyed her for a moment, then grinned widely, causing his eyes to twinkle. "Well, we had better get closer, wouldn't you agree?"

Aurelia smiled. Drest had been her brother's best friend—and recently served as his consult—since they were all children running around the castle together. Drest's mother, Baroness Enya, was a second cousin of King Grannus. She had lived her early childhood in the neighboring Kingdom of Gultero: home to the beautiful, wind-swept beaches that sat on the island across from Venostes's southern shores. The two kingdoms were allies as far back as history was written. However, since young Enya was the fourth child of the then-King Bradan and Queen Iona, and she had no foreseeable way to the crown, she was sent across the rocky and wind-filled bay to Venostes where she settled into the castle as a young lady of the court for the newly crowned Queen Dechtire. Drest's father Louarn had been a soldier in the young King Grannus's army. When the two men became fast friends after a successful war claiming territory along the southeastern shores from the fae, Louarn was awarded Baron, and he and Enya were soon after married. Furthermore, with their parents being such close friends, it was only natural for Drest—Louarn and Enya's only child—to bond quickly with Brennus and Aurelia.

"We do need to move closer." Aurelia licked her lips, eyeing the guards then her good friend. "I was considering a number of spells..." she told him, hoping she sounded confident.

"Going to mend their paper cuts, were you?" Drest smiled at his comment, making Aurelia bite her lip uncertainly.

She held her chin up. "Well, what do you have in mind, if you're so clever?"

Drest crossed his arms. "I was imagining I'd go talk to them."

"Talk to them? And what, bore them to sleep?"

"Very funny, Princess." Drest rolled his eyes. "I will go and start a conversation, something plain that they wouldn't consider a distraction. From there...I'll think of something."

"You'll think of something?" Aurelia said, her voice rushed and low as she peered around the corner again. She wasn't sure how much longer the meeting would go and was afraid of missing her opportunity.

"Do you want my help or not?"

Aurelia turned back to Drest, who was eyeing his fingernails with boredom.

"Fine, yes."

"What's in it for me?"

Aurelia sighed. "Does there always have to be something in it for you, Drest?"

He shrugged. "Only seems fair."

"All right!" Aurelia said, worry rising in her. She racked her mind for a moment, then said, "At the stables tomorrow I'll give you a go with Keller."

Drest narrowed his eyes. "I want Tully."

Aurelia faltered. "But Tully is my best mare!"

"Exactly. Keller is great but only half as fast as Tully. I do this for you now, and you give me half a day with Tully. I'm tired of only being allotted the third rung of the stable's horses."

Aurelia was about to insist his pick of horses had less to do with his station and more to do with his lack of riding skill, then decided she couldn't waste any more time.

"Fine!" she said, waving a frantic hand. "You can have Tully tomorrow. But for half a day, that's it!"

Drest smiled, cleared his throat, and strode past Aurelia into the hallway. Aurelia watched long enough to see Drest wave at the guards, who stood straighter as he approached. She sighed. Aurelia made a mental note to let the stable boy know about the riding changes first thing in the morning. She shook her head and couldn't help but laugh at Drest. He always found a way to get at least part of what he wanted when it came to her and her brother. The three of them together always signaled trouble when they were younger. One time they—and several other children of the castle—had decided to plan an outing to the shore. Aurelia, her brother, and Drest came up with a plan to make it happen, as such a trip was an uncommon luxury with their protective parents. Brennus wrote a flourishing letter of appeal to their mother and father, explaining the benefit of a day outdoors. Aurelia presented it to their parents in a sweet and persuasive speech, and Drest ended the whole ordeal with a showy bit of wind magic he promised to teach to the siblings with the items collected from the beach line. The king and queen had smiled at the eager trio before shaking their heads and sending them on their way. The three spent the day kicking about in the water and gathering shells, rocks, and plants from the beach, something that would not have been possible if not for the magic of the three of them together.

With her mind still wandering along the shores of her memory, Aurelia barely heard her name being called from down the hallway. She frowned and tried to discern where the voice was coming from.

When she turned the corner, Drest stood inches away, and she nearly collided with him.

"Oh! Drest." She lowered her voice, taking a step back. "Were you calling me?"

Drest shook his head, his face set in amused disbelief. "With all respect, Aurelia, I think Brennus inherited all of the common sense between the two of you."

Aurelia frowned and crossed her arms. "I will let that comment go." She peered over his shoulder. "Where are the guards?"

"I told you I would take care of them," Drest replied, puffing his chest, his hazel eyes sparkling.

"I said distract them, not vanish them into the wind!" Aurelia hurried past Drest and down the hallway, her dress kicking up on either side of her against the dark stone floor. When she reached the tall wooden doors, she looked around but saw no sign of the men who were standing there moments before. "Drest," she whispered hotly, "where did you—"

"Relax, Princess." He sighed, strolling across the hall to meet her. "I've nearly mastered wind spells, which means I *do* know when to use them. Besides, it's against the elements to 'vanish somebody to the wind,' as you say." He raised an eyebrow as Aurelia's face flushed.

"Of course. I'm sorry. It's just…well, where are they?"

"I told them my mother requested their presence in the main court."

Aurelia crossed her arms. "Oh, well, that was simple enough."

"Sometimes, it's best not to overthink things, Princess." Drest nudged her arm and adjusted the sword in his pleated belt. "Anyway, this has been fun."

Aurelia's eyes grew wide. "But wait, I thought—"

"My job is done." Drest raised his hands with a grin, then disappeared around the corner of another hallway.

With a huff, Aurelia brushed back her hair. She could handle this. After all, this was what she wanted, why she sneaked all the way across the castle: to be standing here. After taking a deep breath, she pressed her ear against the thick wooden door. One hand lay against an iron rivet, the metal cool against her hand. She pressed closer to the door and strained to listen. Muffled voices came from the other side, but it was hard to distinguish one from the other.

Cursing the thickness of the door, she fought to clear her mind and find another way to listen in. There were no windows into the room, only ones that faced the outside of the tower. Aurelia began to pace in front of the door, worried at each small scratch from a castle mouse or flicker from the wall torch that the guards were on their way back. Her gaze fell on the orange flames flickering against the wall.

"Of course!" Aurelia beamed and pressed her ear once again to the door. She could just make out the distant trail of voices. She forced her mind to move past the noise and focus on the room itself. She heard papers shuffling, the dull scraping of chairs, and even the soft clink of her brother's sword. Finally, the faint crackle from the fireplace drifted over her ear, and she smiled.

With one ear still pressed to the door, she conjured her saol. The glow bounced gently before her, familiar as her own family. Aurelia cupped it in her palm.

The red light glowed brightly for a moment, and she heard the fire from the other side of the door crackle loudly. At the sound, she backed away from the door and crouched in a corner of the tower's hallway. She held the saol to her cheek and listened as the muffled sounds of her family grew more distinct. Her father's voice spoke loudest.

"My dear, it is only more gossip that has everyone so worried. The village border remains secure. I see no reason to send more guards to the north."

"I know, Grannus, but this is the fourth report of unrest from the outlands. I think it would be unwise to ignore such news."

"Father, I still do not understand what all of this means. There has been nothing but peace for the last thirteen years. Why would people want to harm the kingdom...harm us?"

Aurelia's brow furrowed. She cupped the saol closer to her ear.

"My dear son." Her mother sighed. "Unfortunately, no matter when or where you are, people are never satisfied with what they have. Still, it remains our duty as the royal family to ensure our kingdom and its people's happiness."

"But not everyone has the same idea of what that happiness includes," finished their father gruffly.

Aurelia sat quietly, waiting as the conversation seemed to halt. Eventually, her father spoke again.

"In another week's time, I will consider sending a guard party through the Wood to the north. A scouting group should scare off any unruly factions between here and the elves' land. We will move forward from there."

"I will lead them," Brennus said. Aurelia covered her mouth as her mother spoke.

"You will do no such thing!"

"Dechtire," the king said softly.

"Mother, I am of age. I have led guard parties before. Besides, is this not what you were just saying you wanted, to ensure we did not 'ignore such news'?"

"Yes, but, Brennus, this is not the time for heroics."

"I am fully capable," her brother replied, his voice stoic.

"And we do not doubt your capabilities, my son," their mother responded. "You are a great hunter, and an even better rider, but—"

"But when the kingdom is threatened, I am not allowed out of the castle walls? This is exactly like when we were young. Aurelia and I could never set foot anywhere without the watchful eyes of the two of you. Do you realize we are not children anymore?"

"He has a point, darling." Aurelia could practically feel the tension growing between their parents. The fire popped again, signaling her spell coming to an end.

The queen sighed. "This is not up for discussion right now." A chair scraped, and Brennus must have moved to speak when their mother cut him off. "Not tonight. We will reconsider things tomorrow's eve."

Another crack from the flame, and Aurelia knew her time was nearly done. With a grimace, she blew out the flame in her palm, disconnecting from the happenings within the state room. As soon as she did, her head felt heavy. She stood and walked slowly toward the end of the hallway. She had not anticipated this. Daydreaming by the fire earlier, Aurelia had expected exciting news of a visiting royal family or perhaps a new trade treaty. But unrest in the kingdom? Protesting groups seeking to harm her parents? Her mind swam with terrifying thoughts and visions.

Suddenly, Aurelia regretted having ever snuck across the castle at all.

CHAPTER FOUR

Bleak skies and whipping winds strangled Jastyn as she sprinted through the dark Wood. The eerie, echoing laugh of the strange fae surrounded her. Roots lifted, gripping each trembling step. The words he uttered twisted their fingers tight around her mind: "You are an Odium Child." She shook her head, shielding her face from the branches reaching out to scratch her cheek. While the cackling wind grew louder, Jastyn's breath choked within her throat. She tried to scream, but her voice was smothered in the darkness.

With a gasp, Jastyn jolted upright. Her forehead was hot with sweat, and she looked around. The breeze blew through the old wooden window, making the shutter clang against the wall. Moonlight cast shadows across the bedroom. As her breathing slowed, she turned in the small, creaking bed. She watched Alanna sleeping next to her. Her sister had stolen the patched blankets and gripped them tightly despite the warm night.

Careful not to wake her sister, Jastyn got up and walked to the clay basin sitting atop a wooden table next to the doorway. The water felt cool on her face, and she splashed it generously on her neck. Taking a step back, Jastyn stood in the center of the room. Her loose tunic waved as the wind swept once more through the window. With her eyes closed, she imagined herself once again in the Wood. Though dreams of that mysterious fae haunted her mind since their meeting many years ago, Jastyn refused to let them consume her with fear. As the water dried cool on her forehead, she exhaled. The Wood filled her mind, but the rider and his horse vanished. In their place was light and open paths welcoming her.

Eventually, her shoulders relaxed. But as they did, choking coughs erupted from the other side of the room. Jastyn ran to Alanna as her sister's body writhed, and a fit overtook her.

"Shh, I'm here. It's okay."

Alanna sat up and continued to cough, sleep in her eyes. Jastyn watched helplessly as Alanna gripped the blanket tighter, her body doubled over.

"It'll be over soon. It's okay." Jastyn moved to lie behind her sister. Alanna's coughs shook them both. Then Alanna reached for a rag next to her bed and covered her mouth to quiet the coughs. When her body finally relaxed and her hand moved from her face, Jastyn's gaze fell on the dark red splotch crumpled in her sister's hand.

❖

"How is she?"

Jastyn, having settled Alanna back to sleep, walked into the front room of their home and met her mother's gaze. The dimly lit space functioned as a kitchen and common room, with a cluttered hearth always playing host to a burning fire beneath charred and aging pots. Branna, Jastyn's mother, sat in a wooden chair before the flames.

"She's all right. For tonight." Jastyn walked to the fire and warmed her hands.

Silence sat comfortably between them, a sign of a lifetime of easy companionship as friends as well as family. Jastyn nudged the gathered gray ash with the toe of her wool sock, pushing it closer to the crackling logs.

"She's been like this every night for three weeks." Her mother's voice gave the slightest semblance of how tired she was, but her youthful face hardly revealed the long days and even longer nights spent mending another torn pant leg for Jastyn or seeing to Alanna when she was too ill to go into town for a reading lesson. Short and compact, her mother only took up half the chair, and her woolen sleep shirt draped well past her knees. One callused hand brushed aside strands of thick auburn hair, which she wore in a braid twisted loosely down her back. Her sheepskin socks, which Jastyn had made for her three years ago, were beginning to fray at the edges. Coran always told Jastyn she resembled her mother; both had freckled faces and straight, sharp noses set above thin lips. But unlike Jastyn, her mother's fair skin turned pink in the summer sun—a trait she passed on to Alanna.

"The village alchemist gave her another medicine, but I'm afraid it's not working either." Her mother spoke calmly, concerned yet reserved. But Jastyn could see the deep worry in the frown at the corners of her mouth.

Jastyn kept her voice low as she stared into the fire. "No, it's not working. Nothing has." Then Jastyn turned to face her. "She is up with the moon, coughing for an hour each night. And it's only getting worse." She paused. "What about Eegit?"

Her mother sighed. "Jastyn."

"Why not? Nothing the alchemist prescribed her is working. His herbs are nothing but bandages. And each time he gives her something new, Alanna gets even sicker. Eegit might be able to do something that he can't."

"Jastyn, you know I have no problem with you visiting Eegit. In fact, I am grateful to her for keeping my oldest daughter out of trouble… most days." Her mother smiled, and Jastyn couldn't help but return it.

"So, why can't she help?"

"Because, love, she's a brewer of spells and curses—not a learned member of alchemy. Knowing her, she would have your sister dancing nude in the rain while drinking a bowl of wolf's blood."

Jastyn snorted at the image. "But it might work."

Her mother shook her head. "I'm sorry, Jastyn. I don't think it's a good idea. Alanna needs a real healer."

Jastyn ignored the prick behind her eyes at her mother's distrust, even if she had a point. As she knelt to prod the dying flames with a charred stick, she bit her lip and said, "What if we appeal to Queen Diarmaid?"

Her mother was quiet, only shifting one leg up and tucking it close to her chest. Encouraged by the silence, Jastyn went on.

"Everyone knows the queen is a brilliant healer. The entire village speaks of her charity to those who have called upon her. She helped Coran's mom, remember? When she fell into the river three winters ago and nearly froze to death?"

Her mother nodded. "I remember."

"Why not ask if she can do something, anything for Alanna?"

Another moment of silence, then, "You know why."

Jastyn clenched her jaw, stoking the fire more. "It's not fair."

"Jastyn."

"No." She turned on her knee to face her mom. "Why do you continue to let our circumstances confine us to less than we deserve? What happened to you was so long ago." Jastyn reached for her mother's hand. "We are in the light now with Elisedd and Alanna. There is hardly anyone who remembers what we—you—went through."

Her mother watched Jastyn intently. The lines around her eyes crinkled when she cupped Jastyn's face in her free hand. "There is a difference between letting your past define you and knowing where you stand."

Jastyn searched her mother's eyes, and in them, she saw what she would once again have to do. Jastyn nodded and looked at her own hands holding her mother's, or rather, shielding them. She would have to take hold of this situation, like when she and her mother hardly had a scrap to eat after being released from the dungeon and banished to this patch of land near the Wood when Jastyn was born. Or when her mother gave Jastyn her only pair of boots for her tenth birthday so she could go out to practice hunting with Eegit before the harshness of winter was upon them. Or when, Jastyn learned, her mother wasn't entirely turning a blind eye each time Jastyn came home from the market with more than their weekly allowance afforded them.

Jastyn knew, as her mother's gaze drifted toward Alanna's coughs, that she would have to find a way to make her sister better. Slowly, her mother stood and disappeared into the bedroom, carrying a damp rag for Alanna. And as Jastyn watched her go, she knew that her mother would not truly mind if her *gan 'athair* daughter went out and fought for their family's survival once again.

Chapter Five

I can't believe you talked me into this." Coran opened the waist-high wooden gate outside the royal stables where the grazing meadows stretched out and ran into the Wood. Jastyn, having crept from the trees after skirting the castle's walls, grinned and hurried through the gate. Her dark blue cloak covered her hair and half her face. As Coran latched the fence closed behind her, he sighed. "Actually, you know what? I can believe it."

"Hush." Jastyn tugged his gray tunic sleeve as they walked quickly across the field where knee-high grass brushed against their pants. "You owed me one."

"Did I?" Coran glanced over his shoulder. His hazel eyes were clouded beneath a worried brow.

Jastyn shrugged. "Maybe. I don't remember." She bumped his arm. "Don't worry so much."

"Yeah," he said, "last time you told me to do that, we were chased from the brook by an angry water nymph."

Jastyn laughed. "She was too uptight."

Coran rolled his eyes. While Jastyn lowered her hood, he glanced around. She saw a trio of horses nearby. Two were chestnut brown, fit creatures, though small in stature. The third was nearly all black with the exception of a clover-shaped splotch of white on her neck and another above her left front hoof.

"Pretty thing, ain't she?"

Jastyn nodded. "The king's?"

"The queen's. Her name is Keller. Lately, though, the princess has taken her out more." He looked around. "She should be back with Tully any time now."

Jastyn picked at the dirt beneath her nails, half listening. "Tully… her maiden?"

"No, Tully is the kingdom's best mare. She's always the princess's show horse at the summer solstice festivities."

Her gaze was on the stable door that led into the castle. "Never bothered goin' to those much."

Seeming to realize what he said, Coran nodded. "Well, the princess should be back soon. The sun is just over the western hills. Best to wait here."

At this, Jastyn frowned. "You said you could get me in to see the queen."

Coran ran a freckled hand through his shock of red hair. "I want to help you, Jas. I do. But you can't walk in to the castle and expect an audience with Her Majesty."

"Which is why I was going to ask politely."

Coran shook his head. "It's not that simple."

Jastyn's face grew hot, her fists clenched at her sides. "You know how tired I am of hearing that?"

"What?"

"Never mind." Jastyn pulled the hood of her cloak back over her braid. "I'll take it from here." She stalked off, her steps heavy on the grass as she hurried toward the thick doors.

"Wait, Jastyn. You can't just barge in there. You don't even know where to go!"

Watch me. The sound of hooves sounded behind her. She glanced back past Coran. Two horses and riders galloped in from the Wood. But Jastyn was tired of waiting. She needed to get to the queen. She needed to ask for help. She wasn't about to let her family down now.

As Coran cried out for her to wait, she pushed the wooden doors inward and slipped silently into the stables. One way or another, Jastyn would get what she needed.

❖

Aurelia eyed Drest warily as they trotted toward the edge of the stable fence. Throughout their nearly two-hour ride down to the river, she had tried to ignore everything from his kicks to Tully's flanks to the way he tended to lean to the right in his saddle. It wasn't as if she didn't trust Drest with Tully, it was only that *she* knew Tully best. Aurelia huffed as they pulled their reins to slow the horses. She winced when Drest tugged for two seconds too long. She had bitten her tongue long enough, she decided as she dismounted. And that, as her mother would say, was a victory in itself.

"You can leave her to me," she said, stepping over to Tully and reaching for her reins.

Drest raised an eyebrow, then swung his leg over to dismount, landing with a *thud* on the other side of the horse. "Fear not, dear princess. Tully yet stands tall and strong."

Aurelia scrunched up her face, tucking it close to Tully, who neighed when Aurelia patted her mane. She whispered apologies to the horse, prompting a chuckle from Drest. She was about to say something when the stable boy scurried over, reaching for her horse's reins after a quick bow.

"M'lady. Sir," he added to Drest, who was laughing as he removed his riding gloves and brushed a hand through his blond locks. "How was the ride today?"

"Oh, fine. Though I'm afraid Aurelia may never let me near her precious Tully again for fear I may send the beast to the next eastern wind." The stable boy, seemingly confused by Drest's comment, only smiled. Aurelia noticed him glancing toward the doors that led into the stables. Drest was still talking as Aurelia helped the boy remove the saddles. "But fret not, Princess." Drest flourished his gloves after re-buckling his sword, which had been strapped to Tully's side. "Your mare is safe. Thank you, Your Highness, for allowing me the great pleasure of sitting atop a lady such as her." He winked.

Aurelia flattened the skirt of her navy riding dress, not even trying to hide her disgust. "You, Drest, are absolutely revolting. I am ashamed to call you my brother's friend."

"But am I not yours too, m'lady?" He went to grab her hand to kiss it. She yanked it away, prompting laughter from Drest. "Oh, come now, Aurelia. I only jest."

She pulled back her shoulders while eyeing the stable boy as he fidgeted with the reins. He seemed jumpier than usual. When he glanced again at the castle doors, she placed her hands on her hips.

"Boy," she called. "Coran, is it?"

The freckled boy nearly latched his own hand in the gate.

"Look at you, Princess. Getting to know the help."

She ignored Drest's comment and moved toward the boy. "Coran. May I ask you, is there something the matter?" She wondered if there had been more news of the uprisings. Perhaps her father had called another meeting or informed the castle staff of a possible threat. That would explain this boy's look of terror. His eyes were so wide she thought they might sprout legs and trot off on their own.

"M'lady?" he stammered. "I'm not sure what you mean."

She wandered toward the latched gate that opened to a stone-leaden path, which led to the stable doors. Aurelia lifted her skirt as the mud kicked up beneath her riding boots. Upon closer look, she noticed the door into the castle stood ajar. She spun around.

"Who's in there?"

This time, the boy flushed and ducked his chin as he stammered a response. "M…m'lady. I…I only forgot to close the door when I went in not an hour ago to…water the livestock."

"A lie if I've heard one," Drest muttered from the side of his mouth, leaning—amused—against a pile of haystacks.

Aurelia shot him a look. "Coran, tell me the truth. Please. I won't say a word to my father or mother. But if you are helping rebels sneak into the castle—"

"Rebels?" The boy's face went from dread to shock. "Do you mean to say there's war brewing, m'lady?"

"No," Aurelia said quickly. "I…Drest, some help, please?"

Drest was picking mud from his boots with the tip of his sword when he looked up. "Why don't you go inside and look for yourself, Your Majesty?" He grinned and returned to his boots.

"Your Highness, really, there's nothin' to see. I…I may have let a rat past me earlier and I was tryin' to chase it out…"

He trailed off as Aurelia, with a defiant look at Drest, puffed out her chest, pulled up her dress sleeves, and walked across the path to the stable doors. She paused only briefly before nodding to herself in encouragement. Then she pushed into the castle's stables, determined to prove she was as capable as the boys at handling things. Or yet, even better.

CHAPTER SIX

The stables were drafty and musty, and Aurelia imagined it had to do with the open windows that, despite the wind, never actually let any air in or out of the vast, open room full of animals, half-open barrels of feed, and stacks of hay. The air seemed especially stagnant now in the first days of summer. The newly thatched roof groaned overhead, the planks hoisting it up shifting. She resisted the urge to lift her riding skirt over the straw and manure coating the floor, knowing Drest walked behind her. The nearly dozen square-cut windows lining the walls, while seemingly incapable of letting in even the slightest breeze, allowed blocks of fading sunlight to fall on the western side of the large room. Still, overall, the space was dim and growing darker by the minute as Aurelia walked down the dirt aisle running through its middle. Torchlight provided rays of orange across otherwise black shadows.

Chickens clucked in a coop to her left, and a few flapped their wings as she passed, as if perturbed at their evening visitor. Barrels of chicken feed lined the low wall beside the birds, and Aurelia covered her nose when she and Drest approached the pigpen, where two sizeable sows and one gilt grunted and bumped one another on their way to the trough. The boar, half covered in mud and slop, slept in a far corner.

"Look, Princess. Isn't that your great Uncle Harbin in the sty?"

Aurelia glared over her shoulder at Drest, but in doing so, tripped over a stray bucket. The bustle sent the chickens fluttering in a fury, and the contents of the bucket spilled out and onto her freshly shined riding boots.

In a huff, she spun around. "Thank you very much."

Drest cackled, one hand on his waist. "Slop is a good look on you."

Boiling, Aurelia pulled her shoulders back and ignored the stench coming from the hem of her skirt. She briefly wished Brennus was there, if anything to act as a buffer, as he usually did, between her and Drest. It wasn't as if she didn't like Drest or wasn't used to his comments. Sometimes, though, he was simply too proud for his own good. Heading for the horse pens at the end of the room, she imagined Brennus alongside them. Would he have gone barreling into the barn as she did? Come to think of it, she really didn't give Coran much of a chance to explain. She shook her head. Nonsense. Brennus would want to get to the bottom of this, just like she did. Why should she worry? She could deal with this without her brother.

A loud crash followed by a shrill *clang* came from the far end of the stables, not thirty yards from where they stood.

Drest's laughter ceased. "A rat, surely."

Aurelia, her determination shrinking, looked from him to the farthest horse pen: Tully's stable. The horses were all outside grazing under Coran's watch. Unless, he too, had crept in here without her knowing. Perhaps she was hasty in investigating. She closed her eyes and conjured Brennus. *It's all right to be afraid*, he had told her during one of their training sessions. *You can use fear. Harness it and unleash it when you need it most.* Taking a deep breath, Aurelia touched her left index finger to her thumb as she stepped toward the source of the sound. The red saol began to glow within her cupped palm.

Drest, following several steps behind, whispered, "Do you really think that will be necessary?"

"Shh!"

Now halfway to the final, dimly lit stable, Aurelia's gaze fell on the tall door at the end of the narrow dirt path. The door that led to the other side of the castle and toward the servant's kitchen had been tinkered with. Squinting, she saw a pin inside the wide keyhole. It was a simple one, like the kind Roisin used to keep her braids pinned back.

Whoever—or whatever—was in here was unsuccessful in getting farther into the castle. This gave her the slightest push of courage, and she took another step forward before pausing outside the open pen. There was a rustle, like something moving amongst the hay.

Deciding there was only one way to continue, Aurelia leapt through the open gate, her head high as she let a red flame go.

But whoever was crouched in the dark corner of the stable was quick. They had already formed a blue shield the size of the berry shrubs that lined the edge of the woods, and Aurelia's red saol crashed into it. The shield's light flickered and cracked, dimming in places. Still, the light from the two flames colliding had illuminated the stable enough for Aurelia to see a cloak-covered intruder. The cloak was a simple one, and as the blue flame crackled and absorbed the fading red light, she noticed torn, dirt-covered boots and weathered breeches.

The figure rose. Their blue light shrank to fist-size, and Aurelia saw the slight curve of a hip and…was that the end of a braid?

"Thief! Hoodlum!" Drest jumped into the pen, positioning himself behind Aurelia, who turned to see his eyes going clear. The formerly stagnant air picked up. The figure, not seven paces away, stood and readied their arm to throw a fully formed blue orb. Drest scoffed.

"You dare attack royalty?"

At this, the blue flame all but vanished. The figure lowered their arm, their fingertips glowing softly. The air was still picking up, and Aurelia raised a cautious hand.

"Wait."

Drest's eyes returned to their normal hazel. "But, Princess—"

"Princess?"

Aurelia and Drest turned. The voice opposite them was that of a girl. No, not a girl. A woman. Or, just barely one, like Aurelia.

As if to confirm this, the person stepped forward. Drest reached for a torch on the wall, then held it out to better see. The woman pulled back her hood, revealing a narrow face smudged with dirt on one ruddy cheek. Her thin lips were set in a straight line, and her tunic gaped just below her collarbones. Aurelia jerked her gaze up to the stranger's hazel eyes, which were set directly on her.

"You are the princess?" she asked. The now-exposed braid of strawberry-blond dangled over the front of her shoulder when she spoke.

"Yes, she is," Drest responded vehemently, standing with his chest out. "And you will bow before a member of the royal family."

The woman, after what seemed like an eternity of sizing up

Aurelia, glanced at Drest. Her eyes shimmered mischievously, but she bowed. When she straightened, Drest spoke again.

"What did you think you were doing lurking around here? I see your belt; you are a local. From where—"

"Drest," Aurelia cut him off. He opened his mouth to protest, but she said, "I can speak for myself, thank you."

Aurelia swore she saw the hint of a smile on the woman's lips. Clearing her throat, she said, "Well, what business *do* you have here? If you've come to steal our horses, I'm afraid you've mistimed things a bit."

"I'm not a thief."

Drest snorted. The woman's jaw clenched, and she stepped forward. She was nearly a head shorter than Drest but she seemed resolute in her stance. "I came here seeking audience with the queen. I need…my family needs her help."

"Is that why you were trying to break into the castle?" Aurelia asked, nodding to the door.

When the woman only shuffled her feet, Aurelia folded her arms over her chest. "Please, may we know your name?"

"Jaaastyyynn!"

The cry, followed by an uproar from the chicken coop, made them all turn to the front of the stables. A flash of red hair whirled feverishly as a rooster flapped around the stable boy, who crashed through the door. The surrounding torchlight danced in all of the commotion. The boy stumbled forward, emitting irritated groans and muttered swears. "Wait!" he cried, blindly swinging at the chickens whooshing overhead. His foot landed with an unfortunate *thwump* into the slop bucket. When all of the feathers and up-kicked hay finally settled, Coran stood before them, claw scratches along his hands and face and his left foot dragging the bucket half a step behind him.

"Please, Princess Aurelia, let me explain."

"You?" Drest sneered. "I knew you had something to do with this."

"Drest." Aurelia rolled her eyes. "Wait a moment, please."

"Coran had nothin' to do with this," the woman said. Aurelia caught a faint tremble in her voice. "Please, he was only helping me. He told me I could meet with you," she explained, gesturing to Aurelia.

The boy stared at the ground while fingering a tear in his threaded shirt. "But I...I wanted to see the queen. Not you."

Aurelia nearly stepped back into Drest. *They must not teach much in the way of respect in the village.* Working to quell her wounded pride, she placed her hands on her hips. "Oh?"

"The queen is a great healer, is she not?"

"Queen Dechtire is a wondrous healer," Drest answered. "What care you of her abilities?"

The woman kept her eyes on Aurelia when she responded. "My sister is very sick. And we've done everything we can. I'm afraid...I fear we are out of options."

"You've visited the local alchemist?"

"Yes, and we have tried his herbs. But Alanna—my sister— nothing has worked. And she is getting worse." Aurelia noticed the woman's words came in bursts, with deliberate pauses every so often as if she was minding her tongue.

"You're sure you've done everything? Tried the special waters and remedies?"

"Nothing works. Which is why I seek your mother's help. I know she has done things for the village in the past. Helped to heal those in need."

Aurelia pondered this. Meanwhile, the stable boy fidgeted, trying to unstick his foot. She felt Drest brimming with the desire to speak, so she continued before he could.

"Jastyn, is it?"

The woman nodded.

"Please, what is your surname?"

A tint of color swam in Jastyn's cheeks. "I am the daughter of Elisedd Eidhin of Marcra."

"The horse master?" Drest stepped forward. "He has spoken of a daughter, but of a much younger one." His hand drifted to the grip of his sword. Jastyn's eyes followed this carefully.

"Yes, that would be my sister, Alanna. The one who is sick."

Curiosity ran rampant within her, but Aurelia worked to maintain a calm façade. She imagined once again what her brother might do.

"I am sorry for your sister's state," she said. "But I'm afraid my mother and father, well, the whole castle, for that matter, we are frightfully busy at the moment. Things are…" She racked her mind, realizing news of potential war probably shouldn't be shared with villagers. "We are simply handling too many affairs right now. I don't think my mother, or rather, Queen Dechtire, would have time to offer aid at present."

Jastyn's eyes flashed with something, and her jaw tightened.

"Yes," Drest added, "very important matters of the kingdom." He put on his charming smile and moved past Aurelia into the pen. He walked up to Jastyn and placed one arm around her as Aurelia watched, wide-eyed.

"We are terribly sorry at the news regarding Elisedd's daughter," he cooed, and Aurelia cringed as he led Jastyn out of the pen and back to the stable doors. She had never minded Drest talking his way into a shorter lesson, but for some reason, his tone mixed with his arm around Jastyn felt wrong.

Aurelia and Coran, who had extracted his foot and was now untangling feathers from his hair, followed them outside. The sky was nearly dark, and the first few stars shone overhead. Drest was still talking when Jastyn slipped out from under his arm. Aurelia used the darkness to take in her fit figure, the hunting blade tucked against one boot, and the lightness of her hair under the rising moonlight. She had gone down into the village many times, usually on a solstice day or kingdom holiday. Yet she couldn't recall ever seeing a woman like her at any of the events. Jastyn's clothing indicated a lower status, but everything else—from the swagger of her step to her strong-looking hands—exuded pride. There was a hardness to Jastyn, and Aurelia couldn't help but find her intriguing.

"Do not fret," Drest said. "I'm sure the village alchemist can brew something up that hasn't been tried yet. There are breakthroughs every day, you know!"

A single, deep horn blew from within the castle. "Ah, that will be the dinner horn. Come, Aurelia," he said, turning toward the wall that led to a side gate. "We had better be off."

Aurelia's stomach churned. Part of her was angry at Drest for dismissing Jastyn so carelessly, but most of her felt guilty. Here she was, finally with a problem of her own, and she was completely useless.

"I'm sorry," she told Jastyn when Drest was a good ten paces away. She fiddled with the bracelet under the sleeve of her dress. "I truly am. If there was anything I could do, some small token of…"

Jastyn seemed to hardly hear her and was turning to say something to Coran when Aurelia's fingers froze on the silver metal of the bracelet. By the time she pulled up her sleeve and slipped the band from her wrist, Jastyn and Coran were already halfway across the field, heading toward the Wood.

"Wait!" Aurelia took off after them.

Jastyn stopped. Aurelia ignored Coran's bemused face as she sprinted to them. Breathless, she grabbed Jastyn's right arm and placed the bracelet into her upturned palm.

Jastyn looked at her hand. "What…"

"Consider it a small token." Aurelia smiled. "Perhaps it might help your sister."

Still beaming, Aurelia shared one more look with the mysterious Jastyn and hurried back to the castle.

Chapter Seven

The following night, Jastyn fumed over her bowl of cornmeal. She was still so furious at the princess and her gift, she hardly heard Elisedd ask her to clean out the cauldron as the rest of the family stood from their table after dinner. Jastyn met Alanna's eyes while her stepfather grumbled. Her sister, looking suddenly thinner, held intrigue in her gaze. Jastyn gave her what she hoped was an encouraging smile.

Her family retired to the hearth—Mother in the chair, Elisedd in the corner to repair a horse rein, and Alanna lying down by the fire with a book. Meanwhile, Jastyn gathered the old, chipped bowls and black cauldron, then walked outside to the well thirty paces from their home. Gray clouds scattered overhead as if uniting in sympathy for Jastyn's current state. Several raindrops fell on her shoulders as she reached for the rope and pulled up a full bucket. While she rinsed the dishes, she replayed the events following her run-in with the princess.

"Jewelry?" she had exclaimed once she and Coran were halfway back to their village. "And I thought we 'common folk' were ignorant! Does she really think a shiny trinket will heal Alanna?" Jastyn shook with fury as they walked.

Coran shrugged. "Maybe she meant for you to sell it?"

Jastyn halted near a cluster of cypress trees. She could see the rocky hillside where her house was. "Nobody has enough of anything to trade for that bracelet. Look at it!" She held it up under the moonlight. The silver shone, and they admired the three rubies set into its center. "The wealthiest family in the village would have to sell their home *and* their sheep for this."

Coran dug a toe into the earth. "Princess Aurelia was only tryin' to help, Jas."

She sighed. "Maybe. But I'm running out of time." She glanced over at the round, thick walls built into the hillside next to her home. Candlelight glowed softly through the windows. She tucked the bracelet into a pocket sewn into her tunic. "Thank you, Coran. For trying."

He smiled sympathetically, then started off toward his own house. After a moment, he turned. "There's always Eegit."

At first, Jastyn had laughed. She imaged the hedgewitch shoving the bracelet into the nest of hair atop her head, dancing around her meadow with glee. But as she watched Coran greet his mother in their open doorway, she decided that Eegit wasn't such a bad idea after all.

As Jastyn lowered the bucket into the well and collected her clean dishes, she thought maybe it was worth asking Eegit for advice.

❖

Aurelia jabbed at the bits of lamb chop on her plate, thick gravy pooling along its ribbed edges. The usual evening chatter filled the decadent dining hall where twenty people ate and drank mulled wine around a long, narrow oak table in the middle of the room. Located in the dead center of the castle, the room was always warm. Two wide fireplaces topped by snaking chimneys burned brightly on either side of the room. A troupe of village musicians played lilting, cheery music on lutes and lyres while the royal family and their court dined. At the front of the room, in two high-backed chairs, sat King Grannus and Queen Dechtire. Behind them, towering wooden doors, currently open to allow more air into the room, led to the castle gates and out to the markets.

Aurelia glanced around as she rested her chin into her upturned palm. Dozens of torches lined each wall, throwing shadows across the faces of the dinner guests. Laourn, at her father's left hand, spoke somberly, as he was wont to do, especially in comparison to her father gesticulating eagerly over a plate of berries and cheese. To Aurelia's left sat Baroness Enya, caddy-corner to her mother. The women were framed elegantly by pointed deer-skinned chairs. The baroness wore a fitted emerald-green dress that complemented her blond hair and light hazel eyes. Hailing from Gultero, she was taller than most women of the court and had a lither figure compared to the compact ladies who made their way into the kingdom's social circle after working the fields and herding sheep when they were young.

The baroness's style stood out, too. Aurelia heard mutterings that the plunging necklaces and the rings that lined her fingers were the sign of "new wealth." Twenty years ago, she had married the baron and was beside him during his rise in military rank. She stood out in contrast to Queen Dechtire—herself a villager who had captured the heart of the young Prince Grannus—who chose to always don a simple crown and owned a handful of dresses. Baroness Enya adored being able to dress the part. Her dainty fingers tossed a bite of goat cheese into her mouth before she sipped from a goblet of wine. The giant ruby on her left ring finger seemed too big for her bony hand. Her hair was pinned halfway up, the back of it rolled and tucked behind a shimmering dragonfly clip. It became apparent over the years that Drest's handsome and distinguished features, like his proud chin, came from her. Meanwhile, his intimidating stature was inherited from his built and broad-shouldered father.

Across the table from her sat Drest and Brennus, who seemed wedged between his best friend and Laourn thanks to the barrel-chested men. Yet he never appeared uncomfortable. He spoke warmly with Drest, who was recounting their tale featuring the enigmatic Jastyn.

Since their meeting with Jastyn, Aurelia had found it difficult to think of anything else. Last night, not an hour after their meeting, she had asked Roisin if she had any knowledge of the kingdom's horse master and his family. But like Drest, she spoke only of a younger daughter, the one who had been ill for some time. Taking a drink from her goblet, Aurelia wondered where Jastyn was now.

"Come now, Drest," Brennus said. "You speak of her as if she were a common thief."

"Is she not? She snuck into the stables and very nearly picked her way into the castle. Gods know what she would have taken had we not caught her."

Aurelia cleared her throat, and both men glanced across the table.

"Very well." Drest sighed behind a forkful of venison. "If your *sister* hadn't stopped her."

Brennus leaned forward. "Quite the adventure, dear sister." His eyes twinkled, and pride swelled inside Aurelia. She scooted closer to the table, leaning over her plate to ensure her parents couldn't listen.

"It was rather exciting." She poked at a plate of raspberries piled high next to a wax-dripped candle. Then she met her brother's gaze. "Do you think I could have done more to help her?"

Drest snorted into his goblet. "I'm sure the lovely scoundrel is rejoicing as we speak; no doubt her family has bought out the local alchemist with your little gift."

Aurelia was about to protest when Brennus cut in. "She sounds more like a desperate sister doing what she can to help her family."

A bored wave of his hand and Drest returned to his food.

Aurelia slumped in her chair. "You did what you could," Brennus said.

She nodded but couldn't ignore the unease that had settled in her stomach.

Later that night, Aurelia's mind continued to swim with thoughts of Jastyn. Running a silver-handled, horse-hair brush through one side of her hair, she mused over what Jastyn might have done with the bracelet when her chamber door opened. The deep *creak* was followed by the quick tread of her mother's nimble steps. Using the mirror in front of her, Aurelia watched her mother make her way across the room.

"Your father and brother are locked in another meeting in the east tower. I just left them." Her mother strolled across the black bearskin rug, her long red cloak secured at the breast with a gold pin. Beneath it, a deep blue tunic extended to her shins where it fell above a pair of narrow leather ankle boots. Aurelia's own feet were snug inside a pair of brown fitted boots; her woolen robe tied around her waist.

While her mother recounted several conversations from dinner, Aurelia's ears pricked at her mother's mention of Laourn's plans for a scouting party in the coming weeks.

"Scouts? Whatever for?" Aurelia asked casually, placing the brush in front of the foggy glass set in an oval frame atop her chestnut table. She hadn't heard much news of unrest since her quest into the east tower the week before. Perhaps now she could learn more.

Her mother joined her on the bench in front of the vanity. She smiled softly at Aurelia's reflection, then ran her fingers through her hair.

"Your father believes there are some events worth looking into in the Wood. Since our kingdom claimed this land from the elves, many fae have taken advantage of the vacant fields our people have yet to settle." She shifted so that she could reach both hands up by Aurelia's ears and began to twist her hair into a braid. "There have been a few skirmishes in the deeper woods, mostly between fae clans. Nothing to be concerned about."

"And nothing Father and Brennus can't handle, I presume."

Her mother smiled as she threaded the ends of the braid so that it stayed in place. "Precisely. And I believe Drest will be joining them this time."

Aurelia scoffed. "He can make a lot of noise and agitate our best horses along the way."

Her mother chuckled. "They'll be out and back before you can conjure your saol." Aurelia nodded. She looked down as her mother tucked a stray hair behind her ear. "What is it, darling?"

Biting her lip, Aurelia weighed whether or not to tell her mother about the other night, about Jastyn and the bracelet and how she now felt completely silly about the whole thing. Though she wasn't entirely sure why. Thumping her index finger against the table, she decided to ask a question instead.

"Mother, what do you know of our horse master?"

Her mother, who had been pulling her own hair into a braid that she pinned to the top of her head, said, "Elisedd Eidhin? Sweetheart, whatever do you wish to know about him?"

Standing, Aurelia hurried to the other side of the room and jumped into bed, the blankets already turned down thanks to Roisin. Her feet slid under them until they bumped hot stones set in a pan, the warmth emanating from it sinking into her toes. Aurelia spoke slowly, unsure what to say, "I have gotten word that his daughter is unwell."

Her mother stood from the bench, one hand on her hip. "Yes," she said solemnly, "that has been true for some time now. She's such a young thing, too, poor girl."

"Alanna." Aurelia pursed her lips and pulled the blankets closer. She could feel her mother's gaze on her. She settled deeper into the pillows as her mother walked to stand beside the bed.

"You know her?"

Aurelia shook her head. "No, I…I've met her sister. Just the other day."

Her mother blinked. There was something in the back of her mother's eyes, deep within the piercing circles of her pupils, but it vanished so quickly Aurelia was unsure it was ever there to begin with. Dechtire watched her. "Elisedd only has one daughter."

"Oh, for some reason, I thought…"

"Yes?"

Aurelia smoothed the blankets around her. "I must be mistaken. I met a village girl…woman…the other day who claimed to be related. I'm sure they are simply good friends. Like sisters but not quite."

Her mother smiled, though her expression remained cautious. "That must be it." She paused as if considering what to say. "I've known Elisedd for some time. He worked on his family's land when I was little. Before I met your father." Aurelia admired the way her mother's cheeks grew pink at the mention of her father, even after all of these years. "You know I grew up just beyond those hills?" She gestured to the closed window, where rain tapped lightly against the pane.

Aurelia nodded. "I recall the stories."

"Good," she said, patting the post of the bed as if it needed reassuring as much as Aurelia. "Well, Elisedd is a good man. And he's been married for some time. But he and his wife only have one daughter, as far as I know."

Aurelia opened her mouth to protest, to tell her mother everything that happened in the stables and to request she send aid to Alanna. But she considered the other option: *a quest of her own.* Something she knew that her parents did not. This was something she could dig deeper into. Something she could have control over. Somebody *she* could help.

"All right," she said, giving a yawn and an exaggerated stretch.

"I'll let you rest. I'm sure there will be much to hear about in the morning regarding your father and brother."

Aurelia bid her mother good night, and when she closed the heavy door behind her, Aurelia turned on her side to face the trio of flickering candles next to her bed. She watched the flames, her mind dancing as excitedly as the light.

Perhaps Drest was right. Maybe the woman they encountered in the barn was a common thief, looking for a way to their wealth. But Aurelia could hardly think such a thing before she knew it couldn't be true. The way Jastyn carried herself, as if she carried so much in each movement; the look in her eyes when Aurelia told her there was nothing she could do to help Alanna, as if she had encountered another inevitable obstacle in her life. All of this made Aurelia confident that Jastyn couldn't have been lying. She nodded as if to reinforce her final verdict on Jastyn's character, then blew out the candle.

But another thought occurred to her: how was it her mother believed that Jastyn didn't even *exist*?

CHAPTER EIGHT

Jastyn pushed aside a low-hanging branch on her way to Eegit's meadow. Her insides had been in a knot for the last week, and she had finally worked herself up to visit the hedgewitch. For nearly eight days, she had mulled over whether or not to go, her mother's worries at Eegit's ability to take such matters seriously echoing through her mind. But Alanna's cough grew worse. Fits shook her body over breakfast and kept her from sleep in midnight hours. Finally, Jastyn couldn't stand to watch the brave smile her sister wore for another minute.

Thus, after Elisedd left for the castle at dawn, Alanna went to sell woven goods at the market, and Branna took their second chicken to be sold, Jastyn went out into the Wood. She grabbed an apple from a grove she passed along the way. Chewing on it nervously, she checked multiple times that the handful of gooseberries her mother had picked that morning was still tucked into a cloth inside her satchel.

Jastyn fought the unease crawling over her skin and making her fingers tremble. She tried to let the green leaves that hung down heavy with last night's rain—comfort her anxious limbs. But even the quiet of the deep Wood, where she carried herself by memory between trees and over exposed roots, could not lift the heaviness she felt inside. Eventually, she stepped from the shadows and out into the sunlit meadow, where, despite the humidity, an orange fire glowed brightly outside of Eegit's modest hut.

Before Jastyn could greet her, Eegit—crouched in front of a pile of charred bones and crumpled leaves—spoke first.

"Child, if you've come to stomp around my home, now is not the time."

Jastyn replied, "Stomp? Eegit, I could surprise a tree-dweller, I know my way so well."

Eegit guffawed. "Ha! I heard you coming for the last half hour."

Moving to stand beside Eegit, Jastyn crossed her arms over the worn tunic that fell to her knees. "Does this warm welcome mean you're closer to bottling luck?"

Eegit swayed slightly. She extended a shaky hand over the fire, and a fistful of shimmering dust fell into the flames. They smoked and flickered a faint gold, making Jastyn step back at the brightness.

"Not yet," Eegit eventually replied, more to herself than to Jastyn. "But I won a bundle of pixie dust from the tree nymph two knolls away." She stuck her tongue out between her teeth, seemingly transfixed by the fire. "I'm getting closer."

Eegit stood, wiping the rest of the dust on her torn breeches. She shuffled around to the other side of the fire while muttering under her breath. Meanwhile, Jastyn paced nearby, fingering the bracelet inside the pocket of her tunic.

"Out with it, child," Eegit cried. "You're only doing yourself harm biting your tongue like that."

With a sigh, Jastyn pulled the bracelet out and held it in her palm so that the rubies glinted under the warm sun beginning to peek from the clouds overhead. Before she could inhale, Eegit was in front of her, bent over the silver bracelet, a grin stretching from one jutted cheekbone to the other.

"Child! Where did you find such a thing!"

A familiar sense of pride welled in her chest. As a result, the anxiety from her walk here began to dissipate.

"It's from the Princess Diarmaid."

Eegit snapped her head up so quickly that Jastyn was nearly bowled over by the tangled nest of hair atop it. Her eyes lit up.

"Princess Aurelia Diarmaid? Daughter of Grannus and the humble Dechtire Diarmaid?"

Jastyn hastily recounted the tale. As she expected, Eegit only blinked at her story, then glanced back down at the piece of jewelry when Jastyn finished with Alanna growing worse each day.

"I need your help," she concluded, ignoring the way her own voice cracked. "There's no one to trade this with in the village. I could buy out the alchemist, but his remedies are useless. I was wondering if you might know someone who could help. Somebody…in the Wood."

Eegit's chapped lips twitched, and she gestured for the bracelet. She looked it over like a herder mining through a sheep's wool for ticks. She held it up to the sky, shook it, and even licked one of the red gemstones. With her arms crossed, Jastyn watched, resisting the urge to hurry the process along.

"Curious…this princess…to hand such a thing off to a perfect stranger." She squinted, staring into the metal band.

Jastyn let out a laugh. "Curious is right. Here I thought the royals were educated. What could she possibly think something like this could do for Alanna?" She pictured the princess lounging inside a castle chamber, munching on slices of cheese and counting her many fine possessions.

Her face hot with renewed frustration, it took Jastyn a minute to realize Eegit was watching her with a knowing smile.

"What?"

"You'll find out, child."

Jastyn was about to ask what she meant, but Eegit returned her gaze to the bracelet after handing it back. "I may know of someone."

Hardly able to contain her excitement, Jastyn leapt forward. "You do? I knew you would." She paused when Eegit eyed her. "Well, *Coran* knew you would. How *do* you do that, by the way?"

Eegit only waved a hand and strolled toward a collection of rotten apple cores, berry leaves, and crusts of bread lying next to a melon-sized boulder a few paces away. After digging through the pile, she pulled out the remains of a half-eaten apple, picking off bugs and specks of dirt.

"You wish to trade this bracelet, is that right?" Eegit asked, walking back to the fire where an open box of herbs sat near the circle of stones surrounding the flames.

"I do. For Alanna. I don't know how much time she has…" Jastyn trailed off. She cleared her throat and ran a hand down her braid. "Please. I'll do anything."

"Very well," Eegit said, plucking a rectangular vial from the box and standing in front of Jastyn. "I know somebody who may be willing to trade."

"Anyone. I'll go."

Eegit held Jastyn's gaze for a long moment. "What do you know of the Red One?"

Jastyn thought back to the stories her mother told her as a child. They had spent almost every night before her mother's marriage huddled close together by the hearth while her mother told her of the many fae who were said to roam the Wood.

"Do you mean the leprechauns?" she eventually asked.

"Not just any leprechauns…*the* leprechaun. The Red One is the Elder, the head of all leprechaun clans that dwell in the woods of this kingdom and beyond."

"All right," Jastyn replied, rubbing her hands together. "Tell me where I can find this Red One."

"Do you know the brook that lies near the druid's meadow?"

She nodded. Of course she knew that meadow and everything surrounding it. It wasn't far from where, twelve years before, she met the sinister fae from all her mother's tales.

Willing herself not to linger on those memories and the dark rider, Jastyn watched Eegit crouch before the fire once more. She held the apple core, gnawed on and grimy, and dropped two liquid droplets from the vial on it. The core glowed a dull yellow, then all at once, the formerly rotten apple remains became whole again and were coated in gold.

"Craving something expensive?" Jastyn asked playfully.

Eegit grunted and stood. "You'll need this for your trade." She held the golden apple up.

"But I've got the bracelet. That's what I'm offering."

Eegit clucked her tongue. "The Red One is not your everyday barterer for shiny coins, child. You will need to coax it into a deal. Entice it…with this."

"Fine." Jastyn groaned, taking the apple from Eegit's hand. "Anything else I should know?"

Eegit looked into the sky. Thin clouds drifted by, and sunlight shone down between them. "Yes," she muttered. "When the moon is exactly half-full. That is when the Red One will be ready to meet."

"That's in nearly two weeks!" Panic clanged in her chest, and she struggled to keep her composure. "Eegit, that's too long."

Her eyes fixed skyward, Eegit tilted her head as if to see the clouds better. "Yes. Half-full. And you should be grateful, child. The Red

One only appears for trade three times each year." She shrugged and wandered back to the fire, which had faded to dull embers.

Disheartened, Jastyn pictured Alanna shivering beneath her blankets for the next two weeks. Her fists clenched in new rage, and she glared at the clouds. Jastyn felt spiteful looking up at the billowing shapes. Perhaps she could will the sky to change over. Perhaps she could make the moon go through her phases faster. She cursed the endless gray. Couldn't somebody understand how her sister suffered?

"I recommend carrying some of those gooseberries when you go." Jastyn returned her focus to Eegit, who sharpened the end of a brittle bone with a rock. "The Red One always appreciates something sweet."

Rolling her eyes, Jastyn walked dejectedly toward the trees that led her home. She kicked a rock on the matted grass patch with the toe of her boot when all of a sudden, Eegit popped in front of her, clear out of thin air.

"Gods!" Jastyn cried, stumbling back. "I forgot you could do that!"

But Eegit's face was serious. She raised her bony, vein-riddled right hand and spoke in a hurried whisper. "Be warned, child. Do not take this trade lightly. The Red One is one of the cleverest fae to ever live. They survive on wit alone to get what they need. What they want." She held out her hand, and Jastyn was surprised to see the princess's bracelet. Fumbling, she grabbed at her pocket and felt the thin outline of the band.

"But..."

"Do not believe everything you see," Eegit said slowly. Then she flourished, and the bracelet transformed into a thin green snake that slithered up her arm.

A shudder overcame Jastyn, and she swallowed to quench the dryness in her throat.

"The Red One will look into your mind. It will try to offer you more...try to tempt you." She stepped forward, her eyes wide as they looked into Jastyn's face. "Do not allow it to fool you. No matter how enticing the offer appears to be. Do you understand?"

Jastyn nodded. "I will stand my ground. I always do."

Eegit's beady gaze held Jastyn's a moment longer. Then, her eyes flickered, and she yanked a twig out from somewhere on the back of her hair. After examining it for a few seconds, she glanced up as if remembering Jastyn was still there.

"Go on, child!" She waved and hurried away, back to the fire.

Slightly bewildered, Jastyn shook her head. Then she called over her shoulder, "Thank you, Eegit. I won't forget your advice."

Once she was a few paces into the trees, Jastyn smiled when Eegit shouted after her. "And don't forget the gooseberries, either!"

CHAPTER NINE

Please, Roisin. I cannot bear to go through more of this!" Aurelia exhaled loudly, throwing her arms onto the wooden table. Her maiden sat across from her, draped in one of Aurelia's old gray cloaks which she had unclasped over her wide frame to bring some relief from the warm night air. Roisin scooted back in her chair as the princess flung her head down atop her left elbow.

"M'lady," she said sympathetically, leafing through several pages of the leather-bound botanical book open between them, "we've only ten pages left."

Aurelia moaned and looked up imploringly. "You would think I knew enough of this by now that my mother wouldn't require we review such trivial nonsense."

"Trivial nonsense? Is that what you call healing magic these days?" Her mother's voice called from the corner of the room. She stood in front of a floor-to-ceiling bookcase packed tightly with jars and tin boxes containing herbs and crushed plants, the contents of which Aurelia knew so well that she could find whatever remedy within them blindfolded.

Under the gaze of her mother, Roisin shrank in her seat, but Aurelia only sighed and sat up. "No, Mother. You must have heard me incorrectly."

"I must have. Roisin," she added, "kindly resume the lesson."

"Yes, m'lady." She and Aurelia exchanged guilty looks. "Let's see. What if you're out in the Wood and you get bit by a spider? What do you need?"

"Plantain. *Plantago major*. A low, short plant with wide and round leaves. Its veins run parallel," Aurelia stated, running her hand along the edge of the table.

Roisin nodded and turned a page when Aurelia's mother spoke. "That was very good, darling."

Aurelia stood and moved across the room to join her mother, who added several new bunches of yarrow herb to a box wearing the same hand-written label. Seeming to read Aurelia's mind, she said, "Sweetheart, I understand you are anxious to put your skills to practice." Aurelia leaned against the wall near a window that overlooked the stables. "Soon we will go together into the village. We will make a day of it."

"You've said that since I was sixteen."

Her mother's eyes crinkled at their corners. She adjusted the pin at her breast, then reached out to run her fingers through Aurelia's hair.

"I promise," she said softly. Then she grabbed both of Aurelia's hands and held them. "But not right now. It's too much, what with—"

"With everything that is going on. I know," Aurelia finished, wandering back over to where Roisin sat half watching their exchange, half reading.

Her mother was about to reply when the door to the room opened. Brennus strode in, his hair bouncing with each jovial step.

"We head out at first light!" he declared. Even the puffy sleeves of his tunic seemed unable to contain their excitement as they billowed above his shoulders.

"Tomorrow?" Aurelia said after a moment, glancing from him to her mother, then back again.

His smile was wide as he stood beside their mother. "Everything is ready. Baron Louarn will accompany me and Drest to the west. Once we pass through the Wood, it's only a four-day journey to the Mountains of Ionad. After that, we return home."

Aurelia hardly heard Roisin wish him well; her mind was so overcome with pride but even more so, with envy. She smiled, but it was strained, and she hoped her jealousy wasn't as evident as it felt.

Their mother's voice pulled her from her thoughts. "The baron knows the Wood well. He will not lead you astray." The words sounded less like a reassurance for Brennus, and more as a reminder to herself. She reached out and cupped Brennus's cheek. "My dear, brave boy."

Brennus leaned into her palm, then reached up to hold her hand. "Don't worry, Mother. I'm in good hands."

The gleam in their mother's eye allowed Aurelia to focus, and she cleared her throat. "And Brennus is more than ready for such an outing." She gave him an encouraging nod.

Their mother's face shifted, and she wiped her eyes. "Darling, do tell your sister there is a time for everything…and hers will come. I fear she does not believe me."

After throwing Aurelia a knowing look, Brennus said, "Understood. I'll see to it that these two return to your lesson plan."

Their mother gave his hand a final, grateful pat. Then she bid them good night and excused herself, closing the door behind her.

Once she was gone, Brennus turned to them. "Another herbal lesson?"

Roisin raised the book for him to see. "'Fraid so, Your Highness." She gestured to Aurelia, who had returned to the open window. She could just make out the towers of haystacks lining the stable's edge, their dark shadows piled high where Coran left them. Her mind conjured the memory of Jastyn; Aurelia wondered if the stable boy had spoken to her lately. They seemed to be good friends, as far as she could tell from her brief encounter. Perhaps she could ask him more about Jastyn—the mysterious daughter of no one.

"Thinking of anybody in particular?"

Aurelia turned. The nearby torchlight felt as if it was right against her face at the look Brennus gave her. She mirrored his stance, crossing her arms. Tilting her chin upward, she said, "That is none of your concern."

He chuckled and exchanged looks with Roisin, who pursed her lips and pretended to read. Over the past couple of weeks, Aurelia had taken to asking Roisin about their horse master and his family; only now did she realize how often those inquiries ended up back at Jastyn. Jastyn, who left Aurelia with more questions than answers—something she was unaccustomed to.

"Anyway." Aurelia brushed back her hair and pushed the conversation along. "I'm happy for you, Brennus. The adventures you'll have…" She glanced outside once more, her voice wistful. "One can only imagine the things you'll see."

Brennus sifted through several papers strewn across the table. "It's only a scouting party. We'll not have much in the way of fun."

Aurelia sighed. "Nonetheless. You're getting out." She rejoined them at the table, taking her seat. "I'll be here, memorizing plant properties."

"Itching for some real-world practice, are we?" Brennus teased, glancing at his sister.

"Dyin' for it," Roisin answered for her.

Aurelia slumped her chin into her upturned palm, her left elbow planted firmly on the table. "At this rate, I'd settle for a sick calf to tend to in the stables," she muttered.

Brennus reached out, grabbing a letter opener. His eyes sparkled. He flipped the black onyx handle, the blade shimmering. "I may be able to help."

Before she could ask how, Aurelia gasped when her brother stuck out his left arm and—in one swift motion—dragged the tip of the letter opener from his bare, upturned wrist all the way to his elbow.

"Your Highness!" Roisin leapt from her chair, as did Aurelia. Meanwhile, Brennus lifted the blade; its tip dripped blood and the slit left behind in his skin began to seep red.

"Are you mad?" Aurelia cried, standing and shocked. Her brother, grimacing now, leaned against the table with his other hand.

"You want real healing practice?" he asked breathlessly. "Now's your chance."

Aurelia was frozen, watching the gash in her brother's arm grow wider and pouring more blood by the second. The end of his blue tunic, just above the crook in his arm, was now a dark shade of purple where it fell into the blood.

Brennus swayed but held Aurelia's gaze. "Well, what are you waiting for?"

Roisin whispered, "M'lady, what do we do?"

Aurelia, mouth agape, took a deep breath. Then she sprang forward, pressing both of her hands onto Brennus's exposed forearm.

"I've got to stop the bleeding. Roisin, please, go over to my mother's shelves. Near the bottom, look for meadowsweet. It should be labeled. Quickly!"

Roisin, her face awash with panic, hiked up her cloak and rushed to the far corner of the room. As she rifled through various boxes and bowls of herbs, Aurelia stared at her brother.

"Have you completely lost your mind?"

His eyes were growing foggy, but his voice remained strong. "Would you consider this more or less exciting than the time we accidentally set fire to Baroness Enya's favorite dress?"

Aurelia shook her head. "All I've ever known are books." She swallowed. "You put too much faith in others. How do you know I have any idea what I'm doing?"

Roisin was back, a fistful of tiny, white-tipped herbs in hand.

Brennus winced when Aurelia squeezed his forearm tighter; trickles of blood ran between her fingers and down the back of her wrists.

"The same way I know this scouting party will lead to nothing. Aurelia...you are more capable than you know. Trust yourself."

"Miss," Roisin held out the herb, shaking slightly.

"Stop thinking," Brennus said, his voice stern. "Don't dwell on what could be. Just act."

Lingering only a moment more, amazed at the wildness of her brother's methods, Aurelia turned to Roisin. "Here, do as I have. Apply as much pressure as you can."

Bewildered, Roisin obliged. Aurelia gathered the herbs and quickly wrung them together, crushing the petals between her palms. Brennus groaned under Roisin's grip.

"Apologies, Prince Brennus," she said.

"Don't bother," Aurelia said, reaching down to the hem of her blue dress. "He doesn't deserve it, this crazy brother of mine."

Brennus grinned. It looked as if Roisin's sturdy grip had stopped the bleeding some, but his face had lost a lot of color. Aurelia grabbed a seam and tore a long stretch of cloth from her skirt.

"M'lady, your dress!"

Aurelia shot Roisin a look, then spread what had become a floral paste across the cloth with the heel of her palm. She rubbed both ends of the torn strip together to ensure that the herb settled into the material. The dull pink from the blood on her hands mixing with the white herb made her stomach turn.

"All right," she said, brushing away droplets of sweat from her hairline. "When I say, remove your hands."

Roisin nodded, and after a count to three, Aurelia replaced Roisin's hands with a poultice of meadowsweet against Brennus's arm. He cringed at the new pressure but leaned his neck back, relieved.

Aurelia caught her breath, watching carefully as the herb worked to clot the blood. Small rivulets of red halted their path under the cloth beneath her hands.

"It's working," she said, exhaustion replacing the brief wave of relief that washed over her.

"I never doubted you for a minute."

Aurelia looked incredulously at Brennus while Roisin, letting out a bellowing sigh, collapsed into a chair.

"Gods! The two of you will send me on my own mad journey someday, won't you?" She wiped her flushed neck with the end of her cloak, breathing heavily.

Eventually, Aurelia lifted the poultice. She and Brennus examined the line—no thicker than a thumbnail—running the length of his forearm. The bright red stood out so much against Brennus's fair skin, for a second, Aurelia believed it to be drawn on, like a line of crushed berry juice.

Still staring at the self-inflicted wound on her brother's arm, Aurelia's surroundings returned to focus as if she waked from a vivid dream. She could smell the sweat lingering in the air. And she could once again hear the fire crackling in its hearth behind them. The sound filled the silence.

"There are other ways to teach me things," she said eventually, her voice low.

Brennus sat down so Roisin could wrap the wound, using what was left of the torn scrap from Aurelia's dress. Brennus sighed. "I'm sorry. That was rather rash."

Aurelia scoffed. But Brennus continued. "I only wanted you to understand..." He leaned forward. "Mother and Father have their doubts regarding you and me. They believe they know what's best for us by keeping us locked inside this place." He gestured to the high ceiling, the roaring fire. "But we are capable of so much more than they can even imagine." Aurelia hung on his words, forgetting briefly the terror that had overcome her not five minutes before. Brennus had a way of doing that. His eloquence was incomparable. And now, in his voice, she saw the future king of Venostes speaking to his people, reassuring them as he was doing for her now. "That's why it's up to you and me to remind one another of what we can do. Especially when it is most impossible to believe."

After tying the end of the cloth, Roisin excused herself and went to replace the herbs on the bookcase. Aurelia looked at her brother: her clever and patient older brother who had trudged through two decades of castle life by her side. Her brother, who taught her the magic their parents discouraged, who wallowed with her when their mother and father never let them wander beyond the castle's walls. Brennus, who let Aurelia be completely herself even if, at times, she wasn't sure who that self was.

The tears surprised her, and Aurelia blinked to hide them. Brennus's own eyes shined, and he reached toward her.

"One day, you and I will do great things for this kingdom."

"You mean *you* will," she corrected.

"Nonsense. I will marry, certainly. But you will be as much a queen as she."

Aurelia glanced up through bleary eyes. "One day," she echoed, as if saying it aloud might help her see this future her brother promised so eagerly. This future he could see like a rare, clear day along the shore. Yet, despite the brightness in his eyes, Aurelia only saw her own reflection, frightened at the possibilities of tomorrow.

"It will be a grand adventure," Brennus said, squeezing her hand once more. Gingerly, he stood to go.

Once he was at the door, his injured arm close to his chest, Aurelia said, "I will miss you, brother."

Brennus looked back. His face bright with color. She felt a pang of sadness against her heart but also a swelling of joy at what was to come.

Before closing the door behind him, Brennus waved and called out, "You won't even know that I'm gone."

CHAPTER TEN

W hen will you go?"
Jastyn stared at the fire that had been burning in the hearth since midday. She watched the tips of the orange flames as they flickered, emitting soot and ash that clung to the already charred rock. Her mother sat in her chair, and Jastyn sat beside her on the floor, leaning against one side.

"I'll leave tomorrow," Jastyn replied, her voice low. "At sundown."

Her mother, who had been mending a patch in the sleeve of one of Alanna's tunics, nodded while her hands continued to thread together a seam. Despite the near darkness of the house, her hands worked methodically on the worn material.

"Elisedd thinks I'm going to the river for fish?"

Her mother tugged on a blue thread, then cut it easily with her teeth. She eyed her handiwork. "Yes. I've already told him…we need the meat, so he didn't think much of it."

Jastyn pulled one knee up to her chest. Her boot scraped along the earthen floor. Absentmindedly, she ran her fingers along the handle of the blade in its woven sheath strapped to her right ankle. It wasn't uncommon for her mother to weave stories for Elisedd. He disapproved of her outings into the Wood, she knew that, and had for years.

Once, when she was thirteen and just returned from spending a week with Eegit exploring an abandoned dwarf cave, Mother told Jastyn that while she was gone, Elisedd had feared for her safety. That day, her mother had spoken in a hushed voice. She explained that her stepfather once had a brother who sold crystals in the market. According to her, he had gone into the Wood—years ago, before the treaty—after learning of a creek bed said to have a coating of gold at its bottom. He went out in search of it one day, ventured deep into the Wood, and never returned.

Upon learning this, Jastyn had felt sorry for Elisedd. She could only imagine losing a sibling, the reality of which became more of a possibility once Alanna's fits began. But as she grew older, Jastyn felt that Elisedd feared less for her well-being and was actually more afraid of losing an easy target for his overbearing nature. If she wasn't around, Alanna would be smothered under the weight of his need to protect her. As a result, even though she wasn't fond of his berating her each time she left, Jastyn came to the conclusion that their icy relationship drew from the same well: their love for Alanna.

Thus, he scolded her each time for being gone, but Jastyn always came back.

"You'll say good-bye to your sister."

It was not a question. When she explained that she was going to seek a trade with a leprechaun, her mother's forehead had crinkled, but the concern stayed within the lines of her face. This was merely one of many desperate measures Jastyn took to make a life for them. It was not something to discuss, just something that had to be done.

Swallowing, Jastyn said, "Yes. I'll see her before I go."

The torrent of coughs that erupted from the dark doorway leading into the room she shared with Alanna sent a shiver up her back. She shifted to face the fire, extending her hands for warmth. Her mother rested her needle and thread in her lap and watched the flames, too. Then she reached out and ran a hand down Jastyn's braid. They sat like that for a while: mother and daughter idle as they watched the last flames skipping atop crumbling logs. The door swung open behind them, creaking on its shabby hinges and blowing cold night air through the room, nearly chasing away the remaining firelight. Elisedd stomped inside, a pile of fresh logs bundled in his arms. He shook the wet air from his cloak like a dog.

Jastyn turned when he kicked off his muddy boots and made his way across the small living space to drop the firewood next to her. Standing, he clapped his hands to rid them of dirt and tree bark splinters.

"Thank you for collecting more," Mother said, smiling up at him.

He nodded, and the corners of his mouth twitched upward. Then he cleared his throat. "The fire won't make itself." He folded his sleeves and retired to the corner of the room where a table with several broken horseshoes waited for him.

Silently, Jastyn added two fresh logs to the hearth. Once the fire crackled and burned with new life, she bid her mother good night and went to bed.

That night, she dreamt of him again. The Dark Fae and his black horse. In her dream, both of their eyes glowed red like a thousand piercing suns, blinding her until she cried out.

A dull force bumped her shoulder, and she turned, expecting to come face-to-face with the rider and his beast.

"Jastyn, wake up." Her eyes flew open, and Jastyn looked into Alanna's tired eyes. Her sister sat beside her in their bed. She looked pale—or maybe it was only the moonlight throwing itself on her through the cracks in the shudders. "You were dreaming again."

Jastyn propped herself on her elbows and worked to calm her breathing. Alanna tugged one of their shabby blankets over her own shoulders and laid the other on top of Jastyn, who had kicked it off in the night.

"Thank you," Jastyn said.

"Were you dreaming of him?"

Alanna knew of Jastyn's encounter in the Wood. Of course, Jastyn had omitted a few things…like his claiming she was a *gan 'athair*. His accusation of her not knowing who her father was crushed her. And while not completely untrue, such a claim would only prompt more questions than Jastyn cared to have answers to. She kept the worst of her nightmares to herself. Alanna had enough to worry about.

"It was nothing," Jastyn said, pushing herself up so they were face-to-face. She took in her sister's appearance: her oval face looked shallower, and her nose seemed to jut out more than it did before. Yet even the dark circles around her eyes couldn't dull the curious spark lit within them.

"Really," Jastyn said. "I'm all right. Anyway, aren't I the one who should be taking care of you?" Jastyn reached out to feel Alanna's forehead. Her knuckles pressed gently against the warm flesh.

Alanna glanced down, fiddling with one edge of the blanket.

"You're leaving again, aren't you?"

Jastyn lowered her hand. "You really are the smart one. Are you sure you aren't a Seer?"

Alanna giggled but shook her head. "That's what happens when you're stuck in one place. The tiniest details begin to stand out." She paused. "Like the way you take to bringing me more sweets from the market right before your trips."

Guilty, Jastyn bowed her chin. "Nothing gets by you."

They sat in the still air, letting the weight of what was to come fill the quiet. After a while, Alanna took a shuddering breath.

"Jastyn, please, be careful."

Jastyn nudged her arm. "You know I always am."

They shared a smile. "I know. But…this trip is different, isn't it?"

Jastyn bit the inside of her cheek and struggled to hold her sister's gaze. Alanna spoke again. "Mother and Father treat me like a helpless fawn. But I'm not a fool." Her voice grew louder, which triggered a series of coughs. Jastyn moved to fetch her a cup of water, but Alanna shook her head. "I'm okay. Well, maybe I'm not. But…" She met Jastyn's eyes. "That's the point. I know the medicine isn't working. I can feel it." She lifted one hand to her chest and held it there on top of her worn, gray tunic. "Whatever it is you're going after this time, I hope you find it."

Puzzled, Jastyn said, "Alanna, I know what I'm after this time… and it *will* help you."

More coughs sprang from deep within her sister's chest. They were sharp and shook her terribly. Jastyn reached out, holding her knees until they subsided. Alanna looked exhausted when she took a shaky breath.

"You know what I could use?" Jastyn said. "Some of that never-ending strength of yours."

Alanna grinned. "You're the strong one."

"Not all strength is swiftness and cunning."

Her eyes lingering on the window, Alanna said, "I wish I could go with you."

Tears welled in her eyes, forcing Jastyn to look away. Alanna tugged her closer, pulling her into a hug. Holding Alanna, Jastyn grew more determined to get what she needed from the Red One. She would not waver, no matter what tricks they tried to play on her. She would come back with a cure. There was no other option.

"I wish you could, too," Jastyn muttered into her sister's neck. She watched the candle burning dimly on the table beside them and couldn't help but see her sister as the flickering light, fighting against the fast-fading wick.

"Come on," Alanna said, pulling Jastyn from her thoughts. They both wiped their eyes and fell back onto the bed. "We had better sleep. You've got an adventure waiting for you tomorrow."

They lay side by side. Jastyn kissed Alanna's cheek. A cool wind gusted through the cracks in the shudders. Their candlelight blew out. Alanna shivered, and Jastyn tucked a blanket closer to her. Her eyes heavy but her heart light, Jastyn fell into a dreamless sleep.

The next morning, warm air had enveloped the rolling village hills. Gray clouds stretched across the skies. The sun peeking over the horizon signaled the day was nigh for Jastyn's meeting with the Red One.

Elisedd left for the castle early. Mother swept and saw to Alanna's reading lesson after lunch. Jastyn sat beside her sister most of the day, taking in each trail of laughter, each emphatic recitation from her book. The three of them laughed and laughed, and Jastyn dreamed the day would go on forever.

But as the sun set, Jastyn helped her mother tuck Alanna into bed.

"I'll be back soon. And you'll be on your way to feeling better," Jastyn whispered to her sister before placing a kiss on her temple.

Alanna's voice was thick with drowsiness. "Be careful, Jastyn."

❖

The nighttime babble from the druid's brook sent Jastyn into a reverie on the last, long stretch of her journey. She clasped the sack slung over her shoulder and felt through the worn cloth at its contents: the firm exterior of Eegit's golden apple, the suppler bundle of red gooseberries, and at the bottom, the princess's bracelet.

Jastyn exhaled, trying to focus once more on the hypnotizing gurgle of the nearby water. Through the thinning branches, she spotted the meadow. The sight of her destination worked her nerves up into a new bundle so that now, despite hundreds of visits to these woods, she began to tremble.

The blue saol she had conjured hours ago, at the bend of the river that wound around her part of the village, bounced gently in front of her, providing a constant reminder that it, at least, was by her side.

Jastyn walked slowly into the druid's meadow, farther from the comforting conversation of the brook. Her eyes had adjusted to the darkness, and they fell on the pair of trees lying ashen and petrified across the clearing. Not even their leaves had escaped the druid's curse all those years ago; they, too, resembled pale rock, forever caught in an unchanging wind.

Moonlight from the half moon shone down with a dull glow onto the knee-high grass. This meadow was smaller than Eegit's, roughly the length of three village houses. Fairies' nests tucked into the thick tree branches glowed faintly along the perimeter. Their scattered light created a pale, staggered halo surrounding the meadow, and Jastyn was grateful for their presence. Her saol bobbed two paces ahead as she walked toward the center of the clearing.

It hit her then that she was never specifically told where the Red One would meet her, and the realization sent a jolt to her fingers, which clutched the strap of the sack tighter while she turned to scan the nearby tree trunks. She'd had only two previous encounters with leprechauns—if she could even call them encounters. One was with Coran not long after they first met. They had taken to scouting the market together for items that were prime for swiping, and one day, he suggested they hunt for fallen coins along the dirt-laden streets. On a bitterly cold morning when Jastyn could barely feel the tips of her fingers, the two of them crept beneath vendor stalls where merchants and customers often dropped change during a transaction. Jastyn was about to snatch up a gold coin that fell with a dull thud when Coran stretched out his arm.

"Wait," he said. "Look."

Jastyn, frowning, sat back and stared at the coin. There was a flash of green. What looked like the faint outline of a person appeared, only the person was the size of her hand. A face no larger than the pad of her finger held a pair of tiny, beady eyes. Just like that, the figure seemed to gobble up the fallen coin and was gone.

"That," Coran had told her, his voice awestruck, "was a leprechaun."

Jastyn had been less than impressed. To her, they were nothing but thieves with an unfair advantage over her in that they were the size of a pear and nearly invisible. The second encounter had happened when she was twelve and had gone to barter with Eegit. Once again, Jastyn only caught a faint glimpse of the creature while she watched Eegit from a nearby bush. It looked as if she was bargaining with thin air. Any flash of green Jastyn could catch always seemed to be moving, never staying in one spot for longer than a second.

"Slippery creatures," Eegit had said afterward. "Cunning shapeshifters, they are. Can't let 'em talk too much, or before you can sneeze, they'll be off with the shoes on your feet!"

These memories lingered at the front of Jastyn's mind as she waited in the middle of the meadow. She reminded herself that this encounter would most likely be very different from the others. While young leprechauns were small and generally benign, the longer they lived, the more adept at shapeshifting they became. Many took human form, and some even chose to lead a human life and live among the kingdom. The Red One, she had a feeling, would be unlike the others. Jastyn would have to be careful.

Looking up at the moon, she took a deep breath. Her left hand pinched the bracelet at the bottom of the sack, the emptiness of the meadow instilling the need to check that her bargaining items were still there. Feeling the thin band of the bracelet, she smiled. It was hard to believe, still, that the princess had figured *this* as Alanna's best chance to live. She imagined the princess stumbling upon somebody else in trouble, perhaps a man drifted out to sea. She pictured Aurelia, shocked and confused, removing a necklace from around her neck and tossing it at the man's flailing arms.

"Ridiculous," Jastyn mumbled.

A rustling shook the grass, followed by the *creak* of what sounded like an old door opening then closing. She spun around, her saol disappearing, then reappearing in front of her. The edge of the clearing was crowded with shadows, and Jastyn squinted into the darkness toward the source of the noise. She thought she saw the slight outline of someone begin toward her. It quickly vanished, and the gentle fall of footsteps came from off to the right.

"Who's there?" she called.

The footsteps halted, then started from behind her again. She spun around once more, her saol following. She resisted the urge to go for the blade in the side of her boot. When she called out again and received no answer, Jastyn pulled her shoulders back.

"My name is Jastyn," she stated, willing her voice to steady. "I've come seeking the Red One." Peering into the dark, she was sure this time she saw a figure slowly moving closer. The shadow was small, half her height, but seemed to shift and grow with each step.

"I've come to make a trade," she said, but as soon as the words left her mouth, the figure vanished again. Faint laughter echoed over the trees. Growing frustrated, she allowed a hint of desperation into her voice when she shouted, "Please, I don't have much time!"

After a moment, a voice—neither male nor female—answered from the dark. "There never is enough, is there? The more we wish it stood still, the faster it flees from our grasp."

Jastyn's lips pursed in agitation. Her saol drew nearer, and she gazed beyond the blue light. "Show yourself. I don't like games."

Jastyn jumped when the voice spoke from directly behind her. "Oh, but I love them."

Her sack hit against her hip as she stumbled over the thick grass before her gaze landed on the most breathtaking woman Jastyn had ever seen. Her beauty struck Jastyn in a way that stirred something below her stomach. Even in the half moonlight and faint blue glow from her saol, the woman was vibrant. She stood an inch shorter than Jastyn and had incredibly thick, dark hair. She was not from the village or even the kingdom with features like hers. Dark brown eyes—like the riverbank's edge after a heavy rain—were set wide on her broad face. When the woman moved to stand perpendicular to her, a loose pair of red pants swished, and the fabric rustled, and a faint jingle drew Jastyn's eyes to a slim gold chain running around her bare midriff. Sepia brown skin was exposed below a top that barely covered a robust chest and strong shoulders.

Jastyn, still flustered by the woman and the sweet scent coming from the depths of her luscious hair, stuttered.

"You...you are the Red One?"

The woman circled Jastyn, stopping just on the other side of the flickering saol. Her smile revealed a gap between two large front teeth. "I am." She placed one hand covered in intricate black ink designs on her wide hip. Jastyn swallowed. "Not what you were expecting?"

Jastyn shook her head, prompting laughter from the woman. Then her stomach dropped when the woman reached out and ran a finger down her cheek.

"You may call me Rua. Now, what is it you wish to trade?"

The saol cracked as if to reclaim Jastyn's attention. She blinked at the light, then looked back into the mesmerizing gaze Rua had fixed on her. That was when, in the back of her mind, she recalled Eegit's words. The Red One was a shapeshifter. Eegit had said they could look into her mind, perhaps even into her deepest desires. Jastyn's face was hot at the Red One's ability to bring to life something Jastyn had only shared with her mother and Coran. Nevertheless, she reminded herself this was merely a trick of the mind, and she faced Rua.

"I have a feeling you already know what I'm here for," she said.

Rua tilted her head, the moonlight catching the golden hoop wrapped around the right side of her nose. "You need medicine," Rua replied casually, beginning to wander around the meadow. "But not for yourself."

"It's for my sister, Alanna."

Pausing, Rua turned. "Half sister."

Jastyn clenched her jaw, reminding herself to ignore this attempt to rattle her. "She's very sick. I was told you can offer me a cure."

Examining her own body art snaking down her wrists, Rua nodded. "What do you have for me?"

Watching the Red One, Jastyn reached into the sack for the golden apple. When she held it out, a lotus flower revealed itself on Rua's palm before she snatched up the fruit. The image gripped Jastyn's mind, and she remembered something. The sounds of a festival. Smells of roasting meat. Music she had never heard before.

As Rua gleefully admired the golden apple, Jastyn fell back into a nearly forgotten memory. Years ago, a traveling band of musicians and dancers had arrived on the shores of Venostes one summer. Jastyn had been eleven, maybe twelve. She had ventured out on a rare visit to the market with her mother. The crowds were suffocating, but the buzz of anticipation to witness the foreign visitors was contagious. Jastyn had climbed up into a tree when the ship docked, and its inhabitants came ashore. She had never seen anybody like the dark-haired men and women with bejeweled bodies clad in bright clothing. Later, when the eclectic group set up a circle of lute players and dancers, Jastyn had been fixated on one in particular: a woman with lavish black hair, a sumptuous figure, and a gap-toothed smile.

That same woman stood in the meadow with her now, and the cleverness of the Red One washed over her.

Carefully, Jastyn spoke. "I offer you this token to gain your interest."

Rua eyed the apple in her left hand. "The way I've gained yours?" She tossed the fruit skyward, and it vanished. She stepped toward Jastyn. The saol shrank at Rua's closeness, and Jastyn was overwhelmed with the scent of unfamiliar sweetness. She found it hard to look anywhere but into the large pools of brown gazing back at her from behind long lashes.

Slowly, she reached into the satchel and grabbed hold of the bracelet. It was as if the metal knew a spell was being cast over Jastyn's mind because at the mere touch of her fingers, she blinked, and the fog cleared. She walked backward, firmly holding the bracelet and regaining her composure.

"I've come to trade. Nothing else," she added at Rua's inquisitive eyebrow.

"Pity."

Jastyn held the bracelet out. Rua's eyes flickered at the rubies shimmering under the moonlight that had begun to fade behind encroaching clouds. "Well, you do work hard to impress, don't you?"

Jastyn's lips twitched in a smile. "This is from the Kingdom of Venostes, given to me by the Princess Aurelia Diarmaid. This is what I offer for a cure for my sister."

A shadow shifted over them. They both glanced up as the clouds drifted past the moon, leaving them standing in nearly complete darkness. More clouds built overhead, dulling the stars. The air grew heavy, signaling what was sure to be a storm before the night was over.

Rua pulled Jastyn back to their conversation. "It's rare that I'm offered something as precious as this." Her eyes soaked up the rubies, then jumped to Jastyn. "You care for your half sister deeply."

Jastyn nodded. "She doesn't deserve to live half a life."

Rua clucked, once again eyeing the bracelet. "Such a curse…to be so young and suffer as she does."

Jastyn wondered how much the Red One knew of Alanna. It was

common knowledge through the kingdom that many fae had the gift of Sight. Some could See stronger than others. There were hundreds of stories featuring humans making deals with or trying to outsmart different fae. Only a few people ended with the upper hand. It was difficult to deal with those who knew one's strengths and weaknesses upon first glance.

It was quiet as Rua paced again, bracelet in hand. The sky rumbled, and drops of rain began to fall. Itching with irritation, Jastyn asked, "Well, what do you say?" Her boots were beginning to stick to the quickly dampening grass as more rain fell.

Rua, who had placed the bracelet on her own wrist, was taking in the jewelry under the increasing rain. After several moments, she said, "All business, you are. Don't you get tired always working for something? It seems exhausting, constantly thinking two steps ahead only to fall three behind."

The words hit Jastyn hard in her chest.

"Enough," she said, her voice growing louder. "Do we have a deal? The bracelet for a cure."

Rua sighed, her arm dropping to her side. "Very well." She turned, then vanished on the spot. Jastyn searched the dark in a panic, but there was a flash from behind her. Rua wrapped one hand around Jastyn's waist while the other stretched out below Jastyn's left arm. A clear vial stoppered with cloth was held between her thick thumb and forefinger. Her voice tickled Jastyn's ear when she said, "Here you go."

A clatter of thunder sent the rain into a steady downpour, and Jastyn blinked through the thickening strands of water before reaching out to take hold of the vial. Rua shifted again and reappeared before Jastyn, her fingers pushing the vial into Jastyn's grasp.

"This will cure my sister?" Jastyn looked at what appeared to be faint green smoke swirling about the inside of the glass.

Rua, who was now swaying with her eyes closed and her neck craned to allow the rain to dance along her face, said, "It will lead you to the cure for what ails Alanna."

Jastyn froze.

"This...this isn't a cure?" She tightened her grip on the vial. The rain made it hard to see. "But we had a deal."

"And I am a woman of my word," Rua cooed, stepping close again, her bare feet nearly stomping out the dim saol until they stood chest-to-chest. Jastyn swiped at the rain falling into her eyes. Droplets ran from Rua's temples and settled in the crease of a smile. Jastyn was about to respond when the bag slung over her shoulder shifted. There was a *pop*, and Rua held the bundle of gooseberries in her palm. She plucked one from inside the cloth, examining the bright orange of its skin. "To think, you weren't even going to offer me these. Where are your manners, Jastyn Cipher?"

Furious now, Jastyn could only stand and watch Rua toss several gooseberries into her mouth, emitting a joyful moan with each bite. Through gritted teeth, Jastyn finally muttered, "We had a deal."

Rua nodded. "Yes. This will help on your way to the cure. There is a journey ahead of you now."

"But—"

"Our trade is done. Your bracelet for this. Take the vial to your half sister. Once emptied, deliver it to the western caves. There, a noble sacrifice will be required. After that, the cure will be yours."

Each word piled around Jastyn like the heavy raindrops pooling at her boots. They started to drown her, creating once again an insurmountable number of obstacles between herself and a way to help her sister.

Jastyn couldn't stop herself. In a single motion, she pulled the blade from her boot and swiftly angled the point toward Rua, whose full lips lifted higher in a wide smile at the sharp edge against her breast.

"So, there is a bit of spark in you after all? What a delightful surprise."

"This isn't a fair trade," Jastyn said, shaking her head at the rush of water bombarding her face and shoulders. A shiver ran down her back, and another roll of thunder clapped through the sky. Or was that something else? What sounded like swords clashing against shields echoed in the distance.

Rua pricked the blade with the pad of her finger, then disappeared. Jastyn expected her to reappear, but when she turned to look, Rua was gone. Frantic, she scanned the meadow. But her saol was dim in the heavy rain, and even the fairies' nests had been all but extinguished in the downpour. Again, the sounds of a struggle pricked her ears from somewhere to the north, deep in the Wood. Voices called out from between the trees. But Jastyn's eyes stung with tears. Her breathing quickened. She looked at the vial gripped in one hand, her hunting blade in the other. Rua had bested her. The reality of this gripped Jastyn around her stomach, ran up her dry throat and let itself out in a visceral scream. She heaved, and tears raced down her face before she could stop them. She hated herself for letting Rua go. She hated herself for failing her family again.

Bitter disappointment crawled into her lungs and tightened around her heart, and Jastyn fell to her knees. Then, for the first time in a long time, she hung her head and wept.

CHAPTER ELEVEN

Jastyn's feet sank into the muddy earth while the storm continued to release its torrent over the Wood. She had strayed from the path along the brook, the water obstructing her way, overflowing onto the grass in heaping pools. As a result, Jastyn stomped through stretches of sticky dirt, continuing to chastise herself over her encounter with Rua. How could she have been so naïve? She knew the Red One was slippery. Still, Rua got what she wanted, and Jastyn was left with more questions than answers.

Muttering under her breath, Jastyn felt the vial bounce inside the otherwise empty sack—the rest of the items now gone thanks to Rua. She cursed the Red One. But more than anything, she cursed herself for letting down Alanna.

There was another loud crack of thunder, and Jastyn paused to lean under the wide branches of a pine tree. The hundreds of towering trunks tried to shield her from the downpour and ease her anxious mind. Wrapping her arms around herself, she wanted to let the low-hanging limbs lift her up and remind her to be strong. But her body shook, and she had to fight the misery overtaking her mind. Closing her eyes, Jastyn tilted her head back to rest on the moist bark. Raindrops snuck between the needles and dripped onto her face, momentarily relieving the hot frustration. More thunder rumbled, and through her closed eyelids, she saw flashes of lightning.

The brief respite from her frustration vanished faster than she would have liked as she shivered, and the unfairness of the last hour overtook her again. Reluctantly, Jastyn released more cries into her fists, knowing that the only witnesses were the trees reaching down with their long branches to protect her.

Sniffling, she thought of her family. She imagined the warm fire in the hearth, the smell of her mother's stew, even the shadow of her stepfather working in the corner. Part of her longed to be there. But she couldn't go back—not yet. Not after a failure such as this one.

Regaining her breath, Jastyn wiped her face clean with the wet sleeve of her tunic. She ran a trembling hand down her braid, the hair already matted and tangled. She thought about Eegit. Perhaps she could nurse her wounded pride at her meadow before facing the truth of her failures back in the village.

Another loud clash descended upon the Wood. The sound scattered like frightened rabbits between the tree trunks. The tail end of the noise held an unfamiliar echo, and Jastyn opened her eyes to peer through the steady rainfall. She was a good two miles from the village. Yet she thought she heard the sounds of shouting. And what she had thought was lightning was the bright flashes of spell-fire. Crouching, Jastyn moved closer to the noise. Eventually, a gap in the trees revealed a group of thirty men, clad in the kingdom's colors, in full armor and weaponry facing opposite a stampeding horde of—

"Elves!"

Eegit appeared at Jastyn's side so suddenly that they both gasped as Eegit hollered again, pointing toward the skirmish. "Elves have descended from the north!"

Jastyn turned back to the flashes of light, now a bright, streaking mixture of yellows, reds, and blues against the otherwise black night. Moving closer, Jastyn could make out the tall, slender outlines of the elves. The swift slicing sound their arrows made sent a jolt of fear down her back.

Eegit tugged at her tunic. "Come, child!"

But Jastyn pulled her arm away and scurried over the exposed tree roots to get a better look. She recognized the armor worn by the royal guard's scouting party. Toward the front of their box formation stood an older man—incredibly built with a chest the size of the nearby tree trunks—swinging his sword to block an arrow that narrowly missed his left cheek. That same man motioned for a younger soldier with similar blond hair poking out beneath his helmet to advance.

"We must move!" Eegit crouched beside her, but Jastyn's eyes were glued to the chaos unfolding before them.

"Is this the scouting party that planned to explore the west? What happened?"

"None of our concern!" Eegit cried, hopping hysterically from foot to foot.

Jastyn shook off Eegit. Something wasn't right. "But why are the elves attacking? They're a peaceful group."

Eegit sighed, throwing up her hands that dripped with rain. That was when Jastyn's eyes landed on the source of the latest yellow orb hurled across the newly formed battlefield. The young man who threw it was the spitting image of the princess. The pale blue saol floating beside him lit up his face that contorted in a cry before he struck down an elf with his sword. Jastyn saw Aurelia in his proud chin, his thick hair, even in his nose. She was struck by the resemblance when he turned to call after another guard. As he did, an arrow found its target in his left shoulder. He staggered backward while one of the guardsmen cried out, "Your Highness!"

"Eegit—it's the prince!"

Eegit paused to join Jastyn in observing the battle. The elves were gaining ground fast, and more guards crumpled under the onslaught of arrows.

"Why aren't the king's men retreating?" Jastyn's eyes darted around. The prince, she noticed, managed to stand warily. But not one second later, another arrow landed with a sickening *thump* in his side.

"Not good," Eegit muttered. "Come. We must leave."

Jastyn stumbled backward as Eegit pulled her away with surprising strength.

"But, Eegit, that's the prince!" Perhaps if she repeated that fact, her friend would realize the urgency of the situation.

But Eegit's eyes looked past her and were as wide as mouse burrows. Jastyn saw a flicker of fear within them. Eegit's lips parted slowly. "A changing wind howls over Venostes tonight."

A boom of thunder shook the earth. Jastyn turned back to the fight. The older man, who she now presumed was the general, crouched over the prince. He looked to be alive, but his breathing came in shallow, staggered breaths. The king's men shouted over one another frantically, running around while the elves whooped and yipped. The elven leader—the tallest of them all with shoulder-length silver hair and gray eyes—shouted something in their native tongue. Seconds later, his army pulled back.

"What are they doing?" Jastyn muttered, confused. There had been no territory gained by either party. The kingdom's general had not fallen, as he called after the retreating elves while the younger version of himself rushed to the fallen prince. It was almost as if—Jastyn's throat went dry at the thought—the prince was all they were after.

Jastyn caught one more glimpse of the young man stretched out on the muddy, upturned ground. One bloody hand clutched the wound in his side. Meanwhile, the blond soldier, who Jastyn couldn't place, was wrapping the prince's shoulder in cloth from his own tunic. The prince's face looked calm despite the severity of his wounds.

Eegit yanked Jastyn away from the field as more of the elves ran and vanished between the trees. "Child, come now!"

"All right!" she replied hastily. "Let's go."

While the two of them hurried back into the depths of the Wood, the harried battle cries grew distant. But the prince and his sister were now forethoughts in Jastyn's mind, clouding her vision and making her stumble through ankle-deep puddles and over gnarled tree roots.

Trailing Eegit, she had a feeling her friend was right; a new wind was raging over the land, and Jastyn feared it wasn't in favor of the prince.

❖

"Roisin, when is the Autumn Equinox Festival?" Aurelia asked in her most casual tone while finishing off the final crust of bread on her dinner plate. She sat with her maiden in the dining hall, the only two occupants save for the trio of musicians lounging in one corner of the vast room near the roaring fire. The men sat on plush cushions, laughing and occasionally breaking into sweet-sounding melodies on their instruments. Aurelia's mother and father had retired for the evening following dinner. The princess imagined that the idea of Brennus being outside the kingdom's walls was nearly too much for them to handle, and their early turn-in was a way of making the next day, and his return, come faster.

Roisin took a drink from her wooden cup and set it down opposite Aurelia's goblet. The wine left a dull purple stain along her bottom lip. "The equinox? It's not for some time. Seven, maybe eight weeks?" She sat back and crossed her arms. "Why ever do you ask?"

Aurelia stuffed her mouth with goat cheese and shrugged, avoiding Roisin's curious gaze. But Roisin leaned forward, a knowing grin stretching across her face.

"You're hoping to see that girl again, aren't you? The one from the stables."

Aurelia fidgeted in her chair, the wood suddenly stiffer than normal. Roisin giggled at her unease. "You're hoping a kingdom-wide event will bring her out of hiding."

Lifting her chin, Aurelia replied, "See? I knew I never should have told you about her. All you do is tease."

Still chuckling, Roisin washed down a bite of lamb. "Come now, m'lady. It's all in good fun."

"Is it now? It seems only fair that I return the favor. I noticed Coran lingering in the kitchen after breakfast this morning where I happened upon the two of you chatting away like gossiping magpies."

Roisin's face grew as red as the venison on her plate. "Princess! I was only being friendly."

Now it was Aurelia's turn to laugh. She sat straighter, having regained her composure. "Anyway," she said while Roisin bashfully bit into an apple, "what if I do want to see her again? There's no harm in that." She ignored the eyeroll from Roisin. "After all, it would be rude of me not to inquire about the state of her sister."

At this, Roisin's face turned serious. "That poor little thing. So young."

They sat quietly, mulling over the state of a girl neither of them had ever met. Nevertheless, Aurelia felt a deep sympathy for the girl. And the more she thought about the ailing villager, the more she yearned to see Jastyn again.

"What was her name?" Roisin asked after a minute. "The one you gave the bracelet to."

Aurelia looked up from her plate, her lips twitching into a smile. "Jastyn."

Roisin nodded. "Well, I'm sure you'll see her again. The equinox will be here before you know it."

Aurelia was about to reply when the doors to the dining hall burst open.

"Hurry! Over here, quickly!"

Drest sprinted toward the opposite end of the dining table. He wore his armor and helmet, both smeared with mud while dirt and blood mingled together across his breastplate. His right fist clutched the top of an arrow shaft, its tip dark. His face was stricken and pale, his eyes frantic.

"What's happenin'?" Roisin asked. Aurelia glanced from her to Drest, shaking her head. They both stood and started toward the other end of the table when Baron Louarn entered. Aurelia froze.

In his arms lay her brother. His left shoulder was wrapped haphazardly in a cloth soaked with blood. His right arm dangled lifelessly in front of the baron, who wheezed and huffed, his chest expanding against the tight leather of his armor while he rushed to carry Brennus. Her brother's head bobbed awkwardly, his neck pale and limp. His eyes flickered up toward the ceiling, and Aurelia's stomach dropped when she saw the gaping hole in his right side. Blood bubbled out from it, trickling down the back of his breastplate and onto the baron's feet.

"We need help!" the baron bellowed, his own face contorted in panic while he moved toward Drest, who cleared the end of the dining table of its contents in one motion.

"Quick, get him up here." Drest set the arrow down and grabbed Brennus's feet to help his father carefully lay him out atop the wide table. Upon being placed on the polished wood, Brennus winced, and Aurelia rushed to her brother's side.

"What happened?" she asked, taking in his pallid face and the sickening smell of blood that had already hardened in the fabric of his tunic.

Drest answered before reaching to grab a jug of water from the table. "We were ambushed." Roisin, wasting no time, ran out and returned seconds later, a bundle of clean cloth in hand. She and Drest soaked them, then began rinsing the blood from Brennus's arms, chest, and face. When Drest removed his friend's armor, they saw Brennus's navy tunic was completely blood-soaked.

"It was the elves," Baron Louarn added. Aurelia glanced up to find him seemingly stunned, watching the three of them with unblinking eyes. "The elves attacked us. Our allies."

"Elves?" Aurelia asked. "How can that be?"

The baron shook his head.

"Traitors, all of them," Drest said. "Look at what they did." He was leaning over Brennus as Aurelia began to re-dress his shoulder wound. At her touch, her brother groaned and coughed. A spurt of blood erupted from his mouth. The four of them exchanged glances. The musicians whispered to themselves in the corner. Aurelia glanced over her shoulder at them. At the sight of their hands covering gossiping mouths, it only took a second for the fear she felt to turn into anger, and she shouted.

"Go! Don't just stand there. Alert the king and queen!" The stunned men stood quietly but didn't move. "*Now!*" she bellowed.

The trio jumped and ran from the room.

Brennus coughed again, his body spasming with each choking sound. Aurelia ran a hand over his forehead, which burned to the touch. She crouched down so that she was eye level with him. Brennus turned to her. He fought to keep his eyes open. A gurgle sounded deep within his throat when he opened his mouth to speak. Tears brimming in her eyes, Aurelia shook her head. "It's okay. Don't try to talk."

She kept her eyes locked on her brother's. The light within them had grown dim. "Keep pressure on his side," she tearfully ordered Drest, who already had his hands over the wound. "Gods, how could this have happened?"

Aurelia racked her brain for something she could do. She ran every spell her mother had ever taught her through her mind, scouring the annexes of her mental library for any herbs, elixirs, or potions that could aide her brother. But everything she thought of was a temporary fix, a bandage for the surface, not a cure for a wound as deep as the one in his side.

"There has to be something."

"Out of the way!"

They all turned. Her mother bolted through the doorway into the room. Her magenta night robe was coming untied at the waist, revealing a shin-length, navy sleep-tunic that her knees fought against while she rushed toward the dining table. Her hair was braided, but almost half of it had come undone in the night. It flew in thin strands over her pale forehead. Her mother's bare feet seemed out of place when she reached their group.

"Tell me what happened." Her voice was calm and stern, the way it often was during meetings Aurelia listened in on.

Baron Louarn spoke first. "Our troop was headed west, as planned. We were about to set up camp for the night when we were attacked."

Her mother's eyes didn't leave Brennus's nearly unresponsive form, which she scanned from head to toe while her hands did a search of their own on his wounds. "By whom? Who attacked you?" she asked.

Drest spoke through gritted teeth. "Elves."

At this, her mother looked up. Aurelia caught the surprise in her eyes. But her mother's gaze shifted back to Brennus. She ran a hand through his sweat and rain-soaked hair.

"Aurelia redressed his shoulder," Roisin said in a solemn tone once they had fallen quiet save for Brennus's uneven breathing. Her mother's eyes went to the bandages, and she nodded.

"Very good, my darling."

Aurelia smiled despite herself. "That one wasn't very deep. But his side…" Her voice trailed off. Baron Louarn wheezed and moved to sit in a chair near her brother's feet. The red flecks on his boots made Aurelia's stomach churn. Drest muttered under his breath, his hands still pressed against Brennus's side.

Her mother leaned closer to Brennus. Drest moved his hands for her to get a better look at where the arrow struck him, but as soon as the pressure was removed, more blood spurted out. Brennus gasped and moaned. His eyes flickered, then fell closed again.

Aurelia swallowed, watching her mother. Her face was ashen, and her eyes darted around as if searching for an answer. Her mother ran another hand down Brennus's face. "Hold on, my dear, sweet boy."

A clamor of steps sounded from the hallway outside, and Aurelia stood straighter to find her father sprinting into the room. He too wore a disheveled night robe and was barefoot, and his curly hair and beard were wild from sleep. "Dechtire!" he shouted, still running. "I've got it!"

Upon reaching them, he handed her a pear-shaped black vial with a stopper in its top. Her mother took it eagerly, and her father stood beside her, forming a circle around Brennus splayed out on the table below them. When her brother took a labored breath, Aurelia tried to ignore the crackling sound behind his ribs.

"What is that?" she finally asked as her mother yanked out the cork. A scent like mulch wafted from the vial. She, Roisin, and Drest covered their noses.

The baron leaned forward, his face incredulous. "Is that—"

Her father nodded. "Water from the Well of Slaine."

Aurelia gaped, exchanging glances with Roisin. "But the Well of Slaine is a myth. That's what you taught me," she said, looking at her mother, who motioned for Drest to remove his hands again.

"I taught you that as a precaution. The Well of Slaine is dangerous to those who don't know how to use its water properly."

Aurelia was stunned. Her mother had lied to her. But more than that, she was shocked that something she had formerly believed to be a tall tale had actually been sitting inside her mother's medicinal cabinet this entire time.

"The waters are powerful." Taken aback, Aurelia recited the information her mother had read to her years before. "They are capable of reviving the lost. Used most often in…in bringing fallen soldiers back from the dead."

Her mother's hand, which held the tipped vial over the wound in Brennus's side, froze. She met her daughter's gaze. "That's correct."

"But Brennus isn't…"

The look in her mother's eyes told her all she needed to know. Nodding, Aurelia stepped back with Drest as her mother poured three drops from the vial into the gaping wound. The water hissed when it hit the blood, and Brennus's eyes flew open. He screamed, deep and primal, and began to thrash wildly.

"Hold him down!" her mother ordered. She, her father, the baron, and Drest all grabbed on to Brennus as his body spasmed and smacked against the table. Aurelia lifted a hand to her mouth. Pain etched itself into every corner of her brother's face. When his neck bent backward in another yell, she couldn't watch any longer and turned to hide her face in Roisin's shoulder.

"It'll be over soon, m'lady," she whispered. But even Roisin didn't sound as if she believed that to be true.

Brennus's screams continued while the others fought to keep him on the table. Aurelia's tears ran down her cheeks as she clung to Roisin, looking away. The sound was unbearable. After another minute, she couldn't take any more.

"Stop it! Can't you see it's only making him worse?" She turned to her mother and father. They looked up, maintaining firm grips on her brother's limbs. But as they did, Brennus finally stopped. His body heaved in one final spasm, then his mouth fell slack, and his legs collapsed onto the table. For one terrifying moment, none of them moved. They watched his chest. When it didn't rise, Aurelia bit her quivering lip. She was about to reach out to touch him when he gasped.

"My son!" their father exclaimed, crouching down to hold Brennus's hand. Her brother's eyes were open, his gaze clearer. Their mother was crying, and she joined her father kneeling on the floor.

Baron Louarn collapsed back into his chair with one hand on his chest. Roisin moved forward with Aurelia. Drest wiped his brow and looked as shocked as Aurelia felt at the sight of her brother attempting to sit up, the color returning to his face.

"You're all right!" said Drest. Aurelia heard a question in his voice but brushed it off to help her brother.

Still sputtering bits of blood, Brennus managed to sit up with help from their mother and Drest. Meanwhile, the blood that had been gushing from his side halted as if a dam had suddenly been built. Aurelia took in her brother's cracked lips, the deep circles under his eyes…even though he was moving again, he looked incredibly unwell. She wondered exactly how the water from the Well of Slaine worked.

Brennus propped himself up with a grimace. "By everyone's faces, I fear I left the stable gate open again." They all laughed at his first words since he had been brought in. Relief washed over the room and ran from their eyes in grateful tears.

Roisin clapped her hands joyfully. "By the Gods, it's a miracle!"

Aurelia pushed aside more of the dining plates and climbed on top of the table. "I don't believe it." She sat opposite him and stared at his weak smile, his hunched shoulder, and the four-inch hole in his side.

"Neither do I," he breathed, looking around at the bewildered faces surrounding him. Brennus met their parents' gaze. "Did I miss dinner?"

Their father wiped tears from his eyes, and their mother pulled

Brennus into a hug. Aurelia jumped on top of them, embracing her brother with every ounce of strength she had.

"I can't believe it," Drest said, shaking his head. He smiled, and Brennus reached out. They shook hands. "I thought we'd lost you."

Brennus grinned. "You'll have to tell me all about it."

Sitting back, Aurelia sniffled. Everyone wiped their faces clean when the baron asked, "What *do* you remember?"

They sat attentively. Brennus frowned. "I don't…I don't remember much." He reached up to rub his forehead, then pinched the bridge of his nose. "I'm sorry. My head…it aches so."

Their mother stood. "Of course, darling. We can save the investigation for the morning," she announced, shooting the baron a look. "You need to rest."

"That sounds like just what the herbalist ordered," Brennus said tiredly. "Aurelia," he added, "you owe me a duel in the morning, what do you say?"

She nodded. "Absolutely."

But when their father leaned down to lift Brennus from the table, her brother let out a string of coughs. Blood spat from his mouth and into his open hand. His eyes went wide, and his hand flew to his chest.

"Brennus, are you all right?"

He didn't respond. Instead, he fell instantly onto the table, his body shaking uncontrollably once again with spasms.

"Brennus!" their mother shouted. She and their father braced their hands on his shoulders to quell his movements, but it was to no avail. They stepped back and watched helplessly as their son's body shook with agonizing force. When blood trickled from his ears and nose, Aurelia cried out.

"Mother, what's happening? What's wrong with him?"

"I don't know!" she cried. They both looked to her father, who shook his head, his eyes filled with terror. That was when her mother grabbed the arrow that had been cast aside by Drest. "Is this what was in his side?"

Drest, who watched bewildered while his best friend continued to seize, only nodded. She lifted the arrowhead to her nose. Then she licked the tip of it and immediately spat.

Aurelia felt sick. "What is it?"

Her mother's gaze was empty when she said, "Poison."

The air was sucked from the room. Her father took a knee next to his son. Blood ran from every orifice in Brennus's face, and the blood from his wound turned a sickly brown as it bubbled onto the table. Aurelia shuddered when her brother's chest heaved one final time.

Then everything was quiet.

Chapter Twelve

Groaning, Jastyn stirred where she lay on the edge of Eegit's clearing. Her back was stiff, and a creak sprang from her neck when she pushed herself up with her palms, wet grass clinging to them as she shielded her eyes from the sunlight. The sweet smell of damp holly shrubs bombarded her senses. She sat up blinking and leaned against a tree trunk.

"When did I fall asleep?" she called to Eegit, who was hunched over her ever-burning fire. The flames—red today—crackled under what appeared to be an already fading midday sun.

Eegit smashed a handful of elderberries onto the flames, prompting a pop followed by a satisfied hiss. "When the rain let up. After you stopped all of that carrying on about the Red One."

Wiping her face and brushing away strands of hair fallen from her braid, Jastyn frowned. She stood, stretched, and wandered past her nearly empty satchel lying at the base of a tree and joined Eegit.

"The gods almost extinguished all of my hard work with that storm of theirs," Eegit scowled up at the now clear sky. "But my protection spell held strong while I worked to drag you away from the bedlam of last night."

Jastyn shot her a look. Yawning, she plopped next to the fire. Eegit grabbed an expired toad from a tin bucket, yanked off its legs, and threw them into the flames. Meanwhile, the events from the night before returned to Jastyn's mind's eye.

"Don't dwell, child," Eegit muttered, reading Jastyn's mind.

When Jastyn looked, the haze of disappointment from letting

Alanna down last night clouded her vision. Eegit squinted. "Come. We must eat."

"I'm not hungry."

"Nor am I!" Eegit countered, hopping toward her hut. "But, as they say, 'a cured meat cures all!'" Before passing into her dim home, she turned. "Squirrel or rabbit; take your pick!"

❖

Later, Jastyn and Eegit sat opposite each other by the fire, which smelled of meat and singed fur. The sun, beginning its descent, sent shadows across the clearing. Jastyn munched on the thin pieces of meat between the ribs of a roasted squirrel, her gaze unfocused. While her eyes fixed on the lambent fire, her ears pricked at the sounds of the Wood: the settling of birds' wings as they took to their nests, a croaking frog singing to the brook, and the distant, waking howl of a wolf greeting the coming night. Running her tongue over her teeth for any lingering scraps, Jastyn tilted her head at the faint snap of a branch.

Eegit grunted. "That will be your spotted friend."

Jastyn finished her dinner. After several minutes, rustling disturbed the nearby brush. A string of curses followed. Eegit chuckled, and Jastyn, tossing a tiny leg bone into the fire, leaned back.

"You didn't have to come, Coran."

Another stifled curse, followed by stumbling steps. Eventually, Coran fell into the clearing over Jastyn's left shoulder. Thorns stuck to his tunic, and mud coated the bottom of his boots. He ran a hand through his curls—looking more orange under the setting sun—to rid himself of fallen leaves. His light eyes were wide when he said, "How did you know it was me?"

Jastyn exchanged an amused glance with Eegit, who spoke between open-mouthed chews. "You walk like a baby bear in a crowded village market."

Coran swallowed, then cleared his throat, continuing to brush off his pants with a pleading look at Jastyn, who shrugged.

"What're you doin' out here so late?" Jastyn asked, nodding for Coran to take a seat. With a wry smile at Eegit, he took a knee.

Settled onto the grass, he spoke in a low voice. "I went by your house yesterday. Your mom said you had left to fetch somethin' for Alanna."

His face was lit with curiosity, but Jastyn wasn't ready to divulge everything from the previous night. Instead, she asked him, "How is my family? How's Alanna?"

"Worried, of course," he said, eyeing Eegit, who crunched loudly into a skull. Coran paled at the noise. "I figured if you were headin' back after whatever it was you had to do, you might have come here first."

Jastyn tossed the remains of her dinner into the fire. "I didn't find what I was hoping for," she said after a minute. Then she fetched her satchel and sat back down. Pulling out the vial, she added, "But I did get this."

Coran reached out to touch the glass. The green smoke stirred at his touch.

From across the fire, Eegit nodded, seemingly impressed. "Banshee blood, is it? The Red One was generous with you, child."

Both Jastyn and Coran turned to her. "This," Jastyn said, "is banshee blood?"

"Naturally," Eegit replied matter-of-factly. "Banshee aren't corporeal fae. What'd you expect their blood to look like?"

Exchanging looks with Jastyn, Coran mumbled, "Guess I never really thought about it before."

Jastyn tucked the vial away as Eegit licked her fingers clean. "You've got to find the second half of your trade, haven't you?"

"How did you…" Jastyn started, then held up a hand. "Never mind. I should have known."

Coran asked, "What's she mean?"

Reluctantly, Jastyn explained. "This vial of, apparently, banshee blood will help Alanna. But only temporarily. The Red One told me to go west, to the caves, to find the true cure." She bit her lip, hesitant to add that the fae had also mentioned a sacrifice was part of obtaining this mysterious cure.

"How long will the banshee blood last?"

"A couple of moons, I'd wager," Eegit called from near her hut. She rummaged through several wooden bowls, then wandered over to drop an acorn into the flames.

Jastyn stared into the firelight. Coran reached out, placing a speckled hand on her knee.

"Come back to the village with me, Jas."

Jastyn pulled her legs to her chest, resting her elbows on her knees. She stared at her fingers. "I'm not sure I'm ready to go back."

She could feel Coran's unspoken words. He didn't need to tell her that he believed in her, or that he would be there for her in whatever came next. She could feel it in his hand on her knee and see it in his lopsided smile. She could see the years of his looking out for her, taking care of her when she forgot to take care of herself.

A lump rose in her throat. As she opened her mouth to reply, Coran added, "At least come by and let Mum serve you some eggs." He poked at her ribs. "You're lookin' mighty peckish, even after that squirrel."

Jastyn swatted his hand away. "I'd rather my mom's stew."

"Both then. And"—he sniffed, leaning forward—"a bath wouldn't hurt you none either."

At this, Eegit guffawed, surprising both Jastyn and Coran. Wide-eyed, they gawked at her cackling laughter. Eegit threw her head back. "First funny thing you've spoken in years!"

After a second, Jastyn joined in her laughter. For a fleeting moment, she felt lighter. Meanwhile, Coran's neck flushed. "Suppose I'll take that as a compliment."

When Eegit, still snickering, walked back to her hut, Jastyn wiped her eyes, her laughter subsiding. "Very well. I'll head back at first light." She stretched and yawned, her full stomach prompting a sense of ease and renewed sleepiness. She patted the grass beside her. "C'mon and stay tonight, Coran. Eegit can roast something for you."

"I'll pass on dinner," he said before sitting cross-legged beside Jastyn, who lay down with one hand tucked behind her head. "There's one more thing," he said, leaning down to speak low. "I bear news from the castle."

Jastyn's eyes, which had closed briefly in contentment, flew open. The memories from last night, which had drifted to the edge of her mind where dreams lived, rushed back swiftly. She heard the agonized cries from the guardsmen, she saw the slicing of arrows across the night sky, and she watched once more the terror on the face of the general.

Slowly, she asked, "What news has come?"

Coran's face was solemn when he spoke. "Prince Diarmaid is dead."

❖

The dining hall was transformed: long, black curtains hung from every window, shielding the castle's inhabitants from the outside world. Servants and members of the royal court treaded with muffled steps to and from the dark room; those who had not yet paid their respects did so now. Fires burned in their hearths, creating the only light apart from dozens of candles lining the long table, itself now dressed in mourning with a black linen cloth cascading down each of its sides. Groups of three or four, everyone dressed in solemn gray or deep blue, walked with bent heads toward the center of the room and knelt along the table's edges. They spoke in hushed prayer or left a white lily or a plate of berries among the plethora of offerings.

Each person who came to bid farewell was careful to nod their condolences to Princess Aurelia, who had remained now for two days at the head of the table, clad in a midnight-blue cloak over a black tunic, her eyes red from crying and little sleep thanks to the constant vigil she kept over her fallen brother.

One member of the court—a woman Aurelia recognized as a friend of her mother's—whimpered into shaking hands as she knelt a few feet away in front of the fresh leather boots on Brennus's feet. The woman's husband stood behind her. Aurelia knew him as a member of the same guard party who returned that fateful night. After running a hand over his thick auburn beard, the man caught her gaze.

"The prince died an honorable death worthy of a fine warrior," he said in a raspy voice.

When Aurelia only stared back at him, he nodded curtly, wiped his eyes, then left the dining hall, guiding his wife out by her elbow.

Aurelia, who had insisted on being the first to oversee the wake, was exhausted. But not from the lack of sleep. Rather, she felt ragged from the kingdom's endless stream of words for her brother. Nearly every single soldier, chambermaid, or lady of the court had explained to her that Brennus's death had been "honorable," "valiant," or even "of the highest degree of valor."

She shrugged at their well-meaning but ultimately misguided sentiments. Her eyes fell once more to her brother. Even now, it was hard to comprehend the stillness of his face, the unmoving hair, and the stiff hands clutching his sword over his chest. For the hundredth time, her eyes traced the edges of his white tunic and pants, trimmed in elegant black on the cuffs and collar. With such an image as this, Aurelia could not bring herself to seek solace in any of the words that she had heard. What did they know, after all? What pride was there in such a death as this one? Her brother had wanted nothing except to see the world. What had he received in return for that wanting but a premature handshake with Death?

Aurelia's mind festered with the final moments of her brother's life: the excruciating screams, the clenching agony in every bone in his body as he fell, clamoring, into the Otherworld. The contrast was staggering now, looking at his closed eyelids and still frame. As the candles threw shadows across his pale skin, Aurelia grew furious.

"It wasn't supposed to be like this."

"Death rarely comes to us in the manner that we expect."

Startled, Aurelia turned to find her mother standing over her right shoulder. She wore her long hair down, the top half pinned back behind her ears. The skin around her eyes was puffy, and her chapped lips down-turned as she pulled the edges of a gray cloak tighter around her.

Leaning back, Aurelia said, "I feel as if I'm in a dream." Then she shook her head. "No. A nightmare sent to me from the darkest of fae."

Her mother stood beside the wooden arm of Aurelia's chair. She reached out and brushed a hand through Aurelia's hair. "You should rest, sweetheart. The games begin at dawn tomorrow."

"Has it already been two days?"

Aurelia caught a flicker of disbelief in her mother's eyes when she responded. "Yes. We must reopen the doors. The kingdom will spend the next four days honoring him. You know it is our duty to be present for the events."

They were quiet. Through a doorway across the room, the same trio of musicians entered. The men bowed nervously at the sight of their queen, then placed their offerings of gold coins next to the prince before scurrying away.

Aurelia mustered all of the bitterness she could before saying, "I don't understand these silly traditions. Why can't we let Brennus rest peacefully until the seventh day? Does the kingdom actually expect us to partake in such a celebration?" She slouched, her chin landing in her hand. "My brother is dead. There is nothing to celebrate about that."

At this, her mother knelt. Her eyes rested on her son, and she placed a kiss on his forehead.

"I understand your anger. The gods have seen fit to bestow upon me the darkest of dreams these last two nights. I fear they can see the guilt in my heart."

Aurelia frowned. "Guilt? Mother, this was not your fault."

"If I had not given in to your brother's whims so easily—"

Aurelia cut her off. "Brennus lived out a long-held dream. He adored leaving castle grounds."

Her mother nodded. "He did." She ran a finger through his hair, then turned to Aurelia. "Trust me, then, when I say that I know it is difficult to see through to the other side of such a dark time." She took a breath as if steeling herself to continue speaking. "You are not alone in this. Your father and I lost a son. Your dear, sweet brother. The kingdom is without its first heir. You are right, Aurelia: there is no good in losing him. But we can choose to remember the joy wrought from the life he lived. That is the purpose of tomorrow."

Aurelia trembled. Any words she wanted to say stuck in her throat. She could not see the light in this, that "other end" that her mother spoke of. Part of her feared she never would. A vast hollowness had taken root within her. She felt it like a missing limb, a part of her gone that would never return.

"Time will work its healing powers upon us." Her mother's words were spoken to no one, or maybe only to herself. She reached up and grabbed Aurelia's left hand, which rested in her lap.

"Come. Let us ensure Brennus's safe passage to the Otherworld. Then we will get you something to eat. Your father will watch over him until the morning."

Aurelia's legs were numb when she stiffly stood and pushed back her chair. It scraped along the floor. She took a knee beside her mother. With one final look at her brother, Aurelia bowed her head and clasped her hands, and they spoke in unison the traditional farewell prayer:

"The wound was red, the cut was deep, and the flesh was sore; but there will be no more blood, and no more pain till the gods come down to earth again."

CHAPTER THIRTEEN

Alanna finished the last of her cornmeal across from Jastyn at their cluttered kitchen table. Alanna lapped up the sticky yellow mush while Jastyn sipped from her water cup. Their mother sat at the hearth mending a tunic sleeve, humming melodiously. When Jastyn exchanged glances with Elisedd, who sat beside Alanna on the rickety bench in his usual blue work tunic and leather pants, Alanna set her spoon down.

"Will you two *please* stop staring at me?"

Jastyn dipped her chin to hide her smile. Meanwhile, Elisedd wrapped a sinewy arm around Alanna's shoulders. "I'm sorry, my dear. It's been so long since we've seen you like this." His words came out gruff, as if he was trying to keep his emotions from escaping his throat.

As Alanna hugged him, Jastyn felt a swelling of emotion, similar to the way she often did after a successful hunt. Upon returning home three days ago to her mother's relieved embrace and surprisingly, a welcoming Elisedd, Jastyn had rushed to Alanna's room to deliver the vial of banshee blood. Unquestioning, her mother and Elisedd followed at her heels, and the three of them watched with bated breath as Alanna drank half of the vial.

Jastyn had sat beside her on the bed. Alanna coughed after wiping her mouth clean. "Are you all right?" Jastyn asked.

Alanna hiccupped. "It tastes like week-old cabbage."

Within an hour, Alanna was moving about the house like she hadn't done in years. She even went and fetched water from the well to draw a bath for Jastyn. Alanna, bucket swinging gleefully at her side, had tilted her face upward to greet the wind that swept over the hillside.

Now, Alanna finished her breakfast—another feat Jastyn couldn't recall in recent memory. Her sister's face was full of healthy color, and her eyes leapt with new life.

"It's incredible," Jastyn said, reaching out a hand, which Alanna squeezed.

"I always believed in you, Jastyn. Thank you."

Elisedd cleared his throat, and Jastyn shared a smile with her sister.

"It was a gift from one of Eegit's friends, you said?" Alanna asked before carrying her bowl over to the wash basin.

Jastyn straightened, her eyes darting between her mother and Elisedd. They exchanged glances, then her mother quickly shook her head. Jastyn wiped her hands over the table and kept her eyes on the fallen crumbs when she spoke.

"Yes. We got lucky. Eegit managed to make a deal with one of her many customers. She sends her regards, by the way."

Alanna returned to her seat, smiling. "Well, tell her I'm grateful."

Jastyn kept her head down and tried to return her sister's smile. She was thankful when Elisedd spoke.

"You have done well," he said to Jastyn. Her mother stood from her place by the fire and joined them, placing a hand on Elisedd's shoulder. She leaned down and kissed Alanna's forehead, then held Jastyn's gaze.

"I am so proud of you, my daughter."

As Jastyn looked at her family, which included her now-radiant little sister, she was almost able to forget that this moment wouldn't last forever. She willed the pleased faces looking back at her into the recesses of her mind, to the place where her most cherished memories resided. And for a brief second, Jastyn didn't dwell on the impending journey that lay ahead for the rest of the cure, which she wasn't sure how or when would begin. She was almost able to erase the terrible images from the Wood when a distant rumble sounded outside. Three deep, deliberate beats boomed over the moors and humble fields dotting the outskirts of the village. They all turned to the open window.

"The games are about to start." Her mother scooped up their empty bowls and spoons. "That poor family," she added quietly.

Jastyn fidgeted in her seat, fighting the onslaught of images overtaking her mind. Flashes of agonized faces. The tumult of arrows.

"The prince always seemed so kind," Alanna said, brushing crumbs from her tunic.

Elisedd nodded. "He would have made a great king."

"Jastyn?"

Jastyn looked to find both of her fists clenched atop the table, her right leg bouncing erratically.

"Are you all right?" Those formerly proud gazes now eyed her cautiously.

She swallowed, her throat like parched tree bark. "I hate to think what the king and queen must be going through."

"And Princess Aurelia," Alanna said softly.

Jastyn unclenched her hands. Admittedly, she had not thought very highly of the princess upon their first meeting. After all, the two of them had nothing in common and were vastly different people from opposite worlds. Nevertheless, Jastyn *did* understand the reality of playing witness to a suffering sibling. It very well could be Alanna on her way to the Otherworld, not the prince. So, despite her aversion to the princess, perhaps she should find a way to pay her respects. After all, Jastyn reluctantly admitted, she did help to attain the banshee blood with that bracelet of hers.

Jastyn fiddled with a wide gap in the wooden boards on the table when Alanna asked, "May we go to the games? Please?" Outside, another round of steady drumming beckoned.

Elisedd sat in his corner chair, pulling on his boots. "I'm not sure that's a good idea."

Alanna ran to her mother by the wash basin. "Mother, may I go? Please? I feel better than ever!"

Their mother looked at Elisedd, who shook his head. Then she tilted her own head sympathetically. "Not today, my love. You should regain the rest of your strength first. There will be three more days of remembrance before his funeral."

Alanna's entire frame slouched, and she returned to her seat on the bench. With one hand under her chin and her elbow propped emphatically on the table, she stated, "Then you must go."

Jastyn straightened. "Me?"

"Yes, and come back and tell me all about it."

"But I never go to these things."

Elisedd stood. "You can come with me. I'm to join the rest of the stable hands in a ceremonial song as an ode to Prince Brennus. Of course, you wouldn't have to sing." He said this last part so seriously that Jastyn, after being momentarily stunned by his talking to her, had to laugh. Her mother soon joined in, followed by Alanna's quick giggles.

"Did I say something?" he asked, staring at them all. This only prompted more laughter from the girls.

Once they caught their breaths and wiped their eyes, their mother said, "You should go, Jastyn."

The air in the room was dizzy with the unfamiliar trails of laughter. Jastyn felt so light she couldn't protest. Additionally, her stepfather had spoken directly to her more times this morning than he had in the last five years. And when his own face pulled up in a smile, the pointed end of his beard suddenly less severe, she was sure she had to be dreaming. And if that was the case, why let such a blissful morning end? She would hold on to this enjoyment as long as she could.

"Let's get moving. I don't want to be late."

With a quick hug to her mother and Alanna, who handed her a cloak from beside the front door, Jastyn waved good-bye and followed Elisedd outside.

The meandering path that led to the market streets in front of the rolling castle lawns brimmed with people on their way to the festivities. Jastyn and Elisedd joined the trickling lines of villagers funneling into thicker groups near the abandoned market where throngs of eager sympathizers greeted one another.

All around them, men with long, full red beards strolled beside women in plaid skirts with shoulders just as broad from working the fields. Wild-haired young children, recently scrubbed and dressed in their best clan colors, frolicked at their heels. Most attendees wore thick cloaks of navy and pleated belts over a long tunic to ward off the morning gusts coming from the sea.

Upon crossing the bustling roads and walking through the royal gates separating the village from the castle grounds, Jastyn and Elisedd encountered glistening lawns bejeweled with moisture from the previous night's rainfall. On either side of the sprawling grasses stood two dozen royal guardsmen wearing their war uniforms and playing a glaring cacophony of sound on bagpipes. The lines they stood in created a wide lane. Within it, castle staff milled about at various stations. Some roasted whole pigs or deer on slow-turning spits over fires, others coaxed eager participants into a game of archery, and many circled in small groups to gossip and share never-ending casks of wine.

At the top of the lane, opposite the open gates, four high-backed thrones carved from black rock stood tall. King Grannus and Queen Dechtire sat next to one another. The queen wore a black breast pin atop her golden yellow tunic, which fell over knee-high boots. The king had a matching pin on the shoulder of his cloak. Princess Aurelia sat beside her mother in a slightly smaller throne. The fourth seat was adorned with flowers, wreaths, and candles covering every surface, every item donated from a line of generous villagers, each taking a moment to leave a token of sympathy for the fallen prince.

Passing through the gates, Jastyn pulled the hood of her cloak down and shook back her long braid.

"I can understand why you don't come to these often." Elisedd gestured to the hundreds of people wandering around. "I'm not keen on crowds either." He tossed Jastyn a smile. When she only grunted and scanned the area, he added, "That's why I prefer horses to people most of the time. Less conversation." He chuckled at his own comment. Jastyn scrunched her face up, feigning amusement. Despite Elisedd's sudden turnaround in attitude toward her, it still wasn't the time or place to explain the actual reason why she avoided events such as these.

When she had been little, begging on the street or nicking goods from the market with Coran, she had noticed how women whispered, and men with bulging stomachs grunted at her. Her mother's name always passed between nattering lips. The older she got, the less Jastyn was able to tolerate the hot licks of gossip that trailed her every move, even after her mother married Elisedd to aid in mending their tainted past. Eventually, not showing her face at all became the easier option.

Yet, here she was. Visible.

An older woman picked up her daughter and carried her out of their path. Her jaw clenched, and she resisted the urge to put her hood back on. Elisedd interrupted her thoughts.

"By the way, I want to thank you."

She slowed, her mind still in a heated haze. They paused next to an exuberant horde of men Jastyn recognized as the family of pig farmers that lived two hills from her home. They drank from wooden cups, and one particularly skinny boy around her age with a pierced ear continuously refilled everybody's drink.

Elisedd said something to one of them and quickly had two cups of his own. The same skinny boy filled them with wine.

Handing her a cup, Elisedd raised his. "Here's to you, Jastyn. Thank you for helping Alanna."

Jastyn blinked at the liquid sloshing in her cup. She was so unaccustomed to her stepfather even acknowledging her existence that words faltered on her tongue. Seeming to realize this, Elisedd continued.

"Your mother thinks I am oblivious. She thinks that because I spend my days in the castle stables, I don't notice things." He ran a hand over his goatee. "But not everyone would venture into the Wood at night to deal with a fae. Especially the Red One."

Jastyn coughed on her wine. "How did you know?"

Her stepfather chuckled. "Your mother talks in her sleep."

Jastyn shook her head. "I love Alanna. I'll always do whatever I can to help her get better."

In response, Elisedd clinked his cup to hers. "Cheers, then. You did well for our family."

Another swell of emotion surged inside Jastyn. But this was different than this morning. This entire interaction with her stepfather was so foreign. So new. Her insides clamored with unfamiliarity, and Jastyn felt compelled to share more of the story with him.

"Elisedd, about the Red One's gift…"

"Banshee blood. Yes, I'm familiar. Based on scrolls and what is known from those who have used the drink before, I'd wager Alanna has three, maybe four months until she returns to her former state."

Jastyn blinked. She had no idea he knew so much about fae properties. Granted, she never asked. Seeming to read her thoughts, he added, "When my brother disappeared, I tore the kingdom apart to find him. I grew knowledgeable of the fae that roam these lands and of their magic."

She could only nod and take another drink. The liquid warmed her throat. "Does my mother know?"

"I told her my estimation, yes."

Before Jastyn could respond, there was a chorus of cries from the archery targets to their left. Somebody hit a bull's-eye.

Elisedd bent to speak over the noise. "Drink up. I'm going to join the stable men. I will see you at home no later than midday."

This was the borderline intimidating talk Jastyn was accustomed to. She caught a flash of Elisedd's former unapproachable self within his blue eyes before he disappeared into the crowd.

Jastyn, still stunned by the show of gratitude from her stepfather, not to mention his awareness of the Red One's gift, gulped half of her wine down. Smacking her lips at the unfamiliar taste, she scanned the lawn and pushed her way between rowdy musicians and a group of young girls swooning over them. When she came to a gap in the masses, Jastyn breathed deeply, inhaling the scent of freshly roasted meats. Looking around, she realized she was standing at the end of a line shuffling slowly forward, the end point the four towering thrones hosting the mourning royal family.

She peered over the shoulder of a wide man carrying a bushel of potatoes. From her vantage point, she could see the king: hunched and staring solemnly at an elderly woman bowing before him. The queen, meanwhile, sat straight up, looking bewildered, her clear eyes unable to mask what had to be disbelief while she greeted each passing villager.

It was the princess, though, who looked as if she was taking the prince's passing the hardest. As the line inched along, Jastyn watched Aurelia lift her gaze to acknowledge each sympathizer. Yet her eyes seemed to look through every face, beyond them and into the mass of activity in the distance. Her skin was splotched and red. Jastyn noticed a handkerchief tucked in the sleeve of her long blue tunic. She was mildly surprised the princess had decided to wear a tunic and pants rather than the dresses her mother had mentioned she often wore at public events. Perhaps it was an homage to her brother. At the idea of this, a pang hit in her chest. The princess was a lot of things: ignorant, sheltered, and presumptuous. But, Jastyn decided, swiping at her nose, she was still human. The pain of losing a sibling had to be unbearable.

Her gaze lingered on the mourning princess. Then, faster than she expected, Jastyn found herself next in line, standing only a few feet from King Grannus. She had never been this close to the royal family, and the intrigue of the moment held Jastyn in place. The last time she had attended an event like this was at the fifteenth anniversary of the Fae-Diarmaid Treaty seven years ago. She had gone with her mother, but they had lingered near the edges of the lawns. From such a distance, the king and queen had looked like gods on their thrones, the sun at their backs stunning the villagers gazing upon them.

But now, the king looked much less godlike. He and the queen looked weary as the man placed the overflowing bushel of potatoes at their feet. King Grannus's grizzled face was thin in comparison to the queen's, and his gaze was cloudy. His knuckles were swollen, and pink scars ran along his forearms when he reached out to shake hands. He seemed small beneath his billowing cloak and large boots. The queen, too, seemed alarmingly approachable, which was perhaps why a woman with a thick waist and pudgy hands spoke openly to her between choked sobs. Queen Dechtire patiently smiled at the woman, making her clear, almond-shaped eyes crinkle at their edges. Jastyn wondered how she must feel after losing her son. Wasn't she supposed to be the most powerful healer in all the kingdom? How did she feel knowing that her abilities were not enough to save the prince?

There was a sharp elbow in Jastyn's back. Behind her, people muttered restlessly while the potato man and large woman continued to barrage the king and queen with words of reverence. It hit her that she really had no idea what she would even say once it was her turn to speak. Jastyn bit her lip and glanced over at the princess. Aurelia bid farewell to a family of four: a buzzing, freckled bunch Jastyn recognized as fishermen who lived near the shores. Once their troop of frizzy redheads retreated, Jastyn shuffled sideways and, upon standing in front of the princess, suddenly felt at a loss for words.

Swallowing, she knelt and bowed her head.

"My deepest sympathies, Princess."

Aurelia sniffled, and Jastyn heard her hastily stuffing the handkerchief back up her sleeve. Her voice cracked when she said, "Thank you; that is very kind."

Jastyn lifted her head.

The princess's face shifted from anguish to shock.

"Jastyn?"

Whispers sprang up like weeds all around. Jastyn ignored them and straightened. "I came to say, well, to say that I am sorry for your loss." She glanced sideways. The king and queen now held armfuls of potatoes, their faces bewildered as the man smiled broadly at his gift. When she looked back at the princess, Jastyn wasn't sure what to make of the look in those blue eyes.

Aurelia wiped her tear-streaked face and straightened her posture. "Thank you. Your words mean a lot."

Jastyn nodded. She shuffled her feet. All of a sudden, she wanted to explain everything that had happened since their last meeting. She wanted to tell the princess all about the Red One and her bargain and the banshee blood. The desire to tell her that she had actually helped Alanna overwhelmed Jastyn. Why she felt this way, though, she couldn't be sure.

Instead, she only said, "I wanted to thank you, too. For the bracelet."

A flush rushed to the princess's cheeks. "You must have thought me a fool. Handing you jewelry to aid your ailing sister." Aurelia scooted forward in her seat. "How is she, by the way? I have been so concerned for her."

Jastyn raised an eyebrow but stepped closer when another push from the lines forced her forward. *What an odd thing, a Diarmaid who cares.* "That is why I wish to thank you. I was able to use the bracelet to obtain a cure. Well, a temporary one. But Alanna is doing much better now."

The last sentence stumbled out of her mouth, and she bit her tongue as the words skidded to a halt. What was she thinking? Here she was, boasting a happy, healthy sister while the princess mourned the passing of her brother. But if Aurelia felt any sense of bitterness about this, she didn't show it. Rather, she said, "I am pleased to hear such happy news."

An angry shout came from behind her. "Keep moving!"

Her neck grew hot, but Jastyn forced herself to keep her composure. Aurelia sniffled again. "Well, thank you for coming." She paused. "It is good to see you."

Aurelia reached out. It was only after Jastyn took the pale, thin wrist in hand that she realized the princess was going for a handshake. But she couldn't halt her actions, and when her lips kissed the soft skin along the princess's knuckles, Jastyn's entire body felt red hot. The feeling was only magnified when she looked up. The princess's eyes were wide, but her thin lips curved in a smile.

Not waiting another second, Jastyn mumbled her good-byes, yanked on her hood, and dashed back into the folds of the crowd.

CHAPTER FOURTEEN

Aurelia didn't hear the woman standing in front of her. Her head buzzed like a beehive in springtime. Slowly, the buzz scattered and chased away the fog that had overcome her mind the last two days. She pushed herself up in her seat, craning her neck to follow where Jastyn had gone. But elusive as ever, Jastyn was nowhere to be seen.

"Darling, what is it?"

Her mother's curious expression made Aurelia falter. She tried to respond, to explain that Jastyn had been here, that she was real, but before she could do so a high, piercing whistle swooped over them from the clouds. Hundreds of eyes drew skyward.

The sound washed over the lawns, then morphed into a shrill shriek. People covered their ears. A few searched the sky, slack-jawed, eager to find the source of what was surely a surprise for the festival. But the clouds took on a gray hue, and the formerly cerulean sky fell to a foreboding green.

The whistling grew louder.

"Dechtire! Grannus!"

Aurelia's parents gaped as Baroness Enya ran full speed up the knoll toward them, her crane-like neck bobbing atop her small shoulders. She leapt over piles of discarded pheasant bones and shoved through confused onlookers.

Her eyes were fearful when she shouted. "Elves! Elves are coming!"

Somebody screamed. Aurelia's father jumped from his throne,

knocking over the bushel of potatoes at his feet. They scattered and rolled like awkward stones. People ran. More screams mixed with the piercing sound from overhead, and Aurelia spotted the nearly invisible set of arrows bulleting through the air. When twenty arrowheads found their targets in the legs, stomachs, and backs of unsuspecting villagers, her heart sank.

"Sound the drums!" her father roared.

The alarm went off in a matter of seconds, shaking the ground as the drums beat out their warning, but it was miraculous anybody heard it. Chaos had broken loose over the Kingdom of Venostes. Wailing children were scooped up and borne under their father's strong arms. Cups and string instruments lay overturned, quickly trampled and crushed by thousands of frightened feet. Fires spurted, their smoke choking the lawns. People crawled with tear-streaked cheeks, shouting for loved ones and a way out.

Aurelia managed to stand but stumbled when a group of women sprinted through her on their way to one of the musicians. Her gaze followed their frantic flight. The man lay unconscious, an arrow lodged in his throat.

Aghast, Aurelia rushed over to her parents. Her father spoke hurriedly to a guardsman. Her mother grabbed her daughter's hands.

"What is happening?" Aurelia cried.

"I don't know."

Her mother's honesty rocked Aurelia back. "I don't understand."

Her father gave a final order to the guardsman, who rushed off barking at the nearby troop of soldiers already at attention. More shouts erupted behind them. A new sound rumbled in the distance: an army of footsteps drawing near.

When her father spoke, he paled. "It doesn't matter why they are here. We won't let them near you or your brother."

Aurelia's jaw dropped. *Brennus*. She saw the disbelief in her father's eyes, but that was nothing in comparison to the rage burning bright in her mother's gaze.

"They will not touch him." Her mother spun around to the baroness, who had been helping villagers under nearby low-hanging trees for shelter. "Who is with him now? I thought it was you."

"Drest is watching over him. He won't let anyone near him, I assure you."

Her father nodded. There was a flash of something in her mother's eyes, but before Aurelia could pinpoint it, she was ushered toward the other side of the thrones.

"Come," her mother said quickly. She, Aurelia, and the baroness darted behind the backs of the chairs, shadowed by a trio of guardsmen.

"What about Father?"

"He will be fine. We must get you to safety." She glanced around. The lawns were beginning to clear, but many people still scrambled about, frightened and confused. A dozen or so lay unmoving on the grass. "The elves will be here any minute."

Pursing her lips in a deep breath to steady herself, Aurelia said, "I want to help."

Her mother's eyes came to a quick halt on Aurelia. "You will do no such thing. You will go with Baroness Enya. She will take you to the castle." The baroness nodded and said something to one of the guardsmen.

"Mother, please." Aurelia's legs trembled as they crouched behind their stone barrier. Groans of pain and agonized pleas from men and women engulfed them, but she refused to dwell on the sound. She focused instead on the quickly swelling desire to act. "I want to help," she said again.

Her mother held up a hand. "No. You must go, now." She nodded toward the baroness, who grabbed Aurelia's elbow.

"Come, Your Highness. We need to move."

The baroness's grip was tight, but Aurelia shook her off. "I will not cower in fear while the ghouls who killed my brother come for the rest of him. I refuse to let them take him." She pleaded with her mother. "Please. Let me defend him with you."

Her mother had undone her cloak and laid it over a woman nearby whose knee had been the target of not one but two arrows. When she stood, her hands shook, which Aurelia could feel as her mother grabbed both of her arms.

"Aurelia. Please. I will not lose you, too."

The words fell in Aurelia's throat. That same prick of motivation that screamed out for her to help, to do something, to not be useless continued to roar. But in her mother's grasp she felt a parent's deepest fear coming to fruition. She smelled it in the air, ripe with fresh blood and thick smoke. When her own eyes stung with tears, Aurelia nodded.

Her mother kissed her forehead brusquely, then pushed her toward the baroness. "Now go!"

The last glimpse of her parents saw her mother standing alongside her father, both of them accepting swords and shields from two guardsmen. Then they were gone in the crowd as the baroness dragged Aurelia to the edges of the Wood, back to the castle.

❖

"Hurry, keep pace!"

"I'm trying!"

Aurelia's calf cramped, and she grimaced as she raced to stay at the baroness's heels. They had snaked in and out of crowds behind a pair of guardsmen for what seemed like ages, though Aurelia knew it had only been a matter of seconds. Part of her was ashamed at her poor physical shape; Baroness Enya could have run to the castle and back in the time Aurelia's labored stride had gotten to where they were now. But what had truly slowed her down was the agonizing scene around them. They had to jump over fallen villagers. Children sat alone, wailing for their lost mothers or fathers. Bodies lay across the lawns, and Aurelia's shoes sank into puddles of blood. She averted her eyes in order to continue moving. And though the sound of the impending army hadn't dimmed, she took faith in the fact that they were moving farther from the inevitable next round of arrows. Not one second later, though, guilt at the idea of abandoning the kingdom hit her like a shovel. She gritted her teeth and willed herself to keep moving.

A troop of guardsmen in full armor sprinted past, and one from the duo leading the baroness took off with them. Several village women tended to the wounded on the edges of the lawns. Men carried children toward the Wood. The gates ahead of them were open, and people streamed out, fleeing for their homes.

A stitch pricked Aurelia's side, making her stumble. Then a colliding force took her off her feet, and she was flung sideways.

"Your Highness!" Baroness Enya cried.

Aurelia's shoulder stung with the ground's impact. Wincing, she cried out at the pain. On her side, Aurelia found the baroness twenty paces away. But another crowd ran by, forcing Baroness Enya and the guardsman backward. Aurelia shielded her face as people stampeded past.

"Baroness!" she called, trying to stand. But her cramp had worsened. She tried to put weight on her left leg but fell instantly. "Gods be damned!" she shouted. "Baroness Enya!" she called again, scanning the lawns, peering over heads and shoulders.

"Aurelia!" The baroness's shouts were distant now.

Holding her shoulder, Aurelia stood slowly, forcing her weight to her right side. She stumbled forward. Several people knocked against her.

"Your Highness?"

A squeaking voice sounded from her left. She glanced through layers of smoke to find a familiar face.

"Coran!"

"M'lady Aurelia!" He scampered closer. There was blood on his cheek, and his pants were torn on the knee. His wild orange hair, however, remained unscathed.

"You must return to the village, Coran. It's not safe! The elves," she said, then swallowed. "They're coming."

Coran ignored her. "You're hurt," he said, slipping an arm under her and around her back. "Let me help you, Your Highness."

He hitched her up beside him. More agonized cries flew up from the murky ground. At the same time, new figures emerged in the distance. Tall. Lean. Moving quickly in their direction.

Aurelia gasped. "They're here."

"Come, you need to get back to the castle, m'lady."

Together, they ran. Aurelia stared at the mottled lawns. When fingers reached out to brush her hand or her hip, or grazed desperately against her ankle, she didn't look down despite the ache in her heart. There was no time.

Eventually, she could see the outline of the stables.

"Almost there, m'lady."

A horse thundered out from the smoke, cutting across their path. They both fell backward. The rider wore a thick navy cloak bearing the kingdom's colors. The horse neighed and reared up, its hooves kicking the air.

Coran shielded her, but Aurelia stood quickly.

"Drest? Keller!"

Her horse whinnied in recognition while Drest removed his hood and extended his left arm. "Aurelia! Thank the gods I found you!"

"Found me?" Aurelia bent to help Coran to his feet.

Drest shook his head. "I saw my mother. She said you two were separated. Come! I'll take you to the castle."

Aurelia's mind, which had been stuck in slow motion, finally kicked into gear. The image of her brother lying in the castle flew to her mind's eye.

"Brennus!"

"We must make haste!"

Aurelia grabbed Drest's hand. She spun back to Coran.

"You, too!"

But Coran looked past her toward the horse and rider. Slowly, he shook his head. "You go, m'lady. I've got to find my mum."

She released Drest's hand. Awash in relief and exhaustion, Aurelia flew forward, hugging Coran tightly. "Thank you for your help." She stepped back. "Go, find your mother. Good luck."

He nodded and, after a glance up to Drest, disappeared into the crowd.

Swiftly, Aurelia joined Drest atop Keller. He reared them back, turning Keller toward the edge of the lawns.

Once they were off, Aurelia buried her head into Drest's back, catching her breath. She attuned her racing heart to the steady clomp of Keller's stride. Eyes pinched tight, she tried to comprehend the last hour. Distressed faces and painful cries filled her mind. She didn't even realize she was crying until she leaned back and felt tears on her hot cheeks. Hastily, she wiped them away.

When her vision cleared, she glanced around, still holding on to Drest's waist.

"We've turned too far west. The castle is the other direction."

Drest's reply was delayed. "What do you mean?" He laughed loudly. "I fear you must have hit your head, Princess."

Aurelia smiled at the idea but shook her head. "Now is not the time for games. We need to return to Brennus. Who is watching over him?"

The Wood bounced into view. They were on the other side of the castle, opposite the stables and closer to the border of the village dwellings. The trees were basked in shadows like faceless warriors standing guard.

Why wasn't he turning around?

Their pace grew faster. Drest had a tight grip on Keller's reins. Aurelia could feel the tension in her best mare's strong body.

"Drest, didn't you hear me? Who is with Brennus?" His silence grew eerie. The wind whipped at their ears. She craned her neck in order to see his face. But Drest's blond locks curled around his jaw and forehead like a shield, making it impossible for her to tell what he was thinking.

Aurelia glanced behind them. There was more smoke over the lawns: a screen of gray and black beneath the sickly green sky. Lamented battle cries broke through the air. The castle's faint outline grew smaller in the distance.

Finally, Aurelia spun back around, fed up with his coy attitude. "Drest, this isn't funny," she shouted over the thunderous hooves and harsh wind. "I command you tell me where we are going!"

When Drest turned, Aurelia's stomach dropped.

His eyes were clear as glass, and a sickening smile was etched into his stubbled cheek. His voice matched the maliciousness of his face when he said, "You always did ask too many questions."

Then his elbow swung back, and there was darkness.

CHAPTER FIFTEEN

Aurelia awoke with a pounding headache and an intense throbbing running from her shoulders to her legs, which were numb. She groaned and sputtered, tasting blood and dirt. A blockage of something thick made her choke when she tried to cough, and she quickly realized a rag had been tied around her face, gagging her. She blinked. Her stomach sank at the darkness around her, and she feared she must have been blindfolded. Slowly, though, her eyes adjusted. She wasn't blindfolded; night had fallen.

Heart racing, Aurelia lifted her sore head from where it had been hanging against her chest. How long had she been unconscious? Her legs were tucked awkwardly beneath her, and they slowly gained sensation after she wriggled on the ground. Damp moss and grass tickled her tightly clenched fingers. She could smell the earth—fresh like wind after rain. Her wrists itched, and she felt a crude rope tied around them. It didn't take long to realize her hands were bound behind her back.

As her mind cleared, voices drifted over from behind the hundreds of trees surrounding her. *I'm in the forest. How did I get here?*

Drest.

The memory came back in a jolt, like the feeling of missing a step climbing the tower stairs. Her body lurched, and rage bubbled inside her chest. Drest had done this to her. But why? Why take her away from the castle? Why do this on the day of her brother's remembrance? Nothing made any sense. She scanned her surroundings, hoping to catch a glimpse of Keller. As she did, the voices came to a halt, and rustling sounded nearby.

A towering, slender figure emerged from the dark pillars of trees. Aurelia pushed herself back against the trunk she sat in front of, fumbling her tied hands over the large roots at its base.

"What kind of royalty cowers from the unknown?" an elven voice sneered. Despite the less-than-kind comment, his voice was lovely. It rose and fell like a lyre being plucked. Another elf with the same gray eyes and nearly iridescent skin that seemed to glow in the moonlight followed the first out from behind a tree. Together, they walked toward her.

"The human kind. Remember: they're not like us. They hide behind their magic and high walls out of fear, not power. This one is an example of the many weak members of man."

Aurelia grimaced. She felt afraid but grew angrier with each word the elves spoke. *Who do they think they are? And why are they saying such things?* She had always believed the elves to be kind, stoic fae. At least, that was what she had read about and what she was taught by her mother and father.

Of course, her mother hadn't taught her about the Well of Slaine. Perhaps there were some things she believed that weren't as true as she had originally imagined.

The first elf, wearing a flowing green tunic of light material, rested his forearm on a bow that came up to his chest. "Tell me again why we can't take her back to our queen."

"She's not ours to claim." The next phrase was spoken in their native tongue, and Aurelia recognized one word from the fae's mouth: prince.

She tried to yell, but only muffled cries came from behind her gag. She glared at the elves standing a few yards away.

"That riled her up. I'm pleased to know the humans care about their own kin."

Aurelia fumed, her chest heaving. She felt her entire understanding of the kingdom begin to shift and crumble like the sandcastle she had made on the shore years ago once the tide changed. How could fae like these—arrogant and rude in their demeanor—have ever been allies with their family?

Frustrated, she sank back against the tree. Her mind raced. What had become of Brennus's body? Had the Elves won the battle back at the castle? Surely her parents and their army had been able to hold their ground. She had to believe her brother was safe. It was all too much, and her head ached terribly. A familiar heavy tread stomped out from behind the same set of trees from which the elves had emerged.

"Ah, you're awake. Wonderful."

Drest stood next to the pair of elves. Despite his impressive height and width, the fae were nearly a foot taller than him. He placed one hand on the hilt of his sword before kneeling in front of Aurelia, who locked her gaze on his.

"I do apologize for that blow earlier." He reached out to brush hair from her face, then ran a hand along her cheekbone. At his touch, Aurelia winced at what was surely a nasty bruise. "But I had to shut you up somehow."

Aurelia's jaw clenched, squeezing the rag between her teeth. She tried to work her fingers free from behind her back, but her flame never grew larger than an elderberry before it flickered out again. She was too exhausted; she needed more energy.

"Here, let me help you with this." Drest pulled the rag from her mouth, letting it fall below her chin. Aurelia gasped, inhaling cool night air. "Water," Drest ordered. The elves exchanged glances. Then one stepped forward, pulling a flask from behind his back and offering it to Drest. He took it, unscrewed the top, and held the opening up to Aurelia's lips. She eyed it warily. "It's not poisoned. Drink."

Slowly, she tilted her head back and let him feed her the water. She relished the cold liquid as it ran down her throat. She gulped gratefully for a minute, then sat back.

"Good." Drest capped the flask and tossed it back to the elf, who muttered something to his companion in their native language.

"She's of no use to us dead," Drest replied. "Aurelia stays alive until I get what I need." He cleared his throat when one of the elves stepped forward. "*We.* Until we get what we need."

Aurelia stared at him. "I didn't know you spoke elven."

Standing, Drest wiped off his hands. "There are many things you don't know about me, Aurelia." He rolled his neck to stretch it. "They can speak our tongue, as I imagine you were wondering," he said quickly, waving a hand at the elves. "Though it's a stunted, garbled version. But that's to expect from fae." The elves' eyes narrowed at

Drest, but they remained silent. Drest, meanwhile, was staring at a spot behind Aurelia's shoulder, seeming to forget momentarily that she was even there until she spoke again.

Fearing the worst, Aurelia asked, "Keller?"

His eyes still locked on the tree behind her left shoulder, Drest waved his other hand. "Oh, I let her go once we were deep enough in the Wood. I'm sure she can find her way back to the castle."

Aurelia closed her eyes. *Gods, I hope she can.*

"My companions prefer to travel by foot. It's easier."

"How can you be on their side? Tell me that, at least." She gestured with her chin toward the elves. "They're the ones who poisoned my brother! Because of their arrow, the water from the Well of Slaine was useless. They're to blame."

"Well," Drest said, "I am glad you said that. It must mean Dechtire and Grannus believe that, too."

The buzz of insects and fairies halted. Every sound in the Wood seemed to vanish, caught in a moment's net as Aurelia's skin grew hot, and blood surged in her ears.

"You mean—"

Drest only smiled.

"No. It can't be. I don't believe it. I won't!"

"Believe what you want, Aurelia. It's really none of my concern."

When he turned to go, she shouted, "I believe that you were my brother's best friend! You were *my* friend. You had our trust, our family's trust. And you betrayed us by leaving Brennus for the elves to claim."

Even in the dark, Aurelia could see the lightness overtake Drest's eyes as they went clear. "Wait, Drest," she said, knowing what was about to happen. She had seen him use this spell on drunken villagers who heckled him for money in the street. "Where are you taking me? What do you want?" When he didn't respond, she cried more desperately, "You won't get away with this."

But Drest's smile was wide as the air whipped around them, spinning itself into a tunnel aimed directly at her. Aurelia turned her cheek to shield her face, but it was no use. The wind penetrated her mind and stirred her thoughts until they were a torrent of pain. She cried out until the memories from the last few days overwhelmed her, and she fell unconscious once again.

❖

Two days after the attack, the Kingdom of Venostes was in shambles. The royal grounds—where not forty-eight hours earlier a jubilant festival celebrating the life of a fallen son had been—lay strewn with broken remnants of a disastrous day. Most of the bodies had been claimed, but a handful of poor souls still lay alone on the lawns, tucked haphazardly along the edges of the Wood. Ash-soaked firepits steamed against fog that had settled over the grounds. Empty casks of wine lay beside half-eaten legs of lamb that now played host to eager ravens picking at the bones.

Not even the four thrones escaped unscathed by the surprise elven invasion. The top corners of the king's polished, spiked stone were gone, blown off in a fiery showdown. Queen Dechtire's chair had lost a side of its base. Now the magnificent seat tilted toward her daughter's, which was scorched black on all sides. The prince's throne, however, took the most blows from the enemy: its entire back side had crumbled, demolishing the gifts left along its seat and arms so that now the whole thing resembled an obliterated pastry left decayed and abandoned to the elements.

Jastyn had gone each of the days following the tumult to survey the land and help Coran and their neighbors bring home victims of the attack. Coran's mom had been one of them, suffering a stab wound to her back. Miraculously, there didn't seem to have been any major damage to her spine. Coran had tended to her first, and Jastyn took turns dressing the wound between the hours they roamed the grounds together.

"I hear Queen Dechtire is openin' the gates tomorrow so that the injured can come to her for help." Coran's voice was optimistic when he said this over a shared chunk of bread Jastyn had gotten from her mother on their way out the door that morning.

"That woman must be some kind of saint," Jastyn said between chews. Coran eyed her, and she knew he was surprised, considering her feelings for the royal family. She shrugged and added, "It's a decent thing, to think of others after losing her son."

"And her daughter."

Jastyn swallowed another bite. "They don't know she's lost for good, Coran. She might have simply…I don't know…run into the Wood for shelter during the whole thing and…lost her way."

"Princess Aurelia never did go into the Wood that often."

"I'm sure she's fine," Jastyn said. Though the idea of Aurelia surviving alone in the Wood was hard for her to imagine. If the wild animals and rain-filled nights didn't get her, there were hundreds of unfriendly fae always looking for something new to get their hands on.

They finished their food in silence before heading off toward the market streets. The booths were closed, still honoring the wake period for the prince despite the cancellation of the remembrance ceremonies. The scene on the dirt roads was only mildly better than that of the lawns near the castle. Food scraps lay everywhere, and torn and trampled cloth lay scattered along the paths weaving between sections of the market. The elves had been ruthless in their rampage, only leaving the village homes intact as they stormed over the kingdom like ravenous wolves.

"I still can't believe the prince went untouched." Jastyn's eyes lifted to the towering front gates of the castle to their left. "It felt inevitable that he would be taken."

"The army was able to hold their ground outside the gate. Plus, Roisin told me that the queen had laid an extra protection spell over his body." He handed a small piece of their bread to a hungry-eyed little girl sitting near an abandoned booth. "She is a wise woman, Queen Dechtire."

"Yet she seems to hire staff who are entirely too loose-lipped," Jastyn said with a nudge in Coran's ribs.

"Roisin is a trustworthy maiden," Coran said, defending the girl Jastyn had been hearing about for the last three months. She was glad to know Coran had found somebody in the castle to connect with, but she couldn't resist teasing him. He was like a brother to her.

Jastyn laughed. "I'm sure she is."

Coran's face turned serious as they rounded a corner. The castle's stables came into view. "She's been mighty sad, though, since it all happened. Her charge is gone. She feels as lost as the royal family."

Jastyn stopped. "Roisin is Aurelia's maiden?"

"Princess Aurelia. Yeah. Didn't I mention that?"

Shaking her head, Jastyn said, "She was Aurelia's right hand?"

Coran nodded. "In a sense. She didn't make any big decisions or nothin', but she did have the princess's ear. They've been together since they were young."

Jastyn walked a little faster when they rounded a bend and started for the stables. "Coran, do you think you can get me a word with your fair Roisin?"

He faltered, glancing around. "I don't know, Jas. It's not really a good time."

"Nonsense. Elisedd won't be in for another half hour. That's more than enough time to speak with her."

"What do you need to talk to her for? She's got nothin' to do with anythin'."

Jastyn squared around to face Coran as they reached the low gate leading to the pastures in front of the stable. "I'm not saying she does. But if anybody knows what could have happened to Aurelia, it's gotta be Roisin." Jastyn's body felt light as the beginnings of a plan formed in the back of her mind.

"But the king and queen—"

"Have been mourning their son for the last four days. Think about it. The only one who's really spoken to Aurelia since her brother's passing was probably her maiden."

Coran frowned as he opened the gate, and they wandered across the pasture. None of the horses were out yet, and the grounds were peaceful in the dawning light.

Sighing, he said, "All right. But don't blame me if she doesn't want to talk to you."

Jastyn grinned. "Thank you. I owe you."

Coran eyed her on their way inside the stable. "Yeah. I'll add it to your list."

Ten minutes later, Jastyn leaned against one of the horse pen walls, tapping her foot while she waited for Coran to return. The mare Jastyn had seen the princess ride in on nearly a month ago was missing from the stables, but a chestnut brown stallion stood nearby. Between bites of hay, it whinnied in her direction.

"Don't look at me like that." It neighed again, bobbing its head, seemingly amused. "What do you mean why am *I* here? I'm trying to help find *your* princess."

The horse brayed. "Why?" Jastyn squinted at the horse, then looked down, scratching her boot along the wooden floor. Why *was* she here? She wasn't one to jump in and help right away, especially when it came to the royal family. They absolutely didn't deserve it. Or need it. Especially after what they did to her mother. Except…Aurelia was different.

When the horse whinnied at her again, Jastyn snorted. "I do not feel that way about her, or anyone, thank you very much."

Despite herself, Jastyn imagined Aurelia riding in the fields, carefree and laughing. Her heart ached at the image, then skipped when she pictured herself riding alongside.

"Stop it, Jastyn." She shook her head. "You have no business entangling yourself with a noble."

Noble.

Jastyn's throat went dry as the Red One's words rushed back. *A noble sacrifice will be required.* It couldn't be. Could it? Beginning to pace, Jastyn tried to put the pieces together. "Alanna fell ill. I sought the queen's help, but Aurelia is the one who gave me the bracelet." The horse brayed. She glared into its big, blinking gaze. "You don't mean that. The Red One is vicious, but to intend Aurelia as the means to the cure…"

"Who are you talkin' to?"

Jastyn spun around. In the doorway at the end of the narrow path between the pens stood Coran and Roisin.

Jastyn straightened, running a hand over her braid. "Just myself. Roisin?"

The stocky girl with a wide but pretty face nodded. "Are you Coran's friend? The one from the village?"

Stepping forward, Jastyn shook the maiden's hand, clasping hers around Roisin's muscular forearm. "I'm Jastyn Cipher. It's nice to meet you. Heard a lot about you." She winked, and Roisin blushed before exchanging bashful glances with Coran.

She cleared her throat. "Coran mentioned you wanted to see me?"

"To talk to you, yes. You were close with the princess?"

"M'lady Aurelia? Yes, I'm her maiden. We're together most of the day. Or rather, we were." She looked down and wiped her eyes. "My poor lady Aurelia. The poor family Diarmaid." She began to whimper. Coran reached into his pocket and pulled out a piece of cloth and handed it to Roisin, who blew her nose and took a deep breath. "Apologies. It's been a tryin' couple of days."

Jastyn nodded. "Of course. I wondered if you might have any idea where the princess may have gone. Surely, you don't think she was taken by the elves?"

Roisin's eyes went wide. "Gods, I hope not. And to think, they were our allies! To do such a thing." More tears fell. Coran rubbed her arm supportively.

"Have you heard anything? Or did the princess say anything about any place she might've gone if there was trouble?"

They stood quietly while Roisin thought. "No. I'm sorry." She pointed to the door behind them. "This is where she would go. The castle was the safe ground. I'm certain she would have tried to get back here during the chaos. She would have wanted to know her brother was all right."

"Could she have escaped into the Wood?"

"Not likely." Roisin bit her lip, folding the handkerchief between her hands. "The princess is very capable, but I'm afraid she and her brother were never allowed to venture very far from castle grounds. She wouldn't know her way out there in the Wood."

Coran gave Jastyn a look. "Well, thank you anyway, Roisin. If you hear anything—"

"There is something," Roisin said between sniffles. "It's not about the princess's whereabouts. But I overheard the king and queen last night." Jastyn and Coran moved closer, despite being the only ones in the stables. "There's going to be an announcement first thing tomorrow. They're going to call a kingdom-wide search for Aurelia, for anybody who can help. And they're offering a reward."

Jastyn bit the inside of her cheek. "A reward?" she echoed. Coran shot her a look, and Jastyn tried not to fidget. The kingdom was notoriously stingy with their riches. Of course, a member of the royal family had never gone missing before. Trying to contain her excitement, Jastyn asked, "What kind of a reward?"

Roisin replied, "Queen Dechtire and King Grannus will give five thousand rubies to whoever can find the princess and bring her home."

Chapter Sixteen

Roisin was right.

The next day, Queen Dechtire and King Grannus announced a reward for their daughter's return. The entire kingdom and even a few groups of forest-dwelling fae gathered to witness the proclamation which took place in the middle of the market upon its first open day since the invasion.

Jastyn found herself entrenched in the latest event in the Kingdom of Venostes as she escorted Alanna—still faring well thanks to the banshee blood—to the announcement under the watchful eye of Elisedd. Together, they pushed through the onlookers, eventually finding a spot near the back of the crowd where the three of them watched the king clear his throat and unfurl a parchment scroll.

"Hear me. On this day, I announce a reward to anyone who can return Princess Aurelia Diarmaid—now heir to the Diarmaid throne—to the Kingdom of Venostes and back to her family. Aurelia is believed to be somewhere in the Wood. However, the Wood runs deep. Therefore, we request those who know these lands to lend your knowledge to aid in the rescue and recovery of our fair daughter."

The crowd nodded, and the air filled with eager whispers. Alanna nudged Jastyn, who didn't have to catch her sister's gaze to know what she was thinking. And while the king continued to speak, Jastyn knew her mind was already made up, and Alanna's inevitable encouraging speech would fall on stoic ears. Jastyn had decided hours ago, as soon as Roisin told her of the reward, that she would not miss this opportunity.

Thus, later that day, Jastyn was prepared when her mother pulled her aside at the wash basin after their midday meal and handed her Elisedd's dirty bowl to clean.

"I have a feeling you've made up your mind."

Running the bowl under water, Jastyn stared at her hands, then handed her mother the bowl to dry with a worn rag. "My opinions of the royal family have not changed. You should know that. Anyone who believes banishment to the lowest rung of the kingdom as sufficient consequence for what you did is completely backward. I have no respect for the Diarmaids in that regard."

Her mother took a cup from Jastyn, her hand lingering on her daughter's. Jastyn lowered her voice after a glance over her shoulder. "But the princess is kidnapped. The prince is gone. The kingdom cannot go on the way it should unless Aurelia is returned."

Jastyn ignored the pause in her mother's drying at her use of the princess's first name. "Not long ago, I would have imagined your delight at the crumbling of the royal family."

"I guess I've learned to channel my anger into other things," Jastyn said, hoping her mother didn't see the flush on the back of her neck at the thought of the princess. "Besides, the reward would help us greatly. Making sure Aurelia is safe and brought back unharmed would simply be an additional token of good fortune." She fumbled on her words and tried not to imagine the hopeful gaze of Aurelia's eyes in the reflection of the water. She scrubbed off a piece of stew stuck to a spoon, then wiped sweat from her forehead that had formed in the heat of a rare warm day. As she swiped her sleeve across her face, she caught her mother staring. "What?" She grabbed the rag from her to dry her hands. "What is it with everyone lately? Eegit looked at me that same way when I spoke of Aurelia."

Her mother smiled. "You have the biggest heart, my daughter."

Before Jastyn could ask what she meant, her mother motioned for her to follow. They walked past Alanna and Elisedd out the front door, where her mother dumped their dirty water next to the side of the house. She tucked the now empty basin against her hip, exhaled, and leaned her neck back to take in the clouds that turned the blue sky nearly silver.

"The true cure for your sister lies in the western caves?"

Jastyn leaned against the waist-high wall that separated their home from yards of wild grass that ran right to the Wood. "That's what the Red One said. Eegit believes it to be true."

"What do you believe?" Her mother fixed her gaze on Jastyn, who fingered the end of her belt before responding.

"I believe this whole mess with Aurelia, this search to bring her back, is the perfect path." She paused, wary of sharing thoughts she'd been having for days. They felt personal, despite the fact she wasn't sure why. "It's like the gods have lined everything up. Alanna, the Red One, and now Aurelia. The three of them have come together and aligned to lead me to this day. It feels…"

"Inevitable."

More clouds rolled in and the wind picked up, scattering leaves over their feet. "Exactly."

Her mother moved to stand beside her. Their elbows brushed. Jastyn had forgotten that they were the same height now. Her mother wiped her hands over her apron. After a while, she said, "Jastyn, I need you to understand something before you go. Something about our… about my past." She inhaled deeply, steeling herself for what she was about to say. Jastyn turned to listen.

"Nearly twenty-three years ago, I fell in love with the most beautiful man. He was kind, strong, and had the most ferocious spirit of anybody I had ever known." A smile lit her face. "We met at the summer solstice festival. Those days were filled with laughter and even more love."

Jastyn's heart ran faster. She knew so little about her father, it was hard to believe that she was hearing all of this. Talk of him was rare when she was a child, then vanished altogether as the years went by. She swallowed, fearful the smallest word would break whatever spell compelled her mother to speak.

"Our time together, while wonderful, was bittersweet. You see, your father was not of the village. He wasn't even of the kingdom."

A raven cawed from a tree overhead. Jastyn asked, "He was from Gultero?" Many inhabitants of Venostes had emigrated from the neighboring kingdom set on the island across the rocky shores.

Her mother shook her head. "No."

"Then, he was from a faraway land?" Her chest tightened. "Like the East?"

It was quiet between them, the silence filled only by the growing howl of the wind.

"Jastyn, your father was a fae."

Jastyn laughed. "But I thought...no. You told me he was a fisherman from another land. I always assumed..." Her voice trailed off. She felt suddenly weak. Her hands trembled. Her mother reached out and took one of them, holding it tight in her own.

Finally, Jastyn said, "The family Diarmaid. You told me the banishment they declared on you was because I was born without a father. It's a common law in our kingdom. Was this not true?"

Tearfully, her mother shook her head. "I fought against that law. Oh, Jastyn, did I fight." She reached out, running the back of her hand down Jastyn's cheek. "The royal rules frown upon children like you, but those rules can bend. In many instances, a mother alone can still live a full life, even after she is cast out."

Jastyn's eyes stung. "But that wasn't the only law you broke, was it?"

"The same laws exist today as they did twenty-five years ago. However, the resentment and hatred between the royal family and many factions of fae was much worse. We didn't have the treaty. In those days, any human-fae relationship was unspeakable. Add to that relationship the birth of a child, well..."

Jastyn reeled. For years, she had imagined the faces of men who could be her father. In each fantasy, he was patient and handsome, strong and well-informed. Though he always wore a different face, she consistently imagined an adventurous man at sea, stalwart on a ship far out on the horizon, battling thieves and creatures from the deep ocean. Now, all of that vanished. In its place, a black anger grew.

Jastyn shook. Any hope she had harbored for herself or her family vanished. Not only was she born *gan 'athair*—without a father—but she was also a mixed child. From the second she was born, she had represented a race that, only a century before, had brought famine and destruction to their neighboring kingdom.

The history was clear: Gultero had thrived as a powerful kingdom until a new leader took the throne and decided the mingling of fae and human would be conducive to peace. He had been right, until one day, a ship of local fae returned from a stint at sea with a new crop. The entire kingdom rejoiced. When autumn came, however, no food was yielded. Instead, the earth where they'd planted had grown wretched and unusable. The disease spread across the land, poisoning trees and farmland until hundreds were left hungry. The fae who had brought in the seeds were interrogated and found guilty of treason. It was said they sought the throne and hoped to wipe out the human population. Overnight, the guilty fae were executed, and any mixed couples fled north or sailed east, and the laws changed.

This was why people ran from her. This was who she was: a reminder of a dark past and, if given the chance, the bringer of suffering and pain.

Her mother leaned close. "I know you believe your dislike of the royal family is warranted. And maybe part of it is. Gods know I couldn't spend one more day in those dungeons... But you have to understand, the laws were written before Grannus and Dechtire sat on the throne. And I...I didn't have a say when it came to whom I loved."

Jastyn hardly heard her mother. She stared at the Wood, seething, her shoulders rising and falling with each uneven breath.

Her mother reached out a hand. "Jastyn?"

"He left you." Jastyn stood and began to pace, feeling the pain in each heavy step upon the grass.

"What?"

"My father...he abandoned you. Abandoned us. What kind of a man leaves his family? What kind of a man leaves his newborn child?"

Her mother watched her. "It's not that simple, Jastyn."

She spun to face her mother. "It's not that *simple*? It's never that simple, is it? That's all I've heard from you for years. Our past, my childhood, Elisedd, Alanna—it's all 'not that simple.' Gods, Mother, don't you think that I understand that by now?"

Crossing her arms, her mother said, "Darling, it was a different time. I never wanted this to be difficult for you."

Jastyn laughed. "Are you joking? Our lives have been nothing but difficult! We live in poverty, we work like dogs, and steal like rats, for what? To scrape together a fistful of scraps barely enough for us to survive?"

When her mother moved to speak, Jastyn cut her off. "No, I know. Elisedd. That's why you married. To raise us up from the ditches."

"I love Elisedd."

"What a wonderful convenience."

Jastyn could feel her mother's eyes bore into her. Jastyn's head pounded. She felt as if a tree-dweller had taken up residence in her mind, chattering incessantly until she couldn't think. Her mother's next words, though, proved to be the cure.

"I didn't tell you until now because I wanted to protect you."

"Protect me?"

Her mother sighed. "Jastyn, please, let me help you understand."

"I understand, Mother. I understand everything. You wanted to protect me. That's all you've wanted to do. Protect me from the harsh winters when the only shelter we had was a hollowed-out oak tree at the Wood's edge. Protect me when I was hunted—at seven years old—by royal guardsmen for excessive thieving in the markets. Protect me from the prying eyes of curious neighbors, wondering at the Odium Child with dirt on her nose and scrapes on her knees."

"As a mother it's my job to—"

"Protect me! I know. But what you did *wasn't* protecting me. You denied me a life. You kept me from the festivals, from the ceremonies, from befriending anyone my own age. It's only by sheer luck and a near-death experience Coran came into my life. You did so well at making me feel righteous about our state in life. You fooled me completely. You got me to believe I had no choice in this. No choice but to take your hand and fight for everything. You taught me so well, you turned everything around. I became exactly what you wanted me to be."

Jastyn took a breath, her entire body shaking. "I became *your* protector."

A tear ran down her mother's cheek as the wind whipped hair across her face. "You're wrong."

"Then why did you sit back and let me become this? This lowly peasant whose best qualities are pickpocketing and lying my way into and out of things. *You* made me this way." Jastyn felt as if she was going to be sick. She didn't realize she was crying until her face stung in the harsh wind whirling over them. "You made me this way. And I resent you for it."

"You don't mean that."

Jastyn's head throbbed. She looked at her fingers, pale from being clenched tight. She met her mother's gaze. Finding no words, she turned to go.

"Stop. Jastyn, wait. You need to talk to me. We can't leave things like this."

Jastyn kept walking.

Her mother's voice grew louder. "As your mother I command you to stop!"

Jastyn faltered only a step. More clouds rolled in overhead. Any other words her mother spoke were eaten by the blistering gale sweeping over the village hills, transforming the sky into a sheet of gray. Jastyn conjured her saol and let it lead her as far away from her mother as she could get.

CHAPTER SEVENTEEN

Four days.

For four days they had marched through the wood. Aurelia woke each morning, the world still dark. She was fed a stale lump of bread and allowed one minute of water from their group's shared flask. Then she was yanked to her feet and expected to trail behind Drest until midday. That was when the pair of elves, following behind, would call out in their native tongue, which by day four Aurelia interpreted to mean something along the lines of "It's time to eat." At that point, the fae would locate a small creek or a narrow pond where the four of them settled for an hour. Then the process was repeated. Water, marching, food. Aurelia could request two minutes alone to relieve herself. The elves would unravel their rope snare, which wrapped and unwrapped itself from around her wrists only on their command. Aurelia had never seen such rope before or known of abilities to control it through magic. While the elf with broader shoulders was strict with her time each day, Aurelia noticed that the slender-framed fae with a sloped nose gave her an extra minute and didn't tie her wrists as tight as his companion. She even thought she had seen a glimmer of pity in his gray gaze, though perhaps that was only her desperation conjuring wishful thinking.

Drest, she deduced, was paying the elves to keep a close eye. At night, when they all tucked themselves away in a clearing to start a fire to sleep by, Aurelia had witnessed an exchange. Each evening, around sunset, Drest went on his own into the Wood. Aurelia ate her ration of bread quietly. During this time, the elves spoke quietly until he returned. Moments later, the elves tucked something inside their tunics. What it was, Aurelia hadn't yet figured out.

What Drest was using as motivation for the elves, though, Aurelia didn't really care. By day four, Aurelia only cared about one thing: escape. After the first night in the Wood, the night after the invasion at her brother's remembrance, Aurelia had felt overcome. She had felt helpless and weak and wished all night for her parents to find her. But with each passing day, it began to set in that Aurelia was alone. There was no way of knowing when, or even if, her parents would rescue her. How could they? She had no idea where she was. She hated to admit that she hadn't even known in which direction they were traveling. Between the dense tree cover and the seemingly aimless path they walked each day, it was impossible to know.

So now, as she trudged behind Drest, glaring into his back with all of the hatred she could muster, she planned. And when the sun began to fall and she heard the elves shout from behind her, she knew it had to be tonight. Tonight, she would run. Tonight, she would escape.

Her three captors set up camp for the night. It was the same routine: the elves collected firewood, then invoked magic to spark the flames. Aurelia sat at the base of a tree watching the flickering light, as she did each night. Her hands were still tied but looser than they were this morning, thanks to her less-intense captor. She smiled at Drest, who collected piles of leaves and brush for himself to lie upon. He had to be the laziest kidnapper in history. Since her capture, he had hardly given her a second look. Granted, he disappeared into the Wood for half the day. When he was around, he talked mostly to himself under his breath, only glancing over his shoulder occasionally on their marches to confirm she was still behind him.

Now, Aurelia observed the nightly ritual. When she was certain the three of them were occupied, she unfurled her left hand against her right, making sure to cup her palm so that what was inside couldn't be seen. During their midday meal, she had requested a moment to relieve herself. While the elves stood guard five paces away, she had plucked a fistful of valerian root from a clump of overgrown brush. The pale pink flowers were faded at the tips, signs of the warm summer. The plant's sweet scent wafted over her, and she hoped it wouldn't linger for long.

Looking down at the petals, she took a deep breath. *It has to be tonight.* The fire crackled louder, and Drest barked an order at the elves. Aurelia closed her eyes. She focused on the crackling of the fire and worked to drown out Drest. She focused on the sound of the sparks jumping from the wood, on the hiss of the flames. She let the sounds wash over her mind.

When her mind did clear, Aurelia wasn't surprised to see Jastyn. For the last two nights, Jastyn had been the focal point of her dreams. She even walked beside her in the day when her feet ached within her boots and her knees threatened to give out. Though Aurelia knew this Jastyn was only a friendly hallucination, brought on from lack of food and water, Aurelia nevertheless took comfort in her presence. She lost herself in the confidence in Jastyn's eyes, held on to her quiet strength, which she willed herself to carry her through what she was about to do.

Her mind shifted again, this time to an old memory. She was in the study with her mother and Brennus. Letting the visions engulf her, Aurelia lost herself for a moment in what once was.

"Brennus, what would you recommend for an individual with respiratory issues?"

Her brother frowned, a faint line creasing his young forehead. "Like when father suffered the chills and coughed for three days?"

Their mother nodded. "What would you prescribe?"

Aurelia's gaze went back and forth between them like a hungry hummingbird flitting between blossoms. She raised her hand, bouncing in her seat.

Brennus glanced at her, then back at their mother. "Mullein root?"

Aurelia stuck her hand higher. Their mother sighed. "Not quite, my darling."

Sinking in his seat, Brennus grumbled. "I hate this stuff. When will Father return? I'm eager to go hunting."

Their mother sighed. "Aurelia, what would you recommend?"

"Coltsfoot," she replied. "Crush and boil the plant to create a thick syrup. Administer twice a day until better."

"Know-it-all." Brennus elbowed her, and she stuck out her tongue. Their mother placed her hands on her hips.

"Final question. The winner gets the last piece of loganberry pie tonight at dinner."

Brennus and Aurelia shot up in their seats. They listened carefully as their mother spoke. "In order to make a potent sleeping draught, one needs two small cauldrons of water, a fist of valerian root, and what other sweet-smelling plant?"

"Lemon balm! It's lemon balm!" Aurelia shouted, on her feet and dancing behind Brennus's chair. Their mother laughed at her daughter's frivolity.

Brennus groaned while Aurelia continued to jump, jabbing him with her finger. "I win! I win! I get the last piece of pie-e-e." She drew out her words, teasing her brother for all it was worth.

Something hard hit her shoulder, and Aurelia was snapped from her reverie. She looked to find half a loaf of bread in the grass beside her, already being overrun by a beetle. She grabbed it, flicked off the bug, and looked to find Drest.

When he spoke, his voice was hoarse. She wondered if he was as tired as she was. He might be, if the dark circles beneath his eyes were any indication. "Eat. Sleep. We leave at dawn." She watched him until he disappeared into the Wood. She ate quickly, her gaze on the elves. The broad shouldered one ate a handful of berries while the other sipped from their shared flask of water collected from the creek bed yesterday.

Aurelia's heart beat faster when the elf, the one who gave slack on her rope, stood.

It was time.

When he walked over to her and offered a drink, Aurelia said, "I need to go to the bathroom."

By now, she knew the elves fully understood English. At least, most of it. The elf sighed and called back to his companion. Then he leaned down and helped her up, hoisting her to her feet by her tied wrists. Aurelia made sure to keep her fists closed tight, blocking his view of the valerian root. The elf took another sip from his flask when they reached a dense cluster of trees twenty yards from their camp. She held up her wrists, and he waved his right hand over them, muttering his spell. The ropes loosened and fell. Aurelia glanced over her shoulder as she stepped into the dense shrubbery, then ducked low and out of sight. Crouching, she pawed eagerly at the luscious green leaves sprouting from the plant—native to the kingdom's land—encircling her. She ran her fingers over the bumpy, jagged-edged leaves of the lemon balm plant. She even leaned down to kiss it, the scent of the leaves giving her courage to continue with the next part of her plan.

Carefully, she yanked off a fistful of leaves and shoved them into her palm that already held the half-crushed valerian root. Slowly, she stood.

The elf's face was concerned, which meant her face was doing what she hoped it would: conveying pain.

"Please." She gestured to the flask in his hand. "Water. I need water."

The elf eyed her warily, then stepped back.

"Please. I'm so thirsty. I'm having trouble…" She motioned to her abdomen, rubbing against the now-filthy material of her tunic. "I think water will help me."

After a moment, the elf said something. She could translate one word, "quick," so she took the flask and nodded gratefully.

"I'll hurry. Thank you."

The elf said something else, then turned away as she ducked back into the brush. In seconds, Aurelia smashed the root against the leaves of the lemon balm. The air immediately grew sweet. Once the two were mashed well enough, she undid the flask and dropped as much of her concoction as she could into the water. To her dismay, the flask was already half-empty. She hoped she hadn't added too much. Even the faintest amount could induce drowsiness. She only needed enough to put her captors to sleep.

A thought hit her. What if the draught didn't work on fae like it did on humans? Her studies had consisted almost entirely of human prescriptions and human dosages. Gods, what if they drank it and nothing happened? They shouldn't be able to taste the plants, and the smell disappeared once it hit the water, but what if they knew somehow that she had tampered with the flask?

Aurelia fought back tears. Even if it didn't work, she had to try.

Hastily, she wiped her hands on the back of her leather pants. Eventually, she crept out from the brush and handed the capped flask back to the elf.

"Thank you," she said. "I feel much better now."

He only motioned for her to follow him back to camp. Her heart skipped a beat when she realized he hadn't tied her hands. *What a stroke of luck!* Nevertheless, she kept her hands close together. Then, as she hoped would happen, the elf took one more sip. She watched him, scrutinizing every movement for a change. Once back at their camp, she stood opposite them around the fire, warming her hands as the evening grew colder while still keeping the elves in her gaze.

The one she had been with said something to the other. She couldn't make it out, but the broad-shouldered one raised his voice. Her companion gestured to the flask. Aurelia willed him to drink it. The sky was growing dark, and Drest would be back soon. This had to happen now.

Before she could blink, the second elf was right in front of her, holding up the flask. He said something in elven, but she didn't understand.

She stuttered, feeling incredibly small beneath his tall stature. "I don't know what you're talking about." He gestured to the water, then back to the first elf, who crossed his arms and locked eyes with her. Aurelia's heart pounded. *He knows.*

"I'm sorry, I don't...I don't understand." She swallowed. The second elf appeared beside her, holding out the flask. In perfect English, he said, "Drink."

Aurelia was stunned. She stared at the top of the flask—open and dark. She could smell the lemon balm, or maybe that was just her imagination. When she looked again, the first elf was grinning behind his companion.

Not seeing any other way around this, Aurelia raised her hands, opening her fingers just enough to grab hold of the neck of the flask. Then she drank.

The water was tasteless, though she swore the scent of the plants lingered in her nose. The liquid ran down her parched throat. Lowering the flask, she took a breath, forcing a smile as she handed it back.

The slenderer fae, the one who had walked with her, laughed. He said something to the other, who snorted and turned up the flask, nearly downing the rest of it before handing it back to his companion. They laughed and finished the water, which was precisely what Aurelia wanted.

The one who had made her drink returned to the other side of the fire. Aurelia stepped backward, leaning against a tree trunk. She could feel the draught working its way through her system. A sense of calm came over her, and she fought the urge to yawn.

While the elves chatted quietly across the fire, Aurelia scanned the trees for Drest. He would return soon. He was rarely back after dark. She began to wonder where he went each night, but those thoughts vanished when the broader elf suddenly stopped talking. His head drooped against his chest. His slanted eyes closed shut, and he swayed.

Aurelia's heart quickened, despite the herbs working to slow it. She stood. The second elf said something, reaching out to grab his companion's shoulder. When he did, his friend collapsed onto the ground, motionless.

The second elf stared for a moment, then turned to Aurelia. Their eyes locked across the flames. She could see his beginning to close as he reached out an arm, pointing her way.

"I'm sorry," she said.

When he took a step, his legs wobbled and gave way beneath him. He joined his companion in a heap on the ground.

There was no time to check on just how asleep they really were. If her own body was any indication, she didn't have long before the mixture worked its power on her, putting her into a deep sleep.

So Aurelia ran.

She sprinted like mad between the trees, over fallen limbs and through reaching thickets that pulled at her tunic and tugged on her pants. She tried to conjure her saol. Her fingers glowed bright, and she managed to throw the flame ahead of her, but the light only flickered before going out. She was too weak. She stumbled over a tangle of roots, nearly falling on her blistered hands. Her head felt heavy, but she pushed herself to keep going. The woods around her grew darker as the sun dipped below the trees. She had no idea where she was going but hoped it was somewhere with help.

A distant howl stopped her in her tracks. Aurelia spun around. All around were towering trees and layers of brush packed tight against one another like cards in a deck. More sounds followed the howl. The hoot of an owl. A low screech. Something growled. Despite fear running rampant within her, her breathing slowed.

"Not yet," she said, slapping herself across the cheek. She ran again, reaching out to feel her way through the darkness. She ran for what felt like ages, her body working against the heavy shroud of drowsiness overtaking her mind. The darkness grew taller. It reached out and wrapped itself around her until the darkness was inside her mind. Her eyelids grew heavy. She willed her feet to keep moving.

A shout came from her right. Was it Drest? In a panic, she ducked between a line of trees to her left. The sound of water made her stop. She could barely stand now. Sleep was overpowering her.

Suddenly, out of the night, there was another sound. It was light, like a nightingale's song. She stumbled forward, reaching out into the darkness. She followed the sound like a beacon on the shoreline. That was when she saw it. A light in the distance. That was where the music was coming from. A shimmering, melodious light.

Her breath ragged, Aurelia ran with the final ounces of energy she had toward the light. Something emerged from the darkness. A doorway. Smoke from a fire. She kept her unfocused gaze on the light, bracing herself between the trees until she was nearly there.

She reached out. The light was close enough to grab. But Aurelia's fingers felt only air as she fumbled against the darkness and fell into a deep, dreamless sleep.

CHAPTER EIGHTEEN

The day after the row with her mother, Jastyn was up before dawn. She had hardly slept, her body too restless, tingling with its newfound knowledge. She had lain for hours at the base of a stalwart oak while confusion and fury surged in her veins. During the sleepless midnight hours, she had tried to make sense of what her mother had told her. When each attempt proved futile, Jastyn focused on channeling her rage into what the new day would bring.

She left the edge of Eegit's meadow, where she had spent the night after being unable to bring herself to talk to her about her mother's truth. Her anger left her embarrassed, and now she walked with a new sense of shame back to the village. With her head low, she crept along the rows of dark homes, each silent with sleep in the early hours of the day. She leapt easily through the window leading into the room she shared with Alanna.

Her sister was asleep in their bed, the ragged blanket strewn haphazardly across her. In the first minutes of twilight, Alanna looked stronger. Her legs weren't as thin, her shoulders more rounded thanks to chores being done around the house. Even her pale face looked fuller. Jastyn thought about the Red One's gift. Despite the leprechaun's shifty demeanor, Jastyn was grateful to her. But when Alanna's breath sputtered, the moment of gratitude vanished, and the daunting quest for her sister's cure took center stage once again in her mind.

Silently, Jastyn scratched out a note on a spare piece of parchment. She left it on the table next to their bed before gathering a flask and a deerskin satchel, which she filled with a spare tunic, a wooden cup, the empty vial, and an old apple. After a final glance at her sister, she slipped out through the window and headed for the castle.

As she walked, she thought back to the falling-out with her mother. The revelation felt unreal. As her feet carried her to the market road that led to the castle gates, Jastyn grappled with the contradicting images of her father that swam like summer salmon fighting their way upstream, struggling against the current for a way to calmer waters.

The old image—the one she had built and clung to her entire life—shrank and faded while the new picture took its place. But this new picture was unclear, like looking down at the sand below the sea. Her father's image rippled and stirred in one endless eddy, so that she couldn't make out who or what he really was. His image was a distant distortion that, when she stared too long, only grew more unrecognizable.

The sun rose behind the stalls of the market. Villagers packed for travel trickled into the streets. Curious bystanders were also present, eager to see the start of the search for the lost princess. A couple of men carried satchels similar to her own, and Jastyn imagined them saying good-byes to their loved ones before setting out. For a moment, she imagined her mother waking early with Elisedd and noticing she never came home. Though it wasn't unusual, Jastyn had never left home for the Wood after as heated a conversation as the one they'd had the night before.

Upon reaching the castle gates, shining with morning mist, Jastyn leaned against the wall opposite so that she had a clear view of the streets. She breathed in the damp, early morning air and placed her items at her feet. She ran a hand over her hair; strands of it fell over her face. Sighing, she began the process of resetting her braid. The tedious task sent her mind wandering, and her thoughts went to Aurelia as her fingers worked quickly to twist and intertwine the thick strands of hair. She thought about Remembrance Day, when she had watched Aurelia from afar. The princess had endured dozens of bereaved admirers while she herself was, undoubtedly, in infinitely more pain than the line of villagers combined. Jastyn wondered at her strength, wondered at how difficult it must have been to sit and smile and be gracious despite the unbearable pain at losing her brother.

Despite her efforts, she kept finding that Aurelia continued to escape the mold Jastyn had deemed fit for her. *She's a Diarmaid*, Jastyn reminded herself. *She's privileged. She has no concept of what it means to fight to survive.*

Except now she might be doing just that.

She imagined Aurelia's soft blue eyes. She smiled at the memory of the blush in the princess's cheeks when she had kissed her hand. Raising her own fingers to her lips, Jastyn recalled the soft flesh and sweet scent of Aurelia when a horn trumpeted over the grounds, and the gates opened.

By now the market was packed. Jastyn tied off her braid, gathered her things, and moved to the back of the crowd. She spotted a few familiar faces but saw no sign of her own family. *It's better that way*, she decided, as King Grannus appeared, dressed in a somber navy cloak with a line of guardsmen behind him. Everyone grew quiet when he spoke.

"Good morning, all. It pleases me to see so many members of Venostes here today. Your presence here gives me a renewed sense of hope, hope that we will soon be reunited with our beloved daughter."

A solemn murmur echoed over the sea of spectators. The king seemed to ready himself before continuing.

"Today begins the expedition to return Princess Aurelia Diarmaid to her rightful place in the kingdom. To those who have come here to volunteer your services, Queen Dechtire and I wish to extend our deepest gratitude. The queen has already begun a search to the north with a troop of the royal guard. Your party will head west, through the densest part of the Wood. If you will be joining that search, please step forward and accept a small token of our appreciation."

The crowd separated as several villagers, men and women, came forward to thunderous applause. Each made their way to the king, where they bowed and received a blue pouch the size of a large apple. When the fourth recipient gave an overdramatic salute, Jastyn crossed her arms in a huff. A voice startled her.

"What do you reckon is in there?"

Coran stood at her shoulder. He wore a clean tunic over long pants that looked too big. His thicket of orange hair was still wet and matted from a bath. Even his typically ruddy face was cleaner.

Jastyn frowned. "You smell strange."

Coran snorted. "Thanks. The braid looks good."

Ignoring him, Jastyn eyed the satchel thrown over one of his shoulders. "What's that for?" she asked, glancing back at the applauding villagers as a short woman with red hair accepted another pouch from the king.

"You didn't really think you'd go lookin' for the princess on your own, did you?"

Jastyn's eyes went wide as she turned around. "No." She shook her head. "Coran, you can't. I didn't ask for your help."

"You never do, do you?" He nudged her through the crowd. Stumbling forward, Jastyn protested over her shoulder.

"Coran, this is my responsibility. Not yours."

"Tell that to those people." He motioned to the line of a half a dozen villagers gathered tightly, clutching their pouches. "Besides, since when is finding the princess your job? Since when is she your charge?"

Rolling her eyes, Jastyn ignored the flip-flop of her stomach at talk of Aurelia. "I'm only saying that this journey isn't meant for you. I need to do this." She tugged Coran to the side, avoiding the line shrinking before the king.

"Jas, it's okay. You don't have to explain. I know you need the reward. I can't say I wouldn't be happy with a few more coins in my pocket myself. I get it."

Her eyes met Coran's. What she saw in them at that moment made the air catch in her throat. In his eyes swam the complete belief that this really *was* about the reward. She saw her own desperation looking back at her. It made her shudder. In a flash—like the sun glinting off the sea—she saw what everyone else thought of her, too. She saw her own hunger, her unending quest for respect. She saw how little everyone knew of her and of Alanna's illness. She saw her own desperation for a cure and what she would do to find it. She saw how no one, not even Coran, could ever understand the life her family deserved, the life Jastyn knew they could have as long as she didn't return empty-handed.

She knew then what her plan would entail. Closing her eyes, she accepted the inevitable truth of the Red One's words. She knew that she would find Aurelia. But she would not return the princess to the kingdom. Not right away. Not after what the Red One told her. The noble sacrifice the fae spoke of was the one thing Jastyn hoped it wasn't: Aurelia. She was of noble blood, and now the heir to the Diarmaid throne. Aurelia was the one who gifted her the bracelet.

Whatever waited in the western caves, it required something from the princess. Jastyn would have to use her. The idea sent a shock wave down her spine, and she hardened with determination. This was the only way to ensure the cure for Alanna.

Jastyn tore herself from Coran's gaze. There was no way he would understand. He was loyal and wouldn't question her, but he didn't deserve to be burdened with this. This decision was hers to carry. So she let him believe what he wanted.

"You're right," she finally said. "We need the money. So, let's go find this princess of yours, and I'll split the reward with you. Seventy-thirty sounds fair." She winked.

"It'll be sixty-forty by nightfall," Coran replied as she stepped forward. It was her turn to greet the king. The familiar hush that came with her making an appearance anywhere ran through the crowd like a wave—building higher and higher until silence overcame the market streets.

King Grannus looked behind her at the hushed group. She saw the confusion in his gaze and in the triangle of lines formed between his brow. She crossed her right arm over her chest in a salute.

"Your Highness."

He lowered his chin in return. "You are brave to join the search for my daughter. For that, I thank you." A nearby guardsmen handed him a final pouch, which Jastyn took. "May this guide your steps on the journey through the Wood."

Jastyn began to reply, began to tell him that she wasn't doing this for him, that she was barely doing this for Aurelia, that she couldn't care less for his well-being. But in his tired eyes she saw the princess. She saw Aurelia sitting tall in her throne upon the hill, every fiber of her body resonating with grief over the loss of her brother. The image overcame Jastyn, and she was surprised to feel the sting of tears.

Slowly, she extended her hand, and the king followed suit. As their arms locked in a pact, Jastyn hoped he couldn't see the lies springing from her lips. "I will do what I can to bring your daughter home."

Three days later, Jastyn sat beside Coran several yards from a roaring yellow campfire that blazed in the middle of a rowdy circle of villagers, each one exchanging stories and swapping mead-filled flasks under the cold, clear night sky. They had set up camp about seven miles inland from the kingdom's northwest border, in the direction the king had believed Aurelia's captors had taken. Jastyn, reluctantly, had to agree. The elves were to the north, and they were too smart to bring the princess onto their land. The sea lay to the east, so the only other option was west, toward the Mountains of Ionad.

Coran tore off a chunk of bread. His breath gleamed pale in front of his face when he spoke. "Quite the bunch." He chewed pensively, watching several of the villagers begin an arm-wrestling match.

Scoffing, Jastyn said, "They're going to get us all killed." She threw a fallen branch she'd been sharpening into the grass. "Since not one of them knows the key to finding a missing person is being quiet!" She raised her voice on the last two words, which warranted only a slight pause in the group's jubilation.

"They're just excited. Most of 'em haven't been out of the village before."

"So, this is, what, a vacation for them? Don't they realize these woods are teeming with fae, only half of which take kindly to wandering humans?"

Coran wiped his mouth after drawing a drink from his flask. "Probably not."

There was a rustling sound behind them, followed by the crackling of twigs. Coran and Jastyn exchanged glances, then he shrugged and stretched out on the ground, molding his satchel into a pillow. "Give 'em a break, Jas. Not everyone grew up with a hedgewitch as a best friend."

Jastyn grinned, and her ears pricked at another sound, this one like the soft rush of falling leaves. She listened as her mind drifted to Eegit. She didn't like to admit it, but she missed the old loon. When she had gone to her meadow the other night, she hadn't had the guts to talk to her about the fight with her mother. Still, she hoped Eegit had sensed her presence and understood.

Clearing her throat, Jastyn redirected her gaze to the group of villagers. "They don't even know which direction to go. When we set out each morning, they follow an hour later. If it were up to them, Aurelia would be a goner."

As soon as she'd said the words, a heavy pang hit Jastyn deep in her chest. The idea of Aurelia perishing in the Wood was like being drenched with icy river water. She swallowed, forcing the image of

Aurelia starved and left for dead out of her mind. *I'm not supposed to care this much.*

Coran nudged her knee with his foot. "You okay?" His voice was distant. When she looked over at him, he was already half-asleep.

"I'm fine, Coran. Get some rest." Jastyn pulled her tunic tighter around her. The night air nipped at her neck and hands. Meanwhile, the villagers broke into a series of songs, loud and discordant. Yet their voices trilled with happiness and filled the dark air with sounds of home. Jastyn let herself relax, bowing her chin to her chest in an attempt at sleep.

Chapter Nineteen

The Red One danced in circles around Jastyn, her hips swinging hypnotically. They were in the same clearing where they had met over a month ago. And they were alone. Jastyn knew the leprechaun was using a glamor spell to take the form of the woman from her memories, the dark-skinned dancer from a foreign land. Nevertheless, she let Rua move closer, her intoxicating smell engulfing Jastyn's senses. She desperately wanted to take hold of her hips and feel them sway beneath her hands. Rua smiled, turning slowly. Biting her lip, Jastyn's gaze fell to her waist. The Red One's image shifted. Her features grew dim, and her short stature sprang up until a dark shadow towered over Jastyn, and the Dark Fae of her nightmares stood in the blackness.

"Leave me alone!" Jastyn shouted, looking anywhere but at the vast emptiness beneath the fae's hood. She tried to run, but her feet were like rocks, anchored to the ground. The tall grass laced around her ankles, twisting up her calves until she was trapped.

The Dark Fae tilted his head, amused at her struggle. "Foolish Odium Child. This journey will be your undoing."

Jastyn's body shook. Her hands fought against the long blades of grass twisting around her. Furious, she yelled, "You're wrong! I will find the cure! I will!"

Bellowing laughter shook the meadow. Her body trembled, but she never stopped fighting as the grass grew higher. She managed to take out her knife and swiped furiously at the grass winding around her waist. It clenched tight against her. She continued to shout, forcing the Dark Fae's laughter from her mind.

"You're wrong! You're wrong!" The grass fell where she cut it, but as soon as one leg was freed, more vines shot up around the other. "I will find the cure. I will save Alanna. I'll find Aurelia. You're wrong!" She was screaming, her voice hoarse with rage and fear. She couldn't stop. If she stopped, the laughter would overpower her mind, and she'd be lost in the darkness. "You're wrong!"

"Jastyn?"

Jastyn's hand stopped. The tangled vines that had encased her legs fell to the ground. She stepped forward, free from their grasp. The Dark Fae vanished. Where he had been, the princess stood, her face pinched in concern.

"Aurelia!"

The princess reached out as Jastyn ran to her. It took everything Jastyn had to not pull her close. "You're all right! I knew I would find you." She searched Aurelia's face. The princess's gaze was distant. Her lips curved in a smile.

Carefully, Jastyn reached out her hand. Aurelia took it. Raising her arm, Jastyn led Aurelia in a spin, finishing the dance the Red One had begun earlier. Unable to stop herself, she pulled the princess against her. Jastyn breathed her in, pressed their cheeks close. She wrapped her arms around Aurelia, tracing the line of her spine down to her slender waist.

They stood like that for a while, holding on to one another. Eventually, Aurelia began to giggle. Jastyn smiled into her shoulder. The sound was high and quick, like a chaffinch in spring. She tilted her head to leave a trail of light kisses along Aurelia's neck. This invoked more laughter, and warmth radiated from Jastyn's center. She loved the sound of Aurelia's laughter. Wanting to see her face, Jastyn stepped back.

When she did, Aurelia's laughter stopped. Her face was serious, scared even. When she spoke, Jastyn frowned as Coran's voice came through the princess's lips.

"Jastyn, wake up."

Blinking, Jastyn shook her head. She squeezed tighter to Aurelia's waist. But when she did, Aurelia vanished. Jastyn searched the empty meadow, but Aurelia was gone. Coran's voice echoed around her.

"Wake up, Jastyn. Now!"

With a jolt, Jastyn sat up. She looked around, the lingering image of Aurelia still close enough to touch. It was only Coran standing above her though, panic on his face.

"What is it?" she asked, moving to crouch. The Wood was dark and the air still bitterly cold. "Coran, it's the middle of the night. What's going on?" Laughter tickled her ear. Jastyn shook her head, trying to chase the dream of Aurelia from her mind. But the laughter continued.

Coran stooped beside her, hastily packing their satchels. "Nymphs," he said, pointing to the main campfire. Jastyn rubbed her hands to warm them and focused her gaze on the group of villagers. While some of them still lay asleep, their faces slack with dreams, others, including two women and one burly man Jastyn recognized as a shepherd, were dancing arm in arm with four frolicking wood nymphs.

"I've never been this close to one before." Coran spoke low as they moved behind a tree. "I didn't think nymphs lived in groups."

"They don't." Jastyn splashed her face with water from her flask. "I bet this many humans alone in the Wood was too much for them to resist."

"They won't hurt 'em, will they?"

Jastyn laughed under her breath. "Please, they're nymphs. The best they can do is lull everybody into a stupor so that all any of them can think about is singing and dancing and..."

One of the nymphs—a short, curvy creature with the body of a female and skin the color of wet tree bark—pulled one of the village women from their dancing circle. The nymph's hair was a thicket of tree branches that stood straight up and she wore no clothing. Jastyn could see flowers blossoming along her thighs and shoulders. The villager, who Jastyn knew as a grumpy older woman who sold sheepskin blankets at the market, was suddenly alight with a doe-eyed look on her face. Seconds later, she and the nymph tumbled to the ground together in an embrace.

"Are they—"

Jastyn nodded. "Yes."

Coran flushed. "We really do need to get out of here."

"Come on." Jastyn turned to go but ran right into a nymph. This one was almost her height. Her skin, rough and splintered, was the same color as the others. The flowers blooming on her chest and knees featured bright purple petals and emitted a heady smell. Her hair, each strand a thin branch that curved to her shoulders, didn't move when she stepped toward them.

"Lucky me," she purred, running a knotted finger down Coran's cheek, her eyes dancing between them. "Whatever shall the three of us do?"

Coran stuttered, falling over himself. Jastyn elbowed him in the ribs. "We're not interested," she said, grabbing Coran and moving around the fae. But the nymph was quick and stepped in front of them again. This time, she reached out, her hands stretching to wrap around Jastyn's neck.

"You are such a handsome human," she cooed, her voice mesmerizing. "Come dance with me."

Jastyn felt dizzy and began to lose herself in the nymph's swirling eyes, deep pools of lilac and gold. She felt the urge to fall into them and drift away on a careless wind.

"Isn't that the king? And the royal guard right behind him!"

Coran's voice cut through the nymph's pull, and Jastyn tumbled backward. The nymph hissed and spun around. At the same time, Coran took hold of Jastyn's wrist. "Run!"

They took off. Jastyn threw her satchel around her shoulder. Coran did the same, and they sprinted between the trees, deeper into the Wood.

"What about the others?" he called as they parted around the trunk of a giant tree, careful to leap over its gnarled roots.

Jastyn glanced back. There was no sign of the nymph, and the firelight from their camp was only a gleaming pebble in the distance. "They're on their own now."

They continued to run, dashing between trees and over hunched shrubs dotted with elderberries. Jastyn made sure to note the moss, bright and crawling on the surrounding bark, to point them in the right direction. She glanced up between the thick overhang of leaves. Between them she caught flashes of the night sky; the patterns reassured her that they were continuing west, where the king hoped Aurelia might be found.

After a few minutes, they slowed to a walk, their breath shining in front of them. "I think we lost her." Coran bent over, resting his hands on his knees. When his breathing steadied, he laughed. Jastyn watched him for a second. "What?"

"That nymph nearly ate you alive." His shoulders shook, and he wiped his eyes.

Jastyn straightened. "She did not."

"I thought she was going to unhinge her jaw and swallow you up." Now it was Jastyn's turn to laugh.

"She's not my type."

Coran took a drink from his flask. His eyebrow raised over the end of it. "Right. You go for the taller, more refined type, don't you?"

Jastyn shot him a look. He replaced the cap of the flask, then put his hands up. "I'm just sayin'."

Walking past him, Jastyn made sure to give his shoulder a good punch. Coran chuckled, rubbing where she hit. "Let's keep moving," she said, readjusting her satchel. The night was at its darkest now, and Jastyn knew they needed to find a place to sleep before any more fae decided to make their presence known.

They walked in silence, the only sounds coming from the depths of the Wood and the crunch of leaves beneath their feet. A long, lonely howl pierced the shroud of darkness, followed by a grating screech. Coran and Jastyn exchanged looks, picking up their pace.

After a while, Jastyn paused, holding out her arm. "Do you smell that?"

Coran sniffed. "Smells like smoke."

"Exactly." Jastyn moved forward, hurrying between trees. Coran followed at her heels.

"Jas, what is it?"

Crouching behind a line of boysenberry shrubs, Jastyn pointed to a lodging nestled in a clearing half the size of Eegit's. The trivial structure was made entirely of wood, except for the chimney with its lopsided boulders forming a stack from which a line of sweet-smelling smoke snaked out. Two windows sat on either side of a wide wooden door. Bright light glowed from the open squares. Voices and laughter drifted from inside and rode the night wind. A sign above the door bore the image of a cauldron filled with coins.

"It's a leprechaun lodging. A public house for fae."

"Maybe they know somethin' about the princess."

Jastyn swallowed. "Maybe." She stepped through the brush, making her way to the lodging. Coran called out from behind her.

"Wait, Jas, that's fae territory. What if…what if we're not welcome?"

Jastyn kept walking but turned around, gesturing to the Wood. "Coran, we've been in fae territory for days. Besides, I don't know about you, but I'm starved." With that, she turned back around. Coran's quick steps hurried behind her, and together they made their way to the lodging, the smell of meat and baked bread beckoning like a siren's song in the night.

❖

"Are you *sure* this is a leprechaun lodging?" Coran asked under his breath as they maneuvered between uneven rows of low tables, each packed with patrons. "They look just like us."

"Leprechauns are shapeshifters, remember? I hear most of them prefer to walk in human form these days. Makes things easier."

They walked side by side, careful to avoid eye contact, though most of the pub's clientele had hardly noticed their arrival. Nearly every one of them, fae and otherwise, seemed unfazed by the new customers, even at this hour of night. The place vibrated with conversation, filling the warm air with a steady hum. The main room was larger than it appeared from the outside, no doubt a glamour used in order to fit more customers inside while remaining unassuming to the rest of the world. Torches lined the walls, and a wooden chandelier hung from the beamed ceiling, holding dozens of candles with wax dripping from their sides, creating a welcoming glow. Music drifted from a corner where a flute and lyre played unassisted near the fireplace.

They reached the bar, which was bookended by two large barrels dripping mead, and Jastyn leaned against it to scan the room. Coran pulled up beside her. He struggled to find a good spot for his elbow on the edge of the high bar. A toothless, bearded man with blue skin occupying the stool next to him eyed them curiously.

"Act natural," Jastyn whispered.

"I'm trying." He finally decided on a pose that left one hand on his hip so that he looked like a statue from the market square.

Jastyn shook her head. Scanning the dozens of fae enjoying their late-night socializing, Jastyn wondered if any of them had seen the princess or knew of her whereabouts. They were so deep in the Wood now, she doubted news of Aurelia's kidnapping had even made it this far. But she was hungry, and maybe they could sleep for a few hours before continuing on their journey.

"Something to drink?"

The cheery question interrupted Jastyn's thoughts. Behind the bar stood a tall, redheaded woman. Her arms and hands, covered in freckles, worked deftly to dry a series of mugs before laying two down on the bar for Jastyn and Coran. She smiled, and the candlelight lit her playful green eyes.

"Two meads, please." Jastyn met Coran's gaze. He shrugged as the woman poured frothy mead from a wooden pitcher.

"We couldn't trouble you for a slice of bread, could we?" Coran asked, rummaging through a pouch in his tunic and pulling out three bronze coins. The woman pushed their drinks forward and wiped her hands on a rag. She glanced between them.

"You two from around here?"

Coran's mouth fell open. Jastyn kicked him in the shin before responding. "Just passing through."

The woman squinted for a second, then widened her smile. "Well, wanderers are always welcome. Especially those as handsome as you." She winked at Jastyn before laying out a plate of freshly baked sliced bread between them. There was even a slab of butter melting into the fluffy dough. Jastyn's mouth watered; Coran devoured two slices in less than a minute.

"Thanks," she said, taking a long drink from her mug. When the bartender turned her attention to another customer, Coran shook his head.

"What is it with you? First the nymph, now her."

Jastyn shrugged. "I don't know what you're talking about."

He shoved another piece of bread into his mouth. "You gotta teach me whatever it is you do."

"I'm not sure how Roisin would feel about that."

"Oh, it's her I would use it on." Coran grinned into his mug, chugging the cool liquid and emptying half of it. He wiped his mouth on his tunic sleeve. "Gods, this is delicious. I'll be back." He hitched a thumb back to the front door. "Nature calls."

"Don't be too long," Jastyn called as he swayed happily to the door.

She took another drink when the bartender appeared again. "Can I get you anything else?"

Jastyn licked droplets of mead from her lips, letting the bread and drink settle in her stomach. She hadn't realized how hungry she was. The sustenance cleared her mind, and she thought of Aurelia.

"Actually," she said, fingering the rim of her mug, "I'm looking for somebody. I wonder if anyone here might have seen her."

The bartender leaned forward so that her forearms rested on the bar. Doing so exposed the V-cut of her dress. Briefly, Jastyn followed the trail of freckles that clustered between her breasts. Clearing her throat, she lifted her gaze to the fae's.

"She's been missing for almost a week."

The woman reached one hand out, laying it on top of Jastyn's. "I'm sorry to hear that. Anything I can do to help you feel better?"

Jastyn's face warmed, and she wished Coran would hurry up. Swallowing, she said, "I'm flattered. But I'm not interested."

Pouting, the woman straightened. Within seconds, her form shifted, and a dark-skinned man with curly black hair and beautiful dark brown eyes stood where the redhead had moments before. He wore a vest and loose pants hung low on his muscular hips.

Jastyn raised her mug and took another sip. "Impressive. But you were closer the first time."

The man grinned, then shifted again. His wide shoulders shrank and moved closer together. His skin tone faded to a pale cream color, and his dark eyes became the brightest blue. A slim body fit snugly into a navy tunic and dark pants. Her hair turned long and brown and was pinned messily behind small ears. Jastyn's heart felt as if it was being squeezed from her chest.

Aurelia stared back at her.

The fae grinned. "How about now?"

In one swift motion, Jastyn leapt from her side of the bar to the other, unsheathing her knife midair. She landed behind the bartender. With one hand, she gripped the fae's waist while the other held the hunting blade against her throat.

The room surged with cries of confusion, then grew quiet as Jastyn held tight to the bartender.

"Where is she?"

The fae's glamor was good. But it couldn't master Aurelia's voice when it spoke. "Where is *who*?"

Jastyn dug the blade's point into the pulse of blood just below the pale flesh. She had to remind herself this wasn't really Aurelia as she held the struggling fae against her. "Don't play games with me. The Red One is the only leprechaun powerful enough to shapeshift into any human. The rest of you can only conjure people you've met. People you've seen." The fae wriggled in Jastyn's arms. "So, I'm going to ask you again, where is she?"

A few of the patrons were on their feet now. Several gripped the handles of knives saddled at their hips. Others cupped spell-fire, ready to be thrown. Even the music had stopped so that the whimpering of the fae in Jastyn's arms was the only sound. Quickly, the fae shifted back to her original form.

The air was thick with tension when Coran walked back in. His cheerful face fell at the hushed room, and his eyes grew wide when he saw Jastyn behind the bar.

"What are you doin'? Are you mad?"

Jastyn spoke through clenched teeth. "She knows where Aurelia is."

"Jastyn, the chances they know where the princess is aren't worth a blade to the throat!"

She looked across the room. Coran's eyes begged her to put the knife down. Her hand trembled next to the woman's throat. She had even smelled like Aurelia. Her hair had been the same. Her face. The curve of her jaw. But it hadn't been her.

"I'm going to ask you one more time." The fae began to cry, but Jastyn held tight to her. "Where is the princess?"

A wave of voices washed over the pub. Jastyn tore her gaze from the glint of the blade aimed at the fae's throat. Many of the spectators were pointing to a room adjacent to the fireplace.

"Jas," Coran said quietly. "Put the knife down." His gaze was fixed on a spot she couldn't see.

Reluctantly, she lowered the blade.

"What, Coran. What is—"

"Jastyn?"

This time, there was no mistaking the voice that called out her name. Slowly, Jastyn turned to look in the doorway.

Aurelia.

Chapter Twenty

Jastyn?"

Aurelia stepped into the main room. Jastyn took in her dirty tunic, her pants torn at the knee. Even her shin-high boots were ragged. The scrapes and bruises that covered the princess's face made her bones ache, and Jastyn longed to run to her.

Instead, she sheathed her knife and placed her hands on her hips. "You're all right." Jastyn glanced around the room. The number of fae wielding fists of spell-fire had diminished, but many of them still wore looks of disdain. Coran, on the other hand, looked as if he'd caught the biggest river trout in history.

"Your Highness!" He rushed to Aurelia and bulldozed her with a hug. "You're okay! You're alive!" Aurelia winced at the contact. Coran stepped back quickly.

"Apologies, m'lady. Oh, Roisin will be so glad to know you're well!"

"Your *Highness*?" The bartender's voice was raspy, and she rubbed the spot where Jastyn's blade had been. "You told me you were an outcast from Gultero and needed safe passage."

Aurelia nodded. Her voice was strong, and Jastyn realized she was addressing the room when she spoke. "I did come here seeking safe passage." She paused, her gaze locking on Jastyn's for only a second. "It is also true that I am the princess. My name is Aurelia Diarmaid, heir to the Diarmaid throne."

The room erupted. Someone screamed. Half of the patrons rushed the door, leaving only a handful of curious fae, including the blue-skinned, bearded man at the bar. Aurelia's voice was weaker when she added, "Please, I mean you no harm."

The bartender placed a hand on her hip. "Wish your friend could say the same." She glared at Jastyn.

"I didn't mean to scare you. I..." Her words faltered. Part of her was scared but not at what she had done. Rather, because she knew she would have drawn the blade across that fae's throat had she needed to. She would have done whatever it took to find Aurelia and keep her plan intact.

Jastyn shook her head. "I'm sorry."

The fae sighed, her eyes wet. "Can't say it's the worst thing that's ever happened in here." She turned to Aurelia. "You're welcome to stay. But only until you're well enough to travel. My people respect the Fae-Diarmaid Treaty, but many have never ventured onto royal land. Many cling to the old ways. A lot of them are scared to even be in the same room as a human. Not to mention one of royal blood. So please, make haste."

"Of course." Aurelia smiled, then motioned for Coran and Jastyn to follow her. "My room is this way. I think it's best we retire for the night."

As the remaining patrons returned to their conversations, Jastyn and Coran trailed after Aurelia. Jastyn's mind raced with questions while they followed her to a room around the corner of the bar, near the back of the rickety building. She wondered who had captured Aurelia in the first place. Was it somebody in the castle? Were fae involved? And how, Jastyn wondered most of all, did she get away?

The room's earthen floor featured a worn bearskin rug in front of a stone fireplace piled high with logs already charred from a day's burning. There was a bed of blankets in the far corner. Jastyn noticed the water bowl lying on a table next to the door. Rags crisp with dried blood sat beside it. She imagined Aurelia tending to her face and wrists, which were exposed briefly when she closed the door behind them. Jastyn hated whoever had done that to her. She worked to keep her face calm while the three of them stood alone in the quiet room.

Eventually, Coran spoke. "I am glad this place has taken care of you, Your Highness. We've been worried sick...the whole kingdom has! There's a big search party out lookin' for you. Your dad, er, the king organized several." He wrung his hands. "We were with one party when…well, it's a long story, but we got separated and found this place! What a stroke of luck that was."

As Coran continued with his first impressions of the public house, Jastyn felt Aurelia's eyes on her. She couldn't help but notice how the princess stood a good five paces away, nearly on the other side of the room. Admittedly, holding a knife to another woman's neck wasn't exactly how Jastyn had hoped to see Aurelia again. At the memory of the princess's shocked face, her throat went dry, and heat nipped at the nape of her neck. She rubbed her hand against it as if to ease the shame. Aurelia's voice made her look up from the spot on the floor she'd been boring a hole into.

"I am grateful to both of you. You must be quite brave to venture into the Wood for days." Aurelia's bright eyes locked on Jastyn, and she thought she saw a glimmer of admiration but was too embarrassed to hang on to such a hope.

Jastyn shifted her weight. "The Wood is a second home to me. This was merely another day." .

As soon as she said it, she regretted it. Hurt poured from Aurelia's gaze. The princess, seeming to realize this, lifted her chin. Coran coughed.

"What Jastyn means to say is that she and I know these woods like the back of our hands. Well, I know them okay, and she knows them like an old friend. We were happy to help the kingdom. It's wonderful to know you're well. Isn't it, Jas?"

Jastyn had moved closer to the fire, standing with her back to the others. She feigned warming her hands even though the tiny space left her perspiring. Doubt crept inside her chest. How would she be able to go through with this? She wanted nothing more than to talk to the princess. She wanted to hear about everything that had happened to her. She wanted to make sure she slept safely through the night. Yet, if she was to make sure her plan worked, to ensure a sacrifice for Alanna's cure, she couldn't get too close.

"Jastyn?"

Taking a deep breath, Jastyn turned. "Forgive me." She held Aurelia's cautious gaze. "The journey has been long. I'm tired. As Coran said, we are glad you are safe." She kept her voice cold when she added, "It will bring your parents great joy to see you again."

Jastyn clenched her jaw, the heat from the fire adding a blush to her cheeks. Aurelia, if possible, was even more beautiful in the dim light. This was the closest they had been to one another since the prince's Remembrance Day. Jastyn hadn't noticed the deep shine of her hair and wanted to tuck the stray dark strands behind her ears. While Coran settled into a corner opposite them, laying his satchel down and stretching, Aurelia crossed her arms.

"You said you were tired. I myself am quite famished."

"It's the middle of the night."

Aurelia shot her a look. "I wasn't allotted much to eat while I was…there wasn't much offered the last few days."

Jastyn gestured to the door. "Of course."

"Please excuse me while I find something to eat. Make yourselves comfortable in the meantime. It's late, and you both should rest."

Jastyn opened her mouth to protest but decided against it.

"Thanks, Your Highness," Coran said. He slumped against the floor, his mouth wide in a yawn.

Aurelia headed for the door. "I'll only be a moment."

"Don't stay up too late," Jastyn called after her. "If you're well enough, we should head out at first light." Maybe then, Jastyn thought, there would be less time together in such close quarters. Less time for her to get to know the princess.

Aurelia paused only briefly to say, "Certainly. We will leave at dawn."

When the princess was gone, Jastyn exhaled.

"I take it back," Coran mumbled after a minute from the corner, his orange hair bright against the dull floor.

"What?"

"I could've sworn the princess was your type. But you two are like fire and ice. I felt cold just watchin' you." He gave a fake shudder.

"Hush, Coran. Go to sleep."

He chuckled, but it was weak, and his breathing quickly grew slow and deep. Jastyn found a spot next to the pile of blankets. She sat, her eyes tracing the place where Aurelia had lain earlier. She stared at the indention where her head had rested. It wasn't long before the exhilaration from the last hour hit her, and Jastyn's body shrugged, and her mind fell into a deep slumber that she hadn't had in weeks.

❖

Aurelia splashed her face at the water basin near the doorway. The room was quiet save for Coran's soft snores in the corner. She rubbed her eyes. They were still tired and dry, but she had begun to feel more like herself in the last twelve hours. For the thousandth time, she replayed her escape. It had seemed certain she was going to be left to the wolves after fleeing the campsite. Fortunately, in her final moments of consciousness before the sleeping draught overtook her, she had managed to conjure her saol out of sheer desperation. It had glided to the public house and through a window. The barmaid sent a pair of customers outside to find the source. They had found her lying thirty yards away, exposed to the elements and covered in cuts under a cold night sky. Not recognizing her as the princess and instead as a weary, starved traveler, they brought her inside where she slept for three hours while the draught wore off. Since then, there had been no sign of the elves or Drest.

At least, not yet.

She extended a thanks to the gods for watching over her. Her first time in a fae public house had been a good one overall. Save for the tumult accompanying Jastyn's arrival. She glanced over at her, curled up on the bare floor next to Aurelia's blankets. Jastyn had one arm tucked under her head, which rested in the crook of her elbow. Aurelia's eyes traced Jastyn's braid down her side, then lingered on her narrow hips. She watched her chest rise and fall with sleep.

She wondered at the difference a couple of hours made. Jastyn had been the epitome of fear and fury behind the bar, her fist clutching the knife to the bartender's throat. Now she was completely serene, her striking face blank as she lay sleeping.

Aurelia moved over to Jastyn. Her knees were still stiff, and she winced as she crouched. It was funny, she thought. Aurelia had ached to see Jastyn again. She smiled at the memory of gossiping with Roisin over dinner. Her head felt light at the idea of Jastyn risking her life to save hers. Perhaps she did care, Aurelia thought, reaching out a hand to run a quick finger down Jastyn's jawline. She swallowed and pulled her hand back when Jastyn groaned and tucked her knees closer to her chest. Aurelia grabbed a nearby blanket and carefully laid it across her legs. She watched Jastyn sleep for a moment, then realized the snoring had stopped.

When she turned around, Coran had his head propped up on his open palm. "Don't worry, Your Highness. I won't tell her you did that."

Aurelia flushed and stood, moving to stand before the fire. "She looked cold." Busying herself by jabbing the crisp logs with a singed branch, Aurelia changed the subject. "You should sleep more. It's only a couple of hours until daylight."

Coran sat up and took a drink from his flask. Aurelia concentrated so hard on the logs her forehead hurt. She swiped hair from her neck. As she did, the scent of her own tunic made her cringe. Almost every inch of it was soiled by rain, dirt, and gods knew what else. She hadn't noticed until now how wretched she must look. Her wrists were pink from the elves' rope, but most of the lashes were starting to heal. The gash on her knee—which she must have acquired during her run through the woods—was deep but didn't look infected. It stung each time she bent to sit or even walk, but it too would heal. Perhaps once they left here, she could collect a few herbs to expedite the process.

Aurelia stopped prodding the logs. Of course, she knew that Jastyn finding her implied they would return to the kingdom. Since her escape, though, she hadn't truly thought about what returning home would mean. Part of her longed to see her mother and father again. But the ache of returning to a place full of sorrow and mourning, a place that echoed with the memories of her brother…it was too painful to even consider.

With another glance at Jastyn, Aurelia gingerly sat cross-legged before the fire.

"Can't sleep either, Your Highness?"

Aurelia gave a small smile. "I'm afraid not. The smell of me is enough to make one want to run the other way."

"You must not get down to the village much."

Realizing what she said, Aurelia stammered. "Oh, I didn't mean…I wasn't trying to imply—"

"I was only jokin'." Coran laughed, digging through his satchel. He paused. "Well, mostly jokin'. Here." He yanked out a clean navy-blue tunic featuring a slim line of gold thread around the trim of the neck and wrists. "Try this one. It's not much, but you might be more comfortable."

He got up and handed it to her before returning to his seat to repack his satchel.

Aurelia fingered the material, coarser than she was accustomed to but lovely nevertheless. Her eyes dampened. "Thank you."

"Don't mention it," he said through another yawn. "Really. Jas will never let me hear the end of it."

They both chuckled. After a minute, Aurelia asked, "Is she always like that?"

Frowning, Coran asked, "A deep sleeper? Actually, no. She has a history of—"

"No." Aurelia interrupted. "Is she always so…" She searched the room for the right word. "Hard?"

With a snort, Coran rested his head back down. "Jastyn hasn't had the easiest life. Her whole family hasn't, actually."

Aurelia nodded. "Her sister. Alanna, isn't it? How is she?"

Coran looked surprised before he answered, "Better, Your Highness."

"That makes me happy to know."

Instilled with a new sense of camaraderie, Aurelia asked, "You've known each other a long time?"

"Me and Jastyn? We were brought up together. No, more like, we brought each other up, you know? We stuck together, helped each other out when things were tough. Which was most of the time."

Aurelia sat quietly, imagining a young Jastyn.

"Eegit helped, too."

"Eegit?"

"She's the hedgewitch who lives near the village border. She and Jastyn are close. Eegit was Jastyn's safe place if something at home was goin' on."

Aurelia's eyes rested on Jastyn. She imagined Jastyn out in the Wood. It made her happy to know she had a friend, but a small river of jealousy trickled in her veins at the idea of somebody else being the one Jastyn ran to.

Coran yawned again as Aurelia asked another question. "Her father, he is Elisedd the horse master, is he not?"

"He's her stepfather," Coran replied, barely audible as his eyes closed tiredly.

Aurelia frowned. "Stepfather?" But Coran was already asleep. Her mind drifted back to the conversation with her mother. Her mother knew Elisedd. She even spoke of Alanna. But when she had mentioned Jastyn, the conversation had come to a screeching halt.

The pieces began to fall together, but Aurelia had to be sure. Moving to lie beside Jastyn on the bed of blankets, she imagined the many ways to ask about who she really was. Dozens of questions swam in her mind. Her heart, meanwhile, beat happily as Jastyn slept soundly beside her.

Chapter Twenty-One

Jastyn stirred, her eyes adjusting to the dull firelight. At the sight of the unfamiliar room, she bolted upright.

"It's okay. We're safe."

Aurelia's voice came from the fireside where she sat before it, her left leg extended and the other tucked close. Her right arm propped upon it, she reached her hand out to the fire. A red glow seeped from her fingertips. Seeming to notice Jastyn's gaze, Aurelia shook her fingers, and the glow went out.

"Idle magic. It's a silly habit."

Jastyn didn't reply. She only stretched her arms and looked at the blankets beside her. They had been disturbed. Aurelia must have slept. Coran continued to do so in the corner.

There was only one tiny window, but Jastyn didn't need it to feel dawn approaching. Her body rarely let her sleep past the sun. Surprisingly, she felt rested. Visions and warnings from the Dark Fae had come to her in the night, but each time, they had been replaced by more pleasant dreams. Remembering one, she grinned and eyed Aurelia, who gave her an inquisitive look, then refocused on the gash on her left knee framed by the torn leather of her pants.

"That looks bad." Jastyn stood and washed her face. The cold moisture was a welcome relief in the stuffy room. She ran her hands down her cheeks and over her neck. Her hands were dirty, and she cleaned them hastily. Even after a solid scrub, some dirt still lingered.

"It looks worse than it is," Aurelia replied. "I washed it out earlier in the day. It's not wide enough to need stitching, thank the gods. But until I can get my hands on some calendula herb, fresh air and a bandage will have to do."

Noticing a roll of clean rags next to the water basin, Jastyn snatched them up. "Here, let me help."

Aurelia scooted back, her face a blanket of surprise as Jastyn knelt in front of her. It was even hotter by the fire, and she wondered how Aurelia managed to look pristine with bits of perspiration lining her temple.

"You don't have to. I know what I'm doing."

Jastyn unfurled one of the rags, leaving the other in a pile next to them. "I have no doubt your mother passed on her many healing skills to you," she replied curtly, licking her lips regretfully at the sight of Aurelia inching backward again. She sighed. "I'm sorry. I'm normally not this—"

"Rude?"

"I was going to say—"

"Pigheaded? Discourteous?" Aurelia cocked her head. "Insolent?"

Uncertain at the last word's meaning, Jastyn clenched her jaw. "I was going to say, I'm not normally this high-strung. But 'insolent' probably covers it."

It was quiet while Jastyn measured out the length of rag before tearing it easily into a thin strip. Aurelia exhaled.

"I'm the pigheaded one now."

Jastyn began to wrap the strip of cloth around Aurelia's wound. She wound it twice around her knee, making sure to drape the exposed flesh carefully. Aurelia watched her work.

"How is your sister?"

Quirking an eyebrow, Jastyn kept her eyes on her work. "Alanna is doing much better." She recalled Remembrance Day and how she had longed to express her gratitude for the bracelet. "Your gift turned out to be extremely useful."

"Really?" Aurella laughed. "I was afraid you thought me a fool, handing you a silly trinket in your desperate times."

Some trinket. Jastyn pictured the three glistening rubies. "I'm afraid it is lost now. I managed to use it in a trade." Her gaze flickered up. "In exchange for it, the Red One gave me a temporary cure for Alanna."

"The Red One?" Aurelia's eyes lit with curiosity. Jastyn smelled a scent of musky earth and orchids when the princess scooted closer. "I've only read stories. Is it true the Red One can shapeshift into anything? Into anyone?"

Jastyn's fingers slowed their work. "It's true. She's crafty, no doubt about that."

"She?"

"She to me. No one has ever seen the Red One's true form." Aurelia nodded. "But she manifested as a…" Jastyn faltered, recalling the figure from her memories. "She took the form of someone from my mind. The Red One uses temptation as her main weapon in her deals. I had to keep my wits about me, but she was eager to have a token from the Diarmaid family."

Jastyn found it difficult to avoid the inquiring spark that had taken up residence in Aurelia's blue eyes. "She gave me an elixir for Alanna. It's worked, but only for another couple of months. The true cure is still out there."

As Jastyn finished tying off the rag, she felt suddenly self-conscious.

"It's no royal treatment, but it will have to do."

"Thank you." Aurelia's voice was barely above a whisper. "The cure for your sister…do you know where it is?"

"I have an idea. I just hope I can get to it before it's too late." Jastyn held her gaze and found herself falling into the bright, frost-colored pools. Not only were Aurelia's eyes uncommon in the kingdom, they were so startling Jastyn found herself caught off guard with each glance. Finally, the princess dipped her chin, shaking her head as if breaking herself from a spell.

"You are not only brave, Jastyn, but you are kind. Especially when you think nobody is looking." Aurelia's face stretched in a smile as she held out her hand.

Jastyn gripped Aurelia's lithe forearm in a handshake. "Your tunic is clean," fumbled awkwardly out of her mouth.

Aurelia released Jastyn's arm and looked down. "Oh, yes. Your friend was kind enough to lend me his spare tunic. He's rather sweet, if I may say so."

Jastyn licked her lips, noticing how the tunic—which would have been too big on Coran—somehow clung to Aurelia in the most perfect places. What Coran lacked, Aurelia definitely made up for in the way the material settled atop her wide hips. The neck of it hung open, exposing creamy flesh speckled with dirt.

A crackle from the fire made them jump, and they scooted apart on the floor. Jastyn was thankful to find Coran still asleep.

"It will be dawn soon," Aurelia said, her voice a little shaky. "Should we wake him?"

"Let him sleep. We have a long walk ahead of us." She kept her eyes on the fire as she pushed away the task ahead. It was still unclear how she would manage to avoid the royal search party and ensure Aurelia remained close without her knowing they weren't headed back to the kingdom. The king's group—no doubt having heard about the nymph debacle—had to be close behind. Her mind grew foggy, and she watched the flicks of light kiss the top of the fireplace before vanishing in a quick puff of soot.

"What's that?"

Aurelia pointed to the blankets where she had slept. Next to them was Jastyn's satchel. The royal blue pouch holding King Grannus's gift had slipped out from inside it.

"I had forgotten about that." Jastyn collected it and brought it over, sitting so that she mirrored Aurelia's position before the fire. "It was a gift from your father to those of us who left in search of you." Jastyn tipped the pouch over, adding, "I never even thought to look at what it was."

From inside fell a sphere of clear glass, slightly larger than a grapefruit. It fit nicely in Jastyn's palm as they stared intently at the milky light that swirled within.

"It's, um," Jastyn murmured, "very thoughtful of him." She lifted it higher and watched swirls of what looked like watery cream twist inside the glass. "What is it?"

Aurelia's eyes were wide. She tapped the glass, and her lips parted when the light grew brighter. "I don't believe it."

"It almost looks like a saol." Jastyn tilted the glass. "But I've never seen one this color."

"That's because there are no saols like this one. If I'm correct, my father distributed the Light of Triur to each of you." The princess looked dumbfounded. Jastyn racked her mind, but she had never heard of such a thing.

Aurelia's voice took on a wistful tone, as if reciting from a well-read text. "I knew this only as another legend. In the beginning of our world, the first kings of the three kingdoms met in council. Representatives from Venostes, Gultero, and the northern kingdom of Uterni came together to form the laws and create a government for their people. Among their ideas was a recovery plan should outside forces penetrate these lands. It was decided that each leader would contribute a flame from their saols. At the time, elemental magic was new, and these were the first companion flames. It's said each fire burned with the brightness of a dozen suns. Combined, they were even more powerful. Once created, this Light was distributed to each kingdom and kept safely within each ruler's walls. This way, if the world was ever lost to darkness, the light could serve as a guide to reunite the tribes and begin again."

Jastyn listened, enraptured as the light bounced against the sides of the glass. Aurelia took it in her own hands, turning the orb over. Her eyebrows knitted in a frown.

"What?"

Shaking her head, Aurelia said, "I don't understand. The Light of Triur is supposed to be for the direst of times. A war, or mass invasion…" Her voice trailed off.

Jastyn watched Aurelia's face shift from disbelief to pain. She was sure they were both recalling the same images from the prince's remembrance: bloody lawns near the castle gates, bodies strewn helplessly across the grass.

"Your parents care for you a great deal," Jastyn finally said. "If you were not found, the kingdom would be without its heir." Blinking, Aurelia met Jastyn's gaze, whose lips twitched into a smile. "That sounds like a pretty dire situation to me."

Aurelia's eyes swam with something that sent a tremor down Jastyn's spine. Her body grew hot, and she desperately wanted to lean closer, wanted to wrap her arms around Aurelia and hold her until the sadness seeping from her dissipated.

She held out a hand, and Aurelia placed the orb carefully into her open palm. Aurelia's hands cupped Jastyn's, and they sat like that for what seemed like forever.

A raucous shout broke the silence holding them together. Voices, high and worried, rose from the main room. Hurriedly, Jastyn tucked the glass inside the pouch and stood.

"What's happening?" Aurelia rose too, her shoulder brushing Jastyn's.

"I'm not sure."

Sounds of an argument started; voices were quick and heated. Jastyn stepped in front of Aurelia. Coran stirred in the corner.

"Did you make the barmaid angry again, Jas?" He rubbed his eyes, then sat up quickly at the sight of Jastyn and Aurelia frozen together in front of the fire. "What's goin' on?"

There was a sharp splintering, like chairs breaking, followed by fists hitting flesh and the hiss of spell-fire.

"They've found me."

Jastyn glanced behind her. Aurelia's pale lips were tight with fear. Coran gathered his satchel, adding a blanket to his bundle before joining them. Jastyn pulled back her shoulders. "We won't let anything harm you. Do you hear me?"

Aurelia nodded, but her eyes were locked on the doorway. The shouting moved closer. Jastyn recognized the bartender's voice. The three of them stood together, huddled close and barely breathing.

Then the voices stopped.

"Maybe they've gone," whispered Coran.

Jastyn didn't have time to register the soft fingers that gripped hers before the wall next to the doorway blew open in a deafening crash, chunks of wood flying in every direction as dirt and smoke filled the small space. Coran and Jastyn ducked, leaning across one another to shield Aurelia. The earsplitting noise was interspersed with the whoosh of yellow spell-fire, which threw more of the wall against them until the floor was littered with its remnants, and the doorway was three times its original size.

Peeking through the clouds of dust and smoke, Jastyn noticed a limp figure lying in the middle of the floor. Atop a pile of splintered wood lay the barmaid, her freckled arms at awkward angles on either side of her body. Her eyes were open wide, lifeless and frozen.

"Gods," Aurelia whimpered.

"There you are. I knew the wench was hiding something."

Standing within the cragged, sizzling edges of the wall stood a barrel-chested man whom Jastyn recognized from the castle barn all those months ago. His blond curls were longer, wilder and untamed against his broad shoulders. He kicked a piece of broken wood and stepped into the room before swiping two fingers down his goatee.

"Really, Aurelia, the trouble you've caused."

Aurelia shook behind Jastyn. Two silver-haired elves, one several inches taller than the other with slim shoulders, stood behind him. The shorter of the two glared at the barmaid spread on the floor. The other, Jastyn noticed, had his eyes locked on Aurelia.

"Drest. How did you find me?"

He clapped his hands together as if ridding them of the damage he had caused. His left boot kicked the leg of the barmaid when he strode past.

"You thought you were so clever. The sleeping draught was unexpected, I'll give you that. Your mother taught you well."

Aurelia shot out from between Jastyn and Coran, nearly knocking them over as she dug a finger into Drest's chest. "Don't you *dare* speak about my family. You betrayed us. You betrayed my brother!"

"Aurelia." Jastyn reached out, tugging her back. She began to align the story of what happened. This man—Drest—was most likely behind the prince's death. *Was he the one who kidnapped Aurelia?* Jastyn's anger took root, but it was replaced by uncertainty as the man's eyes went clear. She wasn't sure what that meant, but she didn't think it could be good.

"You're despicable," Aurelia finished before spitting in the man's face. He turned his cheek, then wiped his chin clean. The smile he wore churned Jastyn's stomach.

The fire blew out behind them, and the room turned cold. A wind from nowhere picked up, sending several pieces of frayed wood across their path.

"This little reunion has been fun," Drest said, holding out his hands, palms up. Two cherry-sized flames sparked above each one. "Now, come with us, Aurelia. We have unfinished business to attend to."

"I'd rather go to the Otherworld than go anywhere with you."

Coran let out something that sounded like a mixture of a gasp and a squeal. He and Jastyn exchanged glances. What was Aurelia doing? It was the three of them against an extremely unhinged-looking man and a pair of elves. The odds were not in their favor.

"I do suggest you come with us, Princess." Drest's eyes were completely white now. His cheeks jutted out, making his face look unnaturally disjointed.

"Or what?" Aurelia replied, her voice loud over the whipping wind.

The man sneered. The elves stepped back when his voice came out in a yell. "Or else you'll be picking up what's left of these pathetic excuses for peasants with a broom!"

The air left Jastyn's lungs as his head tilted and his voice dropped. "Your choice."

CHAPTER TWENTY-TWO

Aurelia stared into the white emptiness where Drest's pupils once were. She stepped back, flush against Jastyn and Coran. She could feel Jastyn's right hand twitch and knew she was itching for the blade tucked against her boot. Aurelia considered the idea but knew that, ultimately, Drest would have his way. She tore through her mind and tried to conjure every defense spell she knew. But each one had been taught to her by Brennus, who had learned them from Drest. He had always been the best at magic. Everything she knew, he knew first.

She stalled.

"Why are you doing this?" she called over the roar of the wind, now an invisible cyclone lashing at her hands and knees. She slapped aside splinters of wood that blurred her vision.

Drest waited a moment before responding. "Your brother never deserved to be king."

"And you do?"

"I will return this realm to its once great state."

"Once great state?" Coran muttered.

Drest scowled in his direction. "There was a time when humans ruled every inch of these lands. We didn't have treaties delegating fae grounds over nearly half of our territories."

Aurelia frowned. Jastyn, however, spoke before she could. "The fae were here first. These are their native lands."

Drest turned on Jastyn, resembling a menacing predator leering over its food. "This is none of your concern, filthy Odium."

Jastyn's face went pale, then pink when she caught Aurelia's gaze.

Before she could even think about slapping the words from Drest's mouth, the slim-shouldered elf, in a melodic voice that seemed to break the rage spinning around them, called out.

"Princess!" In movements so swift Aurelia felt as if she was witnessing a hawk strike its prey, he sent a ball of spell-fire at his companion, who collapsed. Nearly simultaneously, he leapt onto Drest's back, a string of elven cries filling the air. His nails, suddenly bright blue, dug like daggers into Drest's shoulders, forcing a screech so loud the wind around them ceased, each fragment of wood halted in midair. Jastyn and Coran gripped each of her arms as Aurelia locked eyes with her former fae captor. His thin lips parted.

"Run."

Aurelia grabbed hold of Jastyn and tore from the room. Drest swung at them, but the elf twisted his legs like talons, dragging Drest's mighty torso down to the ground. She caught a glimpse of Drest reaching for his sword before Jastyn pushed her forward.

"Hurry, this way."

The three of them leapt over the still-burning remnants of the wall and sprinted back through the main room. All of the tables were upturned, and one of the mead barrels had been punched in so that the drink flowed like water from a broken dam. Any fae who had lingered earlier was gone.

"Quickly," Jastyn said behind her. Aurelia didn't look back. Once outside, she broke out into a run, Coran and Jastyn flanking her.

"Where do we go?" she asked, glancing between them as they hit the first line of trees.

Jastyn seemed to take in everything at once: the moss crawling over twisted roots, the fading stars overhead, and the approaching light of dawn.

Dipping her right shoulder, she said, "Follow me."

Aurelia and Coran trailed after her. Aurelia tried not to wince with each step on her left leg. She was glad Jastyn had wrapped it earlier, which saved her from the long-reaching branches and thorn-filled shrubs. Each step radiated pain from her knee to her ankle. She pushed the pain to the back of her mind, forcing herself to focus. Eventually, she was able to fall into a rhythm, landing nearly exactly where Jastyn had thanks to her boots leaving deep impressions in the leaf-scattered ground.

After what seemed like ages, they stopped.

"Somebody needs a break," Jastyn said through a grin, one hand on her hip. Coran bent over, both forefingers dug into his sides.

"It's just a cramp," Coran said, exhaling. "Do you reckon we've lost 'em?"

Jastyn nodded. "For now."

Aurelia smiled, catching Jastyn's gaze before she nodded at her leg.

"How are you doing?"

"Fine," Aurelia said quickly. "It feels fine."

Jastyn squinted, then bent over and pinched the knee between her forefinger and thumb. Aurelia cried out, swiping at Jastyn's hand.

"Why in the gods would you do that?" She gripped her knee, which throbbed with such force, her eyes watered.

Crossing her arms, Jastyn said, "I'm impressed you made it this far. I'm afraid the wound is deeper than you thought."

Aurelia huffed and straightened, being sure to put more weight on her right side. "I still don't see why that was necessary."

Smiling, Jastyn wandered a few yards away, digging in her satchel as she walked.

"Don't mind her," Coran said, his breath finally caught. "She's stalling because she's not sure where we are."

He barely put his hand up in time when Jastyn threw an apple at his face. He caught it, took a step, and chucked it back at her.

"I'm not lost," Jastyn said after scooping up the apple from the grass, brushing it against her tunic, and taking a bite. "Just…give me a minute."

They were quiet as Jastyn munched and stared at what seemed to be nothing. Aurelia allowed herself a moment to admire Jastyn, appreciating her strong legs that ran up to a slim waist and even narrower shoulders. Her arms were crossed, and her free hand ran absently down her braid. Despite her slight frame, she looked absolutely majestic against the early light streaming in from the east through the hundreds of tree trunks lined like guards on all sides of them. Drest had to have been spewing lies, Aurelia thought, still watching Jastyn. It was impossible that somebody so proud, so sure of herself, could be what he claimed.

Then she remembered her conversation with Coran. The horse

master, Elisedd, was her stepfather. Aurelia countered her own thought quickly. Women of the kingdom could remarry. Her great-grandmother even did, so she was told. It wasn't uncommon and certainly not against the laws, as long as one's husband was lost to Death. Another memory surfaced, this one of her conversation with her mother. The one where uttering even the smallest implication of Jastyn's existence had resulted in silence and denial.

Jastyn's weight shifted so that she stood with one hip jutted out slightly. The morning light framed her body, making her look completely at one with the Wood.

Aurelia shook her head. It couldn't be. Odium Children were unheard of in modern times. The laws had done their duty and cleared the kingdom of them decades ago. It was silly, she decided, to even consider that they still existed. Especially in the form of the stunning woman standing before her.

Coran took a seat against the base of the tree while Aurelia joined Jastyn. "Perhaps we should continue," she suggested, unable to deal with the whirlwind happening inside her mind. "I don't know how long Drest can be held off, but I doubt he will be occupied for long." Scanning the light dusting of freckles that ran across the bridge of Jastyn's nose, Aurelia watched her watch the depths of the Wood with such concentration, she wondered if Jastyn could see into some other world. Her eyes raced all around as if tracking an invisible creature.

Taking another bite from her apple, Jastyn said, "That's some friend you've got."

Aurelia stiffened. "Drest is not my friend." She shielded her eyes as the sun rose higher, forming beams of light that shot between the trees and cast long shadows that reached toward them in greeting. Her wrists stung, and she absently rubbed the red skin. "It's still difficult to fathom this was his doing."

"He planned this?"

"I think he must have. It was he who took me during the remembrance ceremony. I suppose he has the elves on his side, too." Memories of the invasion sent pain down her leg. She recalled the cries of agony from the villagers as arrows plunged deep into unsuspecting victims.

"Not all of the elves." Jastyn swallowed a bite. "That one from before gave us a head start."

Aurelia tilted her head at the notes of a morning dove. "Yes. I wonder why."

Shrugging, Jastyn threw her apple core out of sight. "Whatever the reason, I'm grateful." She paused, and Aurelia knew the next question before it was even asked.

"Were they the only ones…when you were with them?"

Aurelia, suddenly weary, joined Coran against the tree. He and Jastyn were quiet when she answered. "They were the only three I ever saw. But each night, right before sundown, Drest would disappear. He'd vanish into the Wood and wouldn't return until first dark. I think he was collecting something, but I never could tell what. He would bring whatever it was back and share it with the elves."

Jastyn, who had turned to listen, kept her piercing gaze unblinking. Aurelia, flustered, fingered the rags around her knee. "That's all I know. I'm afraid…I wasn't aware of much else."

"That's okay, Your Highness. You've been through a lot." Coran reached out a grubby hand, resting it for a moment on her arm.

Aurelia smiled, then looked back at Jastyn, who seemed to be looking through her. Her eyes were unfocused, as if she'd lost herself in a dream.

Aurelia yearned to know what was happening inside her mind. She had never met anyone who seemed to think of a million things at once yet show hardly a flicker on her face. What kept Jastyn so preoccupied each second of the day? Surely thoughts of her sister and the cure she needed were enough to worry about. She ached at the idea of Jastyn sitting beside her sister, day after day, unable to do anything. The image shifted, surprising Aurelia with a vision of herself alongside Jastyn. Together, they traipsed through the Wood in the search for the cure. The idea alone sent a stirring to her stomach. Immediately, she shook it from her mind. Aurelia knew Jastyn wasn't the type to trust anybody easily. The mere suggestion that she had something to offer in search for the cure would surely fall on deaf ears. Perhaps, Aurelia thought, she simply needed to try harder to convince Jastyn that she was no longer alone in this.

Crouching, Jastyn ran a stray branch through the fallen leaves. "You're right."

For a moment, Aurelia panicked. Had she spoken her thoughts aloud? Did Jastyn know she wasn't eager to leave her yet?

"I'm right? I didn't realize…"

"We should keep going. I say we walk east until the sun is overhead. Then we'll find food and water and set up camp. Your father and mother were headed north, but I have a feeling they've diverted west. If we camp half a day, that should give them time to catch up to us." Standing, she tossed the branch aside.

Exhaling, Aurelia asked, "What about Drest? What if he catches up to us first?"

"I'll set a protection spell around our site. I know a strong one. It should stave off any unwelcome visitors." She adjusted her satchel and started off.

"Hear that, Your Highness?" Coran said, standing, too. "You'll be back at the castle in no time."

"Wonderful." Aurelia hoped her smile was convincing. The idea of returning home, however, didn't strike the chord of anticipation she had felt only a few days before. She was sure she would be happy to see her mother and father again, yet she could not—despite her best efforts—envision herself in the castle. She could not see herself walking its vast halls, the halls that were now forever devoid of her brother's voice. She could not imagine sitting at their table, dining on legs of lamb while one chair sat eternally unoccupied. She could not see herself being happy in a place brimming with memories of death and destruction.

Worst of all, she suddenly could not fathom what she would inevitably have to do when the time came: ascend the Diarmaid throne and lead the Kingdom of Venostes as its rightful queen.

CHAPTER TWENTY-THREE

L ater that evening, Jastyn shook out the blanket from Coran's satchel, laying it across the ground in the stretch of forest they'd claimed for the latter half of the day following a five-mile march. While the waning sun provided sufficient warmth behind a thick layer of clouds, Jastyn knew that with summer fully upon them, the combination of the coming night and inevitable rainfall would bring the cold.

"Shall I collect wood for the fire?"

Aurelia stood with her hands on her hips, the sleeves of her tunic hiked up above her elbows. The skin around her wrists was a lighter pink now, indicating the raw skin was starting to heal. However, the lashes from where she must have been bound were still visible, a screaming red reminder for what she had been through only days before. Aurelia's mouth was scrunched in concentration, and Jastyn watched, amused, as she bent over a large, rotted log next to a nearby tree. Jastyn waved off Coran, who was about to say something. Aurelia grimaced when she crouched to pick up the log, and Jastyn made a mental note to look for the herb she had mentioned to aid in mending her knee.

Aurelia shrieked and leapt backward. The log she had reached for crumbled in her hands, and a herd of beetles scuttled out.

Upon seeing Jastyn doubled over with laughter, Aurelia wiped her arms in a huff. She marched back over to their spot, brushing her long hair behind her shoulders. Lifting her chin, she calmly stated, "Those were of the *brachinus* species, I believe." She wiped her hands on her pant leg. "The golden ground beetle, if I'm not mistaken."

Exchanging looks with Coran, Jastyn snickered. "I recommend

drier wood, Princess. It'll burn better." Aurelia nodded, then ventured off again. Jastyn watched her, scrutinizing the limp in her gait before scanning the remaining contents of her satchel: the king's gift was next to a bundle of elderberries, her old cup, one apple, and half a crust of bread. She would have to hunt soon if they were going to have enough sustenance to carry on.

Under his breath, Coran muttered, "Are you sure we want a fire?"

Glancing at Aurelia, who was out of earshot, Jastyn felt suddenly defensive. She wanted to ensure Aurelia's safety, but Coran had a point. It would be dark within an hour. While the light and warmth would be welcoming, a fire was risky. They'd be sending up a beacon to Drest and his cronies.

Nevertheless, a miniscule voice Jastyn didn't recognize grew louder in her mind: *What would make Aurelia happy?*

Realizing she hadn't answered, Jastyn gestured to the thick tree line surrounding them. "We've got plenty of cover out here. You'd have to be an eagle-eyed fae to see through these." Coran eyed her. "We'll keep the fire small," she added. "Besides, I know a spell Eegit taught me; it should mask any light or sound coming from our camp."

Coran shrugged, plopping down near his satchel. "If you say so."

Jastyn perused their surroundings as Coran set up a circle of stones for their firepit. There were no obvious signs of activity. She smelled no smoke, heard no breaking of fallen branches, and felt no signs of the Dark Fae. He hadn't appeared anywhere except in her dreams the last two months. Maybe, she thought, he would leave her alone for good. Despite his warnings that her search for the cure would be useless, Jastyn knew there was no other option if she wanted to save her sister. He could try and frighten her all he wanted. It only drove her frustration and desire to see this mission through. Exhaling, she shook out the tension that had built in her arms.

"I'm going to set the protection spell," she called over her shoulder, making her way to the edge of trees around their camp.

Coran gestured to Aurelia, who looked as if she were losing an arm-wrestling match with a knotted pile of branches. "I'll keep an eye on her."

Once she was a good forty paces from their site, Jastyn held up both of her hands. She recalled the incantation Eegit had taught her five winters before, when Eegit was having trouble keeping foxes from stealing her meat. She fell into the memory of her younger self standing next to Eegit, who stood with her arms up and her palms facing out as if she was going to push against a wall. Mimicking the memory, Jastyn focused on the energy inside her own body and the life surrounding her in the Wood. Her saol sparked to life in front of her hands, the soft blue light flickering in greeting. She uttered the incantation Eegit had taught her: *"An fhuaim agus an solas a ghlanadh,"* then began the slow process of encircling their camp, careful not to stray from the path her feet set between the trees.

When she had nearly completed the final iteration of the incantation with her starting point in view, rustling among the low-lying ferns made her falter. Forcing her eyes to stay locked on her saol, she turned her mind to the sound of shuffling feet five paces behind her left shoulder. The step wasn't light enough to be elven but wasn't the heavy tread that would accompany Aurelia's pursuer from the public house. Her left hand inches away from connecting the protection circle, Jastyn froze and listened.

She waited for the half second between footsteps, then whirled around with her saol aimed and ready.

In less than a moment, her flame was extinguished as Eegit waved it away like a bothersome gnat.

"Really, child. How you've managed this long is beyond me."

"Eegit!" Jastyn pulled her into a hug. A startling crack sounded where her arms gripped Eegit's back. She released her quickly. "Are you okay?"

Eegit, one hand on her spine, twisted and bent, a look of relief on her face. "I've needed that one cracked for decades!"

"What are you doing here?"

Eegit shook out her arms like a wolf shaking water from its fur. She glanced up through the few eyelashes she had left. "Child, every fae, witch, and elf south of Uterni has heard about what happened at that public house."

"It wasn't my fault. The leprechauns who run it—"

"The leprechauns." Eegit held up a twisted finger. "You should be mighty careful with them, child. You're making more enemies than allies."

Shaking back her braid, Jastyn huffed. "It's not my fault they'd rather shapeshift then have a normal conversation."

Eegit grunted and motioned for Jastyn to follow her. "I heard you pulled a weapon on an innocent fae."

"She was hardly innocent," murmured Jastyn, recalling the barmaid's suggestive hand on hers. She ducked when Eegit swung a miserly fist her way. Feeling defensive, Jastyn exclaimed, "Is this all you've come for? To scold me for everything I've done wrong?"

At this, Eegit turned, her eyes narrowed. "It would do you well to be more careful. Word travels fast in the Wood."

"I understand." Jastyn stepped back, taking a good look at her friend. She hated to admit it, but she was glad to see Eegit. Did she know that Jastyn slept outside her clearing the night before she left the kingdom? Had Eegit sensed her turmoil? Heard her cries? Momentarily, she lost herself in memories of that night. The image of her mother— standing alone amid the stormy hills—came rushing back.

"How is Alanna?" Jastyn knew Eegit kept eyes on her family and had ever since Alanna fell ill as a child. Perhaps she had news of her mother, too.

Eegit's eyes fixed on the sky, which grew grayer by the minute. Jastyn could smell the moisture collecting overhead, and Eegit seemed to be in conversation with the darkening clouds.

"Your sister remains the same. She misses you." She caught Jastyn's gaze before adding, "Branna does, too."

"My mother has Elisedd to comfort her." Jastyn couldn't resist the bitterness that swam in her mouth. It remained surreal, what her mother had told her. What made her think such a message, dropped like a stone in a calm riverbed, would do? Encourage her? Thrill her? Its effect had been quite the opposite. Jastyn carried the message with her like a dead weight tied around her ankles. She bit her tongue, resisting the urge to spew more hatred toward her mother.

For a moment, it looked as if Eegit was going to start in on her. She opened her cracked lips, and Jastyn noted the familiar look of annoyance pass through her gaze. Maybe Jastyn deserved a lecture. It could do her some good. She was feeling more conflicted the longer Aurelia was with her. She knew that once the royal search party found them, it would be over. Aurelia would return to her family. There would be no noble sacrifice, whatever that entailed. Somehow, she would have to avoid the parties for as long as she could. She knew Aurelia had little to no concept of where they were in the Wood, which helped. They were heading more south than east. If Jastyn could continue to convince her they were headed back to the kingdom, rather than farther away, it would be too late for Aurelia to venture back on her own once she realized.

That was the part Jastyn was dreading. What would happen once Aurelia did understand what was happening? How would she react, knowing that she was a pawn in Jastyn's plan to save her sister? Jastyn balked at the thought of the way Aurelia would look at her. The image was unbearable. This new feeling toward Aurelia was *not* part of the plan.

At what appeared to be a reprieve between herself and the sky, Eegit pouted in temporary defeat. Coran's voice emerged from the depth of trees.

"I'd better get back," Jastyn said, her eyes on the dead leaves sticking out from beneath her boots. "Coran probably sent a piece of spell-fire into Aurelia's hair."

Eegit followed. "Ah, yes. Her Royal Highness. She's tougher than one would expect from a Diarmaid."

Jastyn pictured Aurelia's escape from her captors, a feat she still wasn't sure could have been undertaken on her own. Aurelia's battered hands and legs leapt to her mind. "Eegit, you don't happen to know what calendula herb looks like, do you?"

Without breaking stride, Eegit yanked off two heads of the waist-high flowers flopping lazily nearby atop thin green stalks. She handed the tangerine-colored petals, fanned out around the flower's center like a blazing lion's mane, to Jastyn. "You've been standing in it for the last fifty paces."

"Thank you." Jastyn tucked the herb tightly in her hand. When Eegit followed behind her, Jastyn asked, "You're staying for dinner, then?"

With her eyes back on the sky and her feet somehow missing every rock and stray branch in her path, Eegit nodded. "There's much to sort out."

Jastyn mulled over her meaning as they cleared a line of bushes and thistle and rejoined Coran and Aurelia at their campsite. Much to her surprise, the two had a modest fire burning. Aurelia fussed about beside it, reminding Jastyn of a hen she once raised who happily clucked back and forth in front of her bedroom window each morning. Coran, a look of accomplishment on his face, drank lazily from his flask.

"You fetched water?" Jastyn asked.

Coran wiped his mouth. "There's a creek not far that way." When he noticed Eegit, his smile faltered. "How did she find us all the way out here?"

"Followed your scent, naturally," Eegit replied.

Jastyn gave Coran a shove, unable to hide her laughter. "Apparently, we've been causing quite the stir. Eegit wanted to see what all the fuss was about."

"Eegit?" Aurelia, who had been arranging spare logs into a formation that gave Jastyn the impression she intended them as seats, straightened. "You're Eegit?"

Eyes still skyward, Eegit replied, "For some time now, I'm afraid."

An affectionate smile filled Aurelia's face. Jastyn longed to know what she was thinking as Aurelia stepped around the fire, holding out her arm for a handshake.

"Aurelia Diarmaid. It's lovely to meet you."

Eegit tore her gaze from the sky, now an eerie slate of gray. Her beady, watery eyes took in every inch of the young woman standing before her. They roamed over her like a king surveying his land from the highest hill. Aurelia, much to her credit, never flinched.

Finally, Eegit spoke. "I am sorry about your brother."

Aurelia's hand fell. "Thank you." They stood staring at one another. Coran shuffled closer to the fire, feeding it handfuls of dead leaves. Jastyn wasn't sure whether she should interject or let Aurelia and Eegit continue like this until nightfall. Right as she was about to suggest Eegit help her with a hunt, she spoke.

"Jastyn fetched calendula for your knee."

Aurelia blinked. "You did?"

Holding up her hand, Jastyn revealed the herb.

The look Aurelia gave her sent a flutter in her chest, and she knew Eegit could see the effect Aurelia had on her. To hide it, Jastyn quickly turned and grabbed one of the logs Aurelia had set up in a semicircle. "Decided you wouldn't be much help with only one good leg."

Eegit snorted, which Jastyn ignored as Aurelia joined her. She pretended not to notice the moment's hesitation as Aurelia passed by the closest log, then plopped down beside Jastyn on the same splintered seat.

Self-conscious of her dirty tunic and earth-covered hands, Jastyn fumbled with the clump of flower in her fingers. Unsure how to proceed, she muttered, "Well, you're the expert."

Thankfully, Aurelia seemed to pick up on her uncertainty. "Here. It's best to mash and stir into a paste."

Jastyn grabbed her satchel. Handing the wooden cup to Aurelia, she bit her lip at the surprisingly cool touch of Aurelia's fingers as they grazed against hers. Her gaze flickered up to Aurelia, who smiled before tossing the herb into the cup. After a quick scan of her surroundings, she scooped up a pear-shaped rock, which she used to ground the petals into a sticky paste.

Jastyn sat in silence, watching Aurelia's hands work deftly with the mortar. Once the herb was sufficiently mashed, she frowned.

"Did I grab the wrong herb?" Jastyn asked. It would be like Eegit to mess with her, teasing her like a playmate would.

"It's not that." Aurelia's cheeks gained a tint of blush before she said, "I just remembered that…well, I'm afraid this particular herb, while useful in alleviating infections from wounds, is quite painful upon application."

When Jastyn didn't say anything, Aurelia added, "It's going to hurt."

Unable to hide a smile, Jastyn took the cup. "Stretch out your leg."

Aurelia shifted so that she sat perpendicular to Jastyn, who swiftly moved so that she was straddling the log. Aurelia's left leg in front of her, Jastyn placed the cup between her legs, then slowly began removing the rags she'd wrapped around Aurelia's knee the day before.

Once the knee was exposed, Jastyn couldn't stop the gasp upon seeing the rust-colored gash framed in a garish dark red.

"It looks worse than it is," Aurelia said.

Jastyn looked up, analyzing Aurelia's stoic face. "I've seen you limping. I know it hurts."

Aurelia swallowed. "Let's just get this over with, shall we?"

Leaning back, Jastyn wondered if she had somehow offended her. It continued to surprise her how proud Aurelia could be. When her blue eyes flickered up, Jastyn dipped her fingers into the paste and held them over the wound. "Ready?"

Aurelia nodded. As gently as she could, Jastyn laid two of her fingers—coated in the thick paste—onto one edge of the sliced skin. Aurelia screamed once, her mouth flying shut a second later. When Jastyn glanced up, she found Aurelia's eyes slammed shut, her lips clamped tight together.

While trying to be gentle, Jastyn swiped the herb across the gash as quickly as she could, being sure to add an extra layer over the deepest part. Aurelia's leg was tense beneath her, and she felt Aurelia's entire body relax once she added the final dab of calendula.

"There. Done."

Aurelia exhaled slowly.

Jastyn splashed her hands with water. As the sun lowered over the trees and the world darkened around them, the firelight flickered, throwing shadows over Aurelia's face, which had turned serene. Her high cheeks looked as smooth as a fresh eggshell. Jastyn suddenly felt overcome with the desire to run the back of her hand across that cheek. She even raised her hand between them. Aurelia continued to analyze her wound and didn't notice Jastyn hasten to run that hand down her braid before clearing her throat. "You're pretty brave, for a princess."

Aurelia smiled. "I was thinking of my brother."

The sun had set behind them. Across the fire, Coran skewered a tree-dweller with Eegit, who gesticulated impatiently as Coran, wearing a fearful look, leaned the critter over the open fire. Sensing she and Aurelia could speak without being overheard, Jastyn said, "The village criers said the prince died in battle. They said it was a swift death worthy of a soldier."

Aurelia grunted, the noise startling Jastyn. "You don't agree?"

After a moment, Aurelia said, "My brother was part of a scouting party. We had received news of fae factions growing restless in the Wood. It was my brother's duty to go out, interpret what was happening, and report back to my father."

Jastyn flashed back to that night in the Wood, the one where she had felt helpless to help her sister. She remembered the harsh clashing of swords, the whirlwind of spell-fire, the sickening thump of the arrow landing in the prince.

"It was his first true outing. He had longed to take up arms and serve his kingdom." Aurelia's voice dropped to a whisper. Her eyes were wet as she spoke. "He was eager to be of service. Eager to contribute to the well-being of our kingdom and its people. That was all he wanted—to be useful."

At her last words, Jastyn had a feeling she wasn't speaking of only her brother.

Aurelia shook her head, wiping a tear that escaped. "My brother was murdered. His death was not swift. The last seconds of his life were full of agony and anguish." Her voice was hard when she added, "He deserved so much more."

Before she could second-guess herself, Jastyn reached out to rest a hand on Aurelia's thigh, above the wound she'd dressed moments ago. When she met the eyes looking back at her, Jastyn felt red-hot. She ached to move forward, to pull Aurelia close and hold her. She wanted to tell her she would help her to avenge her brother's death. Aurelia's pain made her chest feel as if it was being torn like used rags and left in pieces on the ground.

"I can't imagine what it's like to lose a sibling." She pictured Alanna, the old quilt they shared wrapped tightly around her frail body. Was the Red One's cure still working? Had the effects began to wane? How quickly would she have to move to make sure her own sister didn't meet a similar fate?

Jastyn was pulled from her thoughts when Aurelia's hand lay on top of hers, her fingers grasping Jastyn's wrist like a lifeline.

A crackling jumped out from the silence. The fire flashed as Coran and Eegit pulled another crispy tree-dweller from the flames, lining it up next to three others ready to eat. Jastyn blinked. She looked at Aurelia's hand. Her fair skin was impeccable, the only signs of life the lashes on her wrists, each a gruesome souvenir from a life that Aurelia was not built for.

What was Jastyn thinking? It was impossible to even imagine a possibility of feelings for somebody like Aurelia. Not only was she not of the village, she was now *the* future queen of Venostes. Jastyn scolded herself for forgetting, once again, that Aurelia was a Diarmaid. She came from a line of royal blood, and Jastyn…she didn't even know who she was. Her mother was deserted, and her father was a fae. There was no use believing in a future where people as different as she and the princess could stand together in front of a crowd. Aurelia had a place, and that place was higher than any one Jastyn would ever be able to go.

It was also useless pretending she could help Aurelia gain

vengeance. The source of Jastyn's own pain had ties to the woman sitting in front of her. She had no business entangling her desires with Aurelia's. It was the Diarmaid family who put Jastyn in the position she was in to begin with. There was no room, she reminded herself, for sympathy toward any of them. Especially Aurelia.

Pulling her hand away, Jastyn stood. "You should eat. We have a long walk tomorrow." Without looking back, she moved around the fire, putting as much space between herself and the princess as she could.

CHAPTER TWENTY-FOUR

*A*urelia reached out. The tips of her fingers caressed Brennus's icy cheek. Her brother lay on the black-draped table in the main hall. His white tunic and pants gave him the image of a ghoul or spirit, floating eerily above the ground in the chamber of darkness. She ran her fingers over his brow, then into the thick locks of hair curling over his forehead.

They were the only two in the vast room inside the castle; the only light in the room was three candles situated at the base of Brennus's boots. Her brother's stiff fingers clutched the sword he was to bear on his way to the funeral pyre. If she listened carefully, Aurelia could hear the construction of the towering structure outside.

Her body ached with grief, and she laid her head down beside her brother's. With her cheek resting on the table, Aurelia stared at the profile of his still face, framed by the soft glow of the candlelight.

Grief turned quickly to exhaustion. Her heavy eyelids closed.

"Aurelia."

She jolted upright. A scan of the room found no one. Her brother lay motionless. It couldn't have been.

"Help me, Aurelia."

Gasping, Aurelia's chair clamored to the floor as she stood, one hand over her mouth. Her brother's eyes flew open.

"Brennus?"

He didn't move. Only his eyes roved from side to side as if searching for something.

"Aurelia?"

She stepped closer, using the edge of the table to steady her trembling hands.

"I'm here." Her voice shook, and she couldn't bring herself to reach out to touch him.

"There's not much time. Drest—"

"I know," she said. "I know it was him."

"Drest is a plaything."

Wiping her eyes, Aurelia breathed through a laugh. "He's not my favorite, either."

Soot from the candles floated over the ankles of Brennus's pants, leaving a dusting of black on the hem. When her brother remained quiet, she leaned closer.

"Brennus?"

"Drest is a plaything."

She frowned. "I don't understand."

Thrice more, her brother repeated himself. Aurelia shook as her brother's words echoed with unnerving clarity. Swallowing, she reached out. When her fingers brushed the collar of his tunic, he screamed.

She leapt back.

With one hand, Brennus raised the sword that had been resting on his chest. Hilt skyward, he gripped the middle of the blade, and Aurelia cried out as blood seeped between his fingers where he held it steady.

She watched in horror as Brennus drove the end of the sharp blade into his side. His screams intensified, filling every corner of the empty room.

"Stop!" Aurelia shrank from the table. She covered her ears to block out the sickening *gush* her brother's body made with each new stab. Blood pooled along every inch of his torso, turning his tunic a shocking red.

"Stop! Brennus, please stop!"

"Wake up, child!"

Thrashing, Aurelia nearly bowled over Eegit, who stood over her in the dark veil of the Wood at night. She sat up, soaked in sweat, parts of her tunic clinging to her chest and back. Slowly, her eyes adjusted to the bright moon overhead, the smell of charred embers in the fire, and the warm body of Coran sleeping next to her.

"I'm sorry," she finally said, taking a drink from the flask Eegit handed her. "I was dreaming." She shook her head, forcing the lingering image of her brother's death from her mind.

Eegit grunted, then plopped next to the dull fire. After adding what looked to be the remnants of their dinner into the flames, she said, "Dreams are the only time the dead can visit us. Best not to be picky."

Deciding not to divulge the horrifying details of her nightmare, Aurelia said, "He's the only person I've ever lost."

Eegit, looking as if she'd already lost interest in their conversation, concentrated on a formation of stones laid out in a semicircle on the grass between them. Sitting cross-legged, she switched one stone out for another, repeating the process several times while Aurelia's heart calmed its beating.

"What are you doing?"

"Runes."

"My mother always said runes was an outdated art…a scheme of nonsensical conjuring brought about by too many steam baths and an overactive imagination."

Eegit's hand froze over her handiwork. She lifted her gaze. "Your mother's not the first Diarmaid to ever say such a thing."

Biting her lip, Aurelia stammered, "I'm sorry. I didn't mean…" She sighed. "I don't agree with my mother, if that's what you're wondering. Actually, in the last six months, I've learned that my mother—and my father, for that matter—are capable of more lying than I thought possible." She grabbed a branch and poked dejectedly at the fire.

A loud guffaw fell out of Eegit's mouth, making Aurelia jump and Coran moan from where he slept.

"Parents lie more to their children than anybody else in this world."

Aurelia propped her chin in her upturned palm. Her gaze drifted to Jastyn sleeping on the other side of Coran. She lay with one arm beneath her head while the other reached out from her chest as if she was stretching it across something or someone. Aurelia imagined herself beneath Jastyn's arm, tucked close against her strong body.

Eegit whistled low.

Aurelia turned. "What?"

"It appears I owe a fairy twelve rabbit's feet."

Jastyn groaned, and her outstretched hand twitched, her previously calm face falling to a scowl.

Eegit spoke quietly. "She's had them for years." Aurelia studied

Eegit, who had returned to her stone reading. "For the last thirteen years, Jastyn hasn't slept well. Not for more than a couple of weeks at a time, anyway." Eegit glanced up, and Aurelia was surprised to see a look of admiration in the old woman's eyes. "She came to me for food, at first. She was smaller than she is now, if you can believe that. Little scrap of a thing."

Aurelia's heart sank. "She was starving?"

Eegit's lips stuck out in a pout. "Her mother is Branna Cipher. Originally Branna Rhinehart. Now wife of Elisedd Eidhin of Marcra. Twenty-two years ago, Jastyn's mother was banished to the outskirts of the kingdom—your kingdom."

Holding up a hand, Aurelia said, "I don't need to hear this." Fear replaced the ache in her heart at the image of a young Jastyn, hungry and dirty and living with nothing. Now, Aurelia had a feeling she knew where Eegit was going with this. She knew her family's beliefs, the beliefs that had dictated the land for centuries. She couldn't bear to think that her family had been responsible for Jastyn's lot in life.

"Jastyn Cipher is the daughter of a woman who broke the laws. The laws upheld by the Diarmaid family. Jastyn Cipher has fought harder than anyone for nothing more than a place in this world. Her journey has not been easy, and what comes next will be even more difficult."

"I never meant—"

Eegit cut her off when she stood swiftly, her stones scattering like mice. Aurelia's throat pinched closed as she cowered beneath her.

"She does not trust easily. She does not understand it. Be ready to forgive her."

"Forgive her? I don't—"

From where she slept, Jastyn cried out, one of her legs kicking against an unseen force. Aurelia leaned over, laying one hand on her shoulder to calm her.

When she looked back to where Eegit had been, she was gone.

"It's all right, I'm here. You're safe."

Jastyn's breathing was too quick, and Aurelia kept her hands on her shoulders while Jastyn regained her composure. Aurelia hadn't recognized the look in Jastyn's eyes when she woke; she seemed completely dazed. Aurelia continued to soothe her until Jastyn's breathing matched her own. A wave of relief washed over her when Jastyn met her gaze, a sheepish smile stretching across her face.

"Are you all right?" Aurelia asked, suddenly aware of her hands gripping Jastyn's shoulders and the way her chest rose and fell with each breath.

Still smiling, Jastyn reached out and poked Aurelia below her collarbone. "You're real?"

"Ouch." Rubbing the spot dramatically, Aurelia scooted back. "I am perfectly real, thank you very much."

Jastyn blinked a few times. "I was afraid…" Seeming to remember who she was talking to, she added, "I'm sorry. I was dreaming."

Adjusting so that she faced the fire and not the incredibly handsome way Jastyn's jaw curved into the point of her chin, Aurelia nodded to the flickering light. "It seems to be contagious tonight." She could feel Jastyn's gaze on her, and Aurelia bit the inside of her cheek so hard she tasted blood.

"Where's Eegit?"

Aurelia looked around. "She…well, she disappeared."

Jastyn laughed. "She does that."

"I see."

Silence sat between them. Aurelia stoked the fire some more while Jastyn splashed her face with water from the flask. From the corner of her eye, Aurelia watched her run a wet hand down her braid, pushing stray strands of light hair from her neck. Aurelia's heart raced when Jastyn lifted both her arms to pull her hair tighter, revealing a taut stomach.

After another minute of silence, Jastyn said, "I think the fire would appreciate a second to itself."

Aurelia blushed, dropping the branch and pulling her shoulders back. Jastyn had one eyebrow quirked when she met her gaze. Overcome with the desire to fill the tense air between them, Aurelia asked, "Have you ever sought medicinal treatment…for your nightmares?"

Immediately, Jastyn's smile vanished. "Who told you I have nightmares?"

Aurelia stammered. "Oh, Eegit only mentioned—"

"Eegit." Jastyn stood, swiping grass from her pants. "I should have known. Wait till she gets back."

"Wait," Aurelia said, standing, too. "She didn't mean anything. We were only talking."

Jastyn's sharp eyes landed on her like a bull's-eye. "About me?"

Aurelia bit her lip.

"What did she tell you?"

What was happening? Not moments ago, Aurelia was sure she had broken through the tough exterior Jastyn wore like a shield against the world. She had caught a glimpse of the kind, thoughtful woman she knew Jastyn was. Why was she being like this?

"I have nightmares, too. It's all right. I only thought that I could help. I know a few herbal remedies—"

Jastyn was stalking off toward the trees but spun around so fast Aurelia stumbled backward. "There are no remedies for what haunts me. Do you understand? He's everywhere. He's with me every day and each night I close my eyes. It doesn't matter where or," her eyes turned resentful, "*who* I'm with. He has never stopped and never will!"

A grumble came from behind them. Coran stirred.

Aurelia lowered her voice. "I'm sorry. I was only trying to help."

For a brief second, Jastyn looked apologetic. She reached one hand out but shook her head and turned again for the trees. When she did, the wind picked up from the opposite side of their campsite.

Coran sat up slowly, one hand rubbing his eyes. "What's goin' on?"

Aurelia turned to reply but froze when a sickening yellow light began to glow from the edge of the trees. The wind grew stronger, whipping the bottom of her tunic against her waist. Coran lifted an arm to shield his eyes as sticks and leaves were thrown across the clearing.

Aurelia's stomach dropped. "Oh no."

The yellow light exploded, sending rays of amber and a tsunami of raging winds across their campsite. The air was knocked from her lungs, and she was tossed backward, landing with a hard thud against the ground. The ripping wind berated her ears, and ringing filled her head, making it impossible to think. She looked around. The world had darkened, their fire extinguished.

"Jastyn!" she called, reaching out into the blackness. She squinted, trying to adjust to the moonlight. A dim figure crawled slowly toward her.

"Jastyn?"

"M'lady! Are you okay?"

"Coran." Aurelia scurried across the grass on her hands and knees. "I'm fine. Where's Jastyn?"

"Here." Aurelia turned and felt a wash of relief at Jastyn crouched behind her. Streaks of dirt covered one side of her face, but otherwise, she looked fine. "What was that?"

The three of them huddled together, Jastyn and Coran on either side of Aurelia.

A blaze like a thousand suns sprang up from the ground. A massive crack, like the breaking of the earth itself, threatened theirs ears and shook the ground. Aurelia shielded her face, leaning into Jastyn. The light burned her skin, and the same wind left her raw.

When the light dimmed, a broad-shouldered figure stood over them. Drest held two fists of yellow spell-fire. Beneath his clear eyes, void of any and all emotion, an eerie grin opened to speak.

"My, that protection spell was terribly sweet, yet I'm afraid left unfinished. Nevertheless, I'm flattered." He brushed off his sleeves. "Now, Aurelia dear, are you going to come with me, or will I have to tear these two apart limb by limb until you do?"

CHAPTER TWENTY-FIVE

Jastyn really hated this man.

Drest's voice was like shards of glass, setting her teeth on edge and sending an unwelcome spasm through her body. "I'm not going to ask you again, Aurelia."

To Jastyn, Drest had looked unwell in their last encounter. Now, he resembled a fire-breather she saw once in a traveling show—after he'd caught himself on fire. His wild blond mane stuck out at odd angles, blown in the tunnel of wind that circled their clustered group like a funnel. His clothes were grimy, and his previously bulging muscles were atrophied. Jastyn wondered if it was worth it, his quest to destroy Aurelia. The toll it seemed to be taking on him was immense.

Managing to stand, Jastyn steadied her shaking legs while the earth settled its quaking. She looked around, half hoping to find Eegit lurking nearby. *Leave it to my friend to take off when things get tough.*

Aurelia's voice pulled her from her thoughts. "As I said before, I'm not going anywhere with you."

The whirlwind intensified. Jastyn felt as if something had wrapped its giant hands around her lungs, making it harder to breathe the longer Drest held his spell in place. She'd never seen anyone use wind power the way he did. Wind was the hardest element to control, at least according to Eegit. Most of the kingdom mastered fire, a few were partial to water, but hardly any human had enough control and strength to conquer the ever-changing winds.

Slowly, Jastyn pulled Aurelia up with her. Coran followed suit, and they clung to one another while Drest towered over them. His spell-fire blazed, reflected in the bare whites of his eyes. His lips—poised in a sneer—parted.

"Very well."

His right arm raised. Jastyn's eyes were drawn downward. Her satchel was strewn on the grass four paces behind him. She had an idea. It was a long shot, but she had to try.

Aurelia said something, but Jastyn didn't hear it. Jastyn leapt forward, tackling Drest at his waist with all of the force she could muster. His spell-fire dissipated, deadening the tunnel of wind as they careened to the ground.

"Jastyn!"

She ignored Aurelia, turning instead to Coran. "Grab my satchel. Go!"

Not hesitating, Coran took off. The element of surprise had worked, but Drest regained composure quickly. She tried to keep him pinned, one of her legs on either side of his broad torso. Looking up at her, he laughed.

"Who do you think you are?" He swung one hand in front of her like an apathetic greeting. An invisible force yanked her off him, and she flew twenty paces in the air. When she landed near the line of trees, she could hardly breathe. Her shoulder, jammed into the ground on impact, throbbed.

Groaning, she rolled onto her side. To her dismay, Aurelia was now climbing atop Drest, her fists pounding against his chest.

"I hate you! You loathsome, vile, bigoted—"

Aurelia couldn't finish her sentence before she, too, was flung from Drest, soaring in the air until she fell next to their fire pit, her legs skidding across the smoking embers.

It required nearly all of Jastyn's willpower not to run to Aurelia. Managing to stand, she watched Drest stalk over to her. Coran, meanwhile, grabbed the satchel and scurried over to Jastyn.

"Are you okay?"

"I'll be fine," she replied, digging through the bag, her eyes still on Aurelia as she rolled quickly up from the ashes, her pant legs now a dark gray. Brushing her hair back, she pulled herself upright to face Drest.

"She's a persistent one, I'll give her that," Coran said.

Jastyn pulled out the pouch containing the king's gift. Thrilled it hadn't been lost in the wind, she kissed the plush velvet. Then she tied the gold strings around her belt so that the pouch dangled against her thigh. "Follow my lead," she said before taking off toward the others. When she was only ten paces away, Drest's wide body blocking her view of Aurelia, she called, "Over here!"

The moment Drest turned, she let a blue fireball go, aimed right at his chest. His hands, astoundingly fast, went up and blocked the impact. Jastyn and Coran dove in opposite directions to avoid the melon-sized yellow spell-fire he threw only a second later. Rushing to her feet and taking aim again, Jastyn was happy to see orange spell-fire from Coran join her blue one before they crashed in front of Drest. His arms went up to shield himself. As he was about to release another shot, his body flew forward, sparks from a red spell-fire framing his shoulders from behind.

When he hit his knees, Aurelia was already reloading another red flame in her hand. Grinning, Jastyn conjured her blue one, and Coran followed suit with an orange orb. Simultaneously, the three of them aimed and fired.

The lights exploded over Drest, who enclosed himself in a yellow shield.

Adrenaline running through her, Jastyn sprinted for Drest. She recalled the image of Aurelia when they first found her: a ragged escapee, bruised and raw, unable to talk about what had happened. Jastyn's jaw clenched. She wanted to make Drest suffer. She wanted to drive her knife into his chest until he couldn't breathe. She wanted to see the life leave his eyes so that he could never lay another finger on Aurelia ever again.

When she was steps away, Aurelia cried out. "Wait!"

A nearly invisible force vibrated from Drest's hands. Jastyn tried to stop her momentum, but his arms pushed forward, and a power like a roaring ocean wave kicked her feet out from under her. She flew skyward, for a moment lost in the night air among the stars. With a sickening smack, the hard ground broke her fall. Her head slammed against the earth, dazzling lights filling the blackness of her vision. A throbbing pounded like drums in her mind.

"This is what was always going to happen." Drest's voice was distant and warped, as if she was hearing him from beneath a riverbed. "You did this to her, Aurelia. All you have to do is come with me now, and all of this will stop."

"Why are you doing this?" Jastyn could hear the façade of bravery in Aurelia's words. She smiled at the stubbornness but doing so shot searing pain through her face. Her body aching, she sat up, one hand rubbing the back of her head.

"Once you are gone, there will be no one left between Venostes and its new king."

Jastyn's head still spun, but the pounding relented in her ears. The sounds of the Wood returned as Drest carried on.

"I told you, Aurelia. The Diarmaids are finished. Their time has ended. It's time to return this realm to its purest form. You can fall in line behind me, or you can cease to exist. Don't make this worse than you already have."

Aurelia was trembling. Jastyn pushed herself up, crouching so that one arm leaned down over her knee propped in front of her. She steadied her breathing, willing Aurelia to meet her gaze. When she did, Jastyn gave her a smile, hoping Aurelia couldn't see the scrambling of her mind while she tried to think of what to do next. They had Drest outnumbered, but his magic contained the power of ten humans. She wasn't sure how long they would be able to hold him off. She felt the pouch containing the king's gift on her leg. She just needed to get close enough...

In the distance, a faint, high noise shifted her gaze from Aurelia to the treetops. She peered into the tree line, nothing more than a series of round shadows in the night's darkness. The sound vibrated through the air, quick and tight. It reminded Jastyn of a harpsichord player from the market tightening her strings before playing.

Dread hit her like a fist. A rustling of leaves confirmed her suspicion. Somebody was in the trees, hidden in the thicket of branches. They were armed, and she knew they weren't aiming at her.

Taking off for Aurelia, Jastyn ran. Her ears trained on the noise, she pushed faster, faltering slightly when the sound paused. Coran shouted behind her. At the same time, she left her feet to dive forward as a streamlined whistle peeled out from the trees.

"Jastyn!"

She shoved Aurelia, who tumbled backward, and for what seemed like the third time in a very short while, Jastyn lost her breath when she hit the ground.

Stretched out on her stomach on the grass, she closed her eyes in relief. It took a few seconds for her to register the searing pain pulsating in her right shoulder.

Everything next seemed to happen at once.

"You fool! How could you miss?"

Somebody jumped down from the trees, landing lightly nearby. A language Jastyn couldn't understand drifted over her like hurried music. She rolled onto her side while a pair of hands landed on her legs, then ran up her waist, treading carefully around her shoulder.

"Jastyn? Gods, Jastyn, no."

She winced. When her vision cleared, Aurelia leaned over her. Her fair skin looked shockingly pale in the moonlight, and her light eyes swam with tears. Another pair of hands gripped her boots while Drest continued to argue with their new assailant.

"Jastyn!" She could feel Coran's hands shaking as they held her. "What are we gonna do?"

Swallowing, Jastyn's voice was hoarse when she asked, "It's an arrow, isn't it?"

Closing her eyes to block out the pain, Jastyn rolled onto her back. Her left hand ran across her chest and found the long end of a shaft sticking out of her shoulder. The arrowhead poked out from its tip about four inches above her punctured flesh. Her stomach churned as Aurelia confirmed her suspicions.

"It went right through you." Her voice was distant. When Drest's voice ceased, Jastyn groaned, leaning her hip toward Aurelia.

"The pouch. Take it."

Aurelia's brows knit together. "What do you mean?"

Drest's heavy tread drew closer. Jastyn gritted her teeth at the spasm the arrow sent through her back. "Your father's gift. The Light of Triur. Use it now."

Aurelia's eyes lit with recognition. She hurriedly opened the pouch, pulling out the small globe.

"Now, where were we?"

Jastyn's eyes followed Aurelia as she gripped the glass in her fist. "Close your eyes," she muttered. Coran looked between them, confused.

"Do it," Jastyn ordered.

Aurelia reared back and threw the orb directly at Drest's feet. Jastyn felt Aurelia collapse on top of her, shielding the three of them in a red shell from the blazing white light that lit up every blade of grass, every fairies' nest, and every fallen leaf in the forest. Drest's screams were overpowered by the light that burst and swallowed him up, encompassing his legs, his waist, and his arms in a sphere of punishing white.

Jastyn's eyes burned, and she squeezed them tight to block out the unfamiliar bright. She could feel Aurelia bury herself lower, her face flush against Jastyn's neck as one arm lay over her protectively.

The smoking, claustrophobic air Drest had left them in was ripped open by the light. A sound like a thousand waves breaking against the sand roared. In a fleeting moment, Jastyn felt a jolt, like a spark, race through her veins as the light washed over them, then disappeared. She opened her eyes. Once again, the world was dark. Night lay over the Wood like a familiar blanket. Stars winked overhead. Everything was quiet.

The sigh that left her throat was echoed by Coran. Lifting her left arm, Jastyn wrapped it carefully around Aurelia. Her neck was wet, and she could feel Aurelia's short, scared breaths.

"It's okay," Jastyn murmured. She forgot about the plan and how she needed to use Aurelia like a pawn in her scheme. She forgot about what it meant to care for her. In that moment, Jastyn pulled her close. Aurelia whimpered, and Jastyn ran a hand down Aurelia's dark hair, still soft as silk despite everything.

Aurelia sniffled, and leaned back. "I'm so sorry, Jastyn."

"Shh." She gave half a smile. "I'm okay."

Coran coughed, swinging his leg in front of him and blinking so fast Jastyn thought he'd gone mad. "What happened? I feel like I've been struck by somethin'."

"Like a thunderbolt," Aurelia explained. "I felt it, too. The Light of Triur. Harnessed the way it was, the compacted light was the brightest force in the realm." She paused. "However, my father only gave us a fraction of his supply. While meant to serve as a beacon for the lost, the light—if focused on a single point—could stun anything in its path of impact. In this case, anyone. According to the texts, the weaponized light penetrates one's mind, causing flashes of instability and a drop into darkness. That's the idea, anyway." She glanced at Jastyn, who nodded.

"That's what I was hoping for. It's similar to spell-fire."

With Aurelia's arm beneath her, she sat up gingerly. Every muscle and bone inside her ached. Reluctantly, she examined the protruding arrow. A thin line of blood trickled down her navy tunic.

All three of them turned to where Drest had stood. He sprawled on the ground, his legs turned inward awkwardly. His barrel chest went unmoving, his face slack.

Next to an empty bow lay a wide-set, silver-haired elf. His chest rose and fell, albeit slowly. Coran kicked Drest's boot. His ankle flopped, then lay motionless. They exchanged glances.

Coran muttered what each of them was thinking. "I think…I think he's dead."

CHAPTER TWENTY-SIX

A re you positive you're ready?"

"Yes. Do it."

Jastyn found herself cradled against Aurelia, tucked against her like a snail in its shell. Her legs were useless, only tired limbs extended over the grass in front of her. She leaned back into Aurelia, who sat behind her like a welcome shadow.

Her arms wrapped around Jastyn, Aurelia gripped the shaft sticking out from her shoulder. When her other hand pinched the base above her skin, Jastyn squirmed.

"Wait." She closed her eyes. "Take me through it again." Jastyn's voice was hoarse, and she hoped Aurelia didn't hear it quiver. Sweat lined her forehead, the brisk night making the sweat cool on her warm face. Coran had restarted their fire, and the low flames flickered lazily in the blissfully still air.

Aurelia sighed, lifting Jastyn's torso as her chest rose and fell. "I have to break this arrow head off. That's the first step."

"Then we're done?"

Aurelia chuckled. "I'm afraid not. I will have to remove the shaft from your shoulder. The only way to do that is—"

"Push it through." Jastyn winced, her eyes slamming tighter. She had to laugh. Occasionally, she had imagined a moment similar to this. She had imagined herself close to Aurelia. She'd imagined Aurelia's hands on her, running down her back in a playful dance. In the middle of the night, in her dreams, Jastyn had let herself fall into a fantasy.

She never imagined it would play out like this.

Coran pulled her from her thoughts. "I'll be right here, Jas. You'll be fine." He sat at her feet. Through her blurry vision she could see the anxiety in his eyes but was grateful for his words.

"Want to switch places?" she joked.

"I'll take the next arrow, how 'bout that?" He patted her boots, and she grimaced when Aurelia shifted.

"Once the arrow is removed," she continued, "we will need to cauterize the wound so you don't lose any more blood."

Her shoulder felt as if it was being pinched between two opposing forces, as if at any moment it might tear and burst into flames all at the same time. Jastyn breathed deeply. She tried to swallow and found her throat dry as tree bark after a drought. "Can I have some water before you start?"

Aurelia's voice was soft when she replied. "Of course." She reached out, and Coran grabbed the flask that lay next to him. His smile fell to a frown. He shook the flask, opened the top, and looked inside.

"'Fraid we're all out." He gave Jastyn a sympathetic glance.

"Then we must fetch you some more." Carefully, Aurelia pulled herself out from behind Jastyn, laying her gently onto a flat-faced boulder so that Jastyn could lean back and keep the arrow from moving. The princess grabbed the flask, and turned back to Jastyn. "I'll only be a moment. Then we have to begin." She smiled weakly, and Jastyn saw worry in the crease between her brows. She knew what Aurelia must be thinking. An arrow was part of her brother's undoing. While Jastyn still didn't understand the depth of what had brought upon the prince's death, she knew Aurelia had to be drowning in memories of her lost brother.

Wanting to reassure her, Jastyn held up a hand. Aurelia took it in her own, brushing Jastyn's knuckles across her cheek. When she turned to go, Jastyn pressed her knuckles against her heart.

"Wait," she said, ignoring the skip in her chest. "Coran, go with her."

Even in the dim light, Jastyn could tell this wasn't what Aurelia wanted to hear. Her hands flew to her hips. "I am quite capable of fetching water."

A spasm of coughs overtook Jastyn. She winced, then said, "Coran knows where the creek is. He'll show you."

Aurelia opened her mouth to protest, but Jastyn shot Coran a look, and he was on his feet. "She's right, m'lady. This way."

Aurelia gestured to Drest and the elf. Reading her mind, Jastyn said, "Drest is out. If the fae wakes, I can handle him."

Aurelia didn't look as if she believed her but thankfully, didn't argue. When she turned, Jastyn mouthed a thank you to Coran, who shook his head as he ushered Aurelia into the trees. "Don't go anywhere now, eh?" he called over his shoulder.

Jastyn gave a half-hearted wave. Once she could no longer hear their footsteps, she collapsed backward, gripping her arm in agony.

With half of her back pressed against the boulder, her right arm hung dully at her side. Her elbow and wrist were starting to go numb. She hoped it was only the shock of the arrow that caused this. She moaned. What had she been thinking?

I was thinking about Aurelia.

In that moment of chaos, Aurelia filled her mind. She had cared only about ensuring her safety. Jastyn ran her left hand over her forehead, resting it for a moment over her eyes.

How did she let that happen? How did she let her feelings get the best of her? *Some good it did.* She dared a glance down at the arrow. Leaning back, Jastyn took in the outline of clouds scattered overhead. Patterns of stars poked through their thin veil, and the edges of the sky began to lighten with the first signs of dawn.

She let her mind wander. Surprisingly, she found herself back in the village. She stood against a wall of her mother's home. She peered in as if she was looking through one end of a shell she picked up from the shore. Her family appeared small and distant. She spotted Elisedd in the corner, mending a misshapen horseshoe. Alanna read by the fire. She stretched out on the floor, her head resting comfortably in their mother's lap. Her mother worked a needle and thread through an old tunic of Jastyn's, one that had been handed down to her sister. Jastyn watched her family go about their evening. She even smelled stew in the cauldron. Her stomach ached with hunger. More than that, it ached to join them.

"I'll be back," she muttered through the shell. "I'll find the cure and save Alanna."

Each member of her family froze. They turned, but their faces had changed. They were empty and cold, like faceless stone.

Elisedd spoke first.

"Don't come back, Jastyn. I never wanted you. You're only another mouth to feed."

The image shifted, and her sister's face came into view. She looked pale and feeble. "Jastyn, you won't make it in time. I'll be gone soon."

"No," Jastyn said. "I will find the cure. Somehow, Alanna, I will find it. Don't give up on me. Please."

Her mother was next. "You did this." Her eyes were dark, unfamiliar. Shadows aged her typically youthful features. "If it weren't for you, Alanna would be well. We would be happy."

"That's not true." Jastyn fought to move closer, but her legs were stuck, tied to the ground. "Mother, please. I didn't mean what I said. I was angry."

"You are no daughter of mine."

"Mother!"

Her mother's words warped into a cackle. The seashell shrank away, taking the image of her family with it. The village disappeared into vast darkness. In its place stood the fae from her nightmares.

"You're not real," she said. "You're only a dream."

Forcing herself to sit up, Jastyn pinched her arm. Her eyes flew open. Relieved, she looked around the clearing. The campfire burned nearby. Drest didn't move, and the elf's breathing came slowly.

"It was only a dream," she said again, using her good wrist to prop herself up.

A set of footsteps rustled behind her.

"Aurelia?" She squinted into the dark. "Coran, is that you?"

But she saw no one. The steps shifted. On her right, the tread drew nearer.

"Who's there?"

Without warning, the darkness sprang up, and the Dark Fae was before her atop his horse. The beast's eyes burned red. Instinctively, she covered her face.

The horse reared, bringing its massive hooves to the ground in a clap of thunder. The Dark Fae directed his steed to the elf. Jastyn scrambled back, moving behind the boulder. From there she could see the fae look down as if analyzing the fallen elf from beneath his black hood. The rider's long fingers, like spindles, reached down from the reins.

An excruciating scream, like a horde of banshees falling from the sky, erupted across the clearing. Jastyn shrank back as the Dark Fae's fingers pulled silver smoke from the elf's chest, which rose like a toy on a string. His body thrashed, his entire being fighting desperately to keep whatever the Dark Fae was taking. The thin, sinewy smoke floated higher, where it slowly took on a shape.

When the elf's soul had completely left its body, the Dark Fae curled the smoke into a circle the size of Jastyn's fist. In horror, she watched as he pulled back his hood, revealing a jagged line where his mouth should have been. There wasn't a face, for Jastyn saw no eyes nor a nose. Only the serrated opening that parted and swallowed the elf's soul.

Next to Drest, the elf lay lifeless.

As if he'd forgotten Jastyn was there, the Dark Fae tilted his head toward her. The horse followed suit.

"Odium Child."

Jastyn scurried back, trying to stand. But each effort proved futile, and she ended up on her side, one elbow propped beneath her while her feet pushed against the earth.

Dismounting, the Dark Fae floated in her direction. She couldn't move. Her entire body was frozen, rooted like the trees behind her. She wanted to run but was locked to the ground with dread and impending doom that accompanied the fae from her nightmares.

"Your journey ends here."

His voice was lighter than she remembered but possessed the echoes of shadows long forgotten.

"Luck does not walk with you this night. Come."

Jastyn couldn't muster the energy to untangle the Dark Fae's words. She concentrated only on pulling herself across the grass, trying to put as much space between herself and the fae as she could.

A familiar whistling pierced the air. Half a second later, a blazing blue arrow scraped the neck of the Dark Fae's cloak, warranting a screech so loud Jastyn covered her ears. Another arrow followed, then another. The arrows narrowly missed the Dark Fae, each landing with a quick thump into the trees around them.

Swiftly, the Dark Fae flew to his horse, which reared back again once he was atop it. Jastyn wasn't sure whether it was the wind or the Dark Fae who let out a monstrous howl. But in the seconds that followed, a dark cloud appeared, sweeping away the vision from her tormented dreams until only the quiet night was left.

❖

"Gods, what was that?" Aurelia sprinted behind the elf, the same slender-framed one who had loosened her ropes the day of her escape. He had found them when Coran was filling the flask with water from the creek. It turned out he had followed Drest, knowing he was after Aurelia. When she had spotted him standing like a statue on the other side of the creek not ten minutes ago, she wasn't sure if the elf was going to plunge an arrow into her heart or bring her back to Drest. She was taken aback when he leapt over to them and bowed.

"Your Highness Aurelia. Please, let me offer my company as compensation for past indiscretions."

Coran, who had stood in front of Aurelia, one hand across her, muttered, "What's he on about?"

Aurelia, however, stepped past Coran and held out her arm. The elf straightened, reaching out to take Aurelia's forearm in his grasp.

"You are forgiven. But please, what made you change your mind?"

The elf's gray eyes turned to slivers. "We were told by our queen that a dark force threatened our lands. When the human offered her a deal to extinguish the force, she could not refuse. Our lives are in her hands. She had no choice."

Aurelia listened intently as he continued. "The human claimed he could offer an unbreakable alliance between the kingdom of man and the elves. There was, however, one stipulation." He paused. "This human would offer this alliance but only if the power to do so lay in his hands."

Aurelia swallowed as the elf's gaze fell. "He came from your kingdom and promised us his protection but only after the heirs to the Diarmaid throne disappeared."

"I don't understand," Coran interjected. "Why would the queen of the elves believe something like that? Drest is hardly a prominent figure in the kingdom."

"The elves respect titles," the fae explained. "However, we are keener on answering to power. The human showed great strength with his frighteningly astute control of wind. He impressed the queen. And her territory was being threatened. She saw this as the only path to ensure our safety."

Aurelia felt as if a bearskin rug had been yanked out from beneath her. "Drest was behind all of this."

"He manipulated many. However, I believe he is under the service of another."

"The dark force? The one threatening your queen?"

Before the elf could respond, a curdling scream split the silence behind them.

Aurelia's heart sank. "Jastyn."

Coran capped the flask, and they took off. The elf bounded beside them through the trees. "Where are you going?" he asked, jumping nimbly over exposed roots.

"Our friend's in trouble," Coran explained.

"You don't have to come," added Aurelia.

The elf smiled. "I am at your service, Princess. Please, let me."

Aurelia nodded as they sprinted through the last lines of trees. Through the towering trunks, she could see what looked like a dark cloud descending over their clearing.

She slowed. "What is that?"

The elf snatched an arrow from his quiver and positioned it in his bow. "The dark force. Stay back."

He jumped into the depths of the tree branches, and Aurelia heard his bow string as it released. She followed the blazing blue of his arrow. Moments later, a piercing howl shook the ground. Exchanging glances with Coran, she ran faster while the fae let a series of arrows go.

When they reached the clearing, the dark cloud had vanished. Aurelia sprinted for Jastyn. When she stood over her, Aurelia's stomach dropped at the paleness of her face. Jastyn's eyes looked through her as if she'd seen a spirit from the Otherworld.

"Jastyn?" Aurelia crouched. "Jastyn, can you hear me?"

Her hands traced down Jastyn's face, running down her freckled cheeks to her chin. "Jastyn, please speak to me."

Jastyn stared blankly, trembling. Frightened, Aurelia turned. "Please, she needs help."

Coran wrung his hands where he stood next to Drest. The fae, who had knelt to examine his former companion, stood and hurried to join Aurelia.

"She's been in the presence of the dark force." The elf held up one hand, running it from Jastyn's head to her feet an inch above her body as if feeling for something they couldn't see. He held both palms over her heaving chest. He closed his eyes, murmuring under his breath. Aurelia glanced at Coran, who shrugged.

The elf finished his incantation, and they all held their breath when Jastyn's breathing stopped. Her eyes closed, and when they opened again, Aurelia was ready to weep with relief at the familiar glint in them.

"Jastyn!"

Jastyn looked around as if unsure where she was. Her gaze landed on Coran, then Aurelia. Upon noticing the elf, she asked, "Who's this?"

Aurelia wiped a tear from her cheek. "He's one of the elves who had worked for Drest."

Jastyn looked from him to her, then lunged. The elf zoomed back, standing five paces away in less than a second.

"Whoa," Aurelia held out her hands, gently pushing Jastyn back. "He's good. He's working with us now."

Jastyn continued to glare at the fae. "So he says." Aurelia couldn't help but smile at her protective nature.

"He's on our side," Aurelia reassured her. "Now, drink some water. And please, let me tend to this wound."

Grumbling, Jastyn drank water and leaned back so that Aurelia could sit behind her. When they were both situated, Aurelia inhaled. She'd seen her mother do an arrow extraction dozens of times. Aurelia was confident in her ability but was not looking forward to the pain that would make Jastyn wish she'd never met her.

Carefully, she gripped the base of the arrowhead, her other hand on the shaft. "Ready?"

She felt Jastyn's body tense. "Ready."

Right as her hand tightened, the ground began to shake.

"What now?" Aurelia exclaimed.

"Horses," the fae said, moving to stand in front of them. Coran, wearing a look of panic, hurried to his feet.

Aurelia dropped her hands, instead gripping Jastyn's shoulders. "Is it the elves?"

The fae squinted through the trees. His nostrils flared. "No. They're human."

Aurelia swallowed. Jastyn fought to sit up against her. "Don't even think about it," Aurelia told her. "We can handle this."

Standing next to the fae, Coran conjured his spell-fire as the elf readied an arrow in the direction of the noise, now unmistakably a legion of horseback riders. Aurelia pulled Jastyn closer, peering between the legs of the fae and Coran as the first pair of horses broke through the trees.

The elf pulled back his bow. Aurelia blinked, uncertain she was seeing correctly. But the colors of the riders belonged to only one kingdom.

"Wait!" she cried, raising her arm to halt the fae's arrow. "Don't."

"Who are they?"

Coran's spell-fire dissipated. He fell to his knees. "Thank the gods. We're safe now."

The elf frowned. "I don't understand."

Aurelia's breath caught in her throat. The swirl of emotions overtaking her chest made it hard to think. Part of her never thought she'd see them again. Now, suddenly, here they were.

Finally, she managed to speak. "It's all right. My mother and father are here."

Chapter Twenty-Seven

Her mother and father led a legion of twenty guardsmen on horseback across the clearing and over to their group as the sun peeked over the treetops.

Aurelia gingerly placed Jastyn back on the ground and couldn't help but notice the way her body shrank away from the incoming royal party. She wanted to reach out and assure her she had nothing to be worried about. Her mother and father were there to help, to bring them back home.

Aurelia's steps faltered. *Home.* The idea of the castle and returning to the kingdom was not a welcome one. As her mother and father approached, Aurelia stared at her parents, waiting to feel elation or joy or the faintest glimmer of happiness. She willed even a whisper of relief to appear. Deep inside her chest, though, she felt only pain.

"Aurelia!" Her mother dismounted first, a flurry of navy cloak and flowing braid. "By the gods, you're all right!" She ran to Aurelia, followed quickly by her father as he practically fell from his horse, clamoring to his feet to join them. Aurelia stepped forward to meet them and was crushed in a long-awaited embrace.

"I'm all right," she muttered against her father's chest. Her mother's arms wrapped around her, and Aurelia inhaled the scent of chamomile and sage, a smell so distinctly her mother she hadn't realized how much she'd missed it.

Her father stepped back. "Darling, we thought we'd lost you."

Aurelia glanced between her parents. In the time she'd been gone, they looked as if they'd aged five years. Her father's beard, which before had only a few gray whiskers, was now peppered with silver. The shadows beneath her mother's eyes startled her, but her voice was as bright as ever.

"Sweetheart, I can't believe it. I'm so happy you're all right. Thank the gods."

Aurelia smiled, stepping back. Her parents' hands held hers, their fingertips outstretched when she let go as if they were unable to stand the space she put between them. She motioned to the trio standing behind her. "They are who you should be thanking. I'm safe because of them." She noticed the elf's inquisitive gaze. "Well, mostly." She smiled at Coran's puffed chest as he wiped his hands on his pants before stepping forward.

"It's an honor," he said, shaking both of their hands. Her father frowned.

"Don't we know you?"

Coran beamed. "I work in the stables," he said before moving past them to pat the noses of the horses, who whinnied in recognition.

Her mother nodded. "Of course. Young Coran Feirmeoir. You are incredibly brave to have come so far."

Coran's cheeks flushed, and he busied himself with adjusting the reins of the nearest guardsman's horse.

"You're too kind, your majesties." He paused. "You wouldn't mind tellin' Roisin that I'm alive, would you?"

Her mother smiled. "I would be delighted, young man." Her gaze shifted to the elf, who hung back behind Aurelia. "Who is that?" she asked warily.

"I am a visitor from the north, currently a servant to the Princess Aurelia Diarmaid." The fae spoke eloquently, drawing himself up until he was almost a foot taller than each of them. Aurelia could tell her parents were intrigued but, thankfully, asked no further questions regarding the fae's presence.

Aurelia cleared her throat, suddenly self-conscious. She stood next to Jastyn, who still lay on the ground. "This is Jastyn. She led the latest party through the Wood to find me."

Her father bowed his chin. "I recall seeing you in the market. I'm glad to know you used my gift well."

"That's how you found us," Aurelia noted with excitement. "The Light of Triur."

Her parents nodded. "We saw it about ten miles to the east. The blaze is unmistakable." Her mother's gaze fell to Jastyn. "Thank you for leading us to our daughter."

Jastyn tried to stand, but her mother shifted closer. "Dear, you're hurt. Please," she glanced at Aurelia, "let me help you."

Before Aurelia could say anything, her mother knelt beside Jastyn, who looked as if she wasn't sure whether to try to run or block her mother's hands as they assessed the arrow. Lips pursed, her mother pricked the arrow tip with her forefinger, slowly bringing it to her mouth. Running her tongue over her teeth, she sighed. "It's not poisoned."

Aurelia sat on the other side of Jastyn. "Thank the gods." She brushed a hand through the strands of Jastyn's hair that had fallen over her sweat-laced forehead. She caught her mother's gaze and ignored the inquisitive look.

"On three, I'm going to break the arrowhead. All right?" her mother asked Jastyn, who hadn't said a thing. Aurelia longed to know what Jastyn was thinking, though she knew this couldn't be easy for her. Still, her mother was helping. There wasn't time for messy politics now.

At the crack of the shaft, Jastyn screamed.

"I know, I know." Her mother tossed the arrowhead aside. Her hands cupped the rest of the arrow, new blood trickling out from Jastyn's shoulder. A soft red glow surrounded the shaft, and Jastyn's breathing steadied.

"You've numbed her?"

Her mother nodded. "Now, Aurelia, brace yourself against her while I get this out."

Aurelia hurried behind Jastyn, holding her while her mother situated herself so that she could push the few inches of wood through Jastyn's shoulder and out her back.

After a few agonizing seconds, her mother lifted what was left of the foot-long arrow. "There," she said triumphantly.

"Do we need to cauterize it?" Aurelia asked.

"No," her mother said, examining the wound. "The spell-fire took care of that."

Jastyn sat back. "Thank you," she said quietly, avoiding the queen's gaze.

"Yes, thank you," Aurelia said as her mother stood. Then she leaned down, placing a quick kiss on Jastyn's forehead before joining her mother near the fire.

"It's the least I can do for the woman who helped rescue our daughter." Her mother's smile was wide, and her eyes gleamed. Coran hurried over to Jastyn, helping her to sit up, bracing her arm against her stomach so that the shoulder could begin to heal in its proper place.

The king wiped his face, which was wet with tears. When he noticed Drest, his bushy eyebrows formed a V. "My, what happened here?"

Aurelia crossed her arms, suddenly weary with the memory of everything that happened. "It was Drest."

Her mother and father looked from his motionless body to her. Her father frowned. "What do you mean?"

"He was behind Brennus's death. He kidnapped me during Remembrance Day. Drest is responsible for this. He's working for somebody…or something. I'm not sure."

Her father's face paled, but it was her mother who seemed to grow with fury. "I don't believe it." Her voice was eerily calm. She turned to her father. "We're going to have to look into this. That means—"

"I know," he replied. "Louarn and Enya will need to be questioned." He motioned to Drest. "Is he—"

"Dead?" Aurelia shrugged. "We don't know. The Light of Triur left him like this."

"Good. He's not dead." Her mother motioned for the guardsmen. Two dismounted and stood on either side of Drest. "He's in a stupor. When he comes to, he'll find himself in chains." She nodded, and the guardsmen lifted Drest, dragging him over to their troop. With some struggle, they placed him over the back of one of their horses, his arms and legs dangling lifelessly.

Her mother wiped her hands. "We will deal with him later." She smiled again and moved toward Jastyn. "Now, I know which family to acknowledge for that young man." She motioned at Coran, who practically danced with glee. "Please, tell me, which family do we have to thank for your outstanding courage?"

Jastyn pushed herself awkwardly up with one hand. Aurelia hurried over to her, wrapping one arm around her waist to help her stand. Jastyn's body was still tense as her mother approached. When

Jastyn didn't respond, Aurelia nudged her. "It's all right," she said in her ear.

"I don't think it will be," Jastyn muttered. Their eyes locked, and Aurelia saw distress rampant in Jastyn's gaze. Despite that, Jastyn sighed. "Very well. My name is Jastyn Cipher. I am the daughter of Branna Rhinehart, who is the wife of Elisedd of Marcra."

A murmur swept over the guardsmen, and Aurelia saw her mother's eyes widen. At the same time, her father's mouth fell open.

Jastyn steadied herself, standing tall. "I am, as your family has deemed fit to call me, an Odium Child."

Her mother stepped back. Her chin lifted, and she motioned for Aurelia. "Come, darling. It's time to go."

Aurelia didn't move. "I don't understand."

"Interactions with an Odium are punishable by law," Jastyn stated. "Your mother is simply following the rules."

Aurelia's face turned hot. She had to be hearing wrong. "Mother, you can't possibly still believe all of that. Those laws were written nearly half a century ago." She laughed, looking around. "A quarter of the village residents are fae."

"That is not the same thing."

"How?"

But her mother didn't seem to hear her. She raised her hands, searching her palms. "I shouldn't have." She stared at Jastyn's shoulder, her voice drifting. "I shouldn't have…"

"You shouldn't have…what? Helped Jastyn?" Aurelia's voice rose. She couldn't believe what she was hearing. "Mother, you don't truly believe that, do you?" Her mother stumbled back under the arm of Aurelia's father.

"I'm sorry, sweetheart, but this is not a discussion to be had. You must come, now."

Anger boiled over inside Aurelia. Her fists clenched, and she stormed forward. "What are you saying?"

Her mother, regaining her composure, pulled her shoulders back. "She is not one of us," she hissed. "I am grateful you are safe. But please, Aurelia, you have to forget her."

Aurelia froze in her tracks. "You can't be serious."

Her parents exchanged glances. Her father reached out a hand.

"It's complicated, my love. We can explain everything once we are home."

Aurelia stared at her parents. She realized how often she pictured them like this, posed as they were, not unlike many of the portraits hanging throughout the castle. Painted in a sympathetic, kind light. Two leaders believed to be the soft hand of justice and strength. Two leaders continuing the long-held reign of the Diarmaids over the Kingdom of Venostes.

Except something was different now. The painting was askew. Aurelia cocked her head, trying to pinpoint what had changed.

Then she saw it. Her mother's desperate grip on her father's wrist. His hunched shoulders. The look of terror about what they did not know staring back at her. Aurelia hadn't noticed before, but now she realized: that fear had always been there. That fear was what drove the Diarmaid dynasty to the throne and kept it there like an unwavering torrent.

"No," she finally said, walking to stand beside Jastyn, who wore a look of shock. "Mother, Father…I'm not going with you."

"Aurelia."

"Jastyn has unfinished business. And I am going with her."

At this, Jastyn faced her. "You are?"

Aurelia nodded. "As the nature of this business is uncertain, I cannot say when we will return."

Her mother hurried forward. "Darling, you don't know what you're saying."

When her mother reached out a hand, Aurelia swatted it away. "I know exactly what I am saying."

"My love, listen to me—"

"No! For years you've blinded me to the truth. For years, you kept Brennus and me locked away in that dreadful castle you call a home, preventing us from knowing anything about the world. We were ignorant of the breathtaking places, the beautiful people," she said, glancing at Jastyn, "the unbridled magic that fills this realm. I will not go back. I will not play the part and be locked away, tied to a throne that's built on lies and deceit."

Her father's voice was the sternest Aurelia had ever heard it when he spoke. "You have no idea what our family has done to manage the weight of bearing this kingdom on our shoulders for as long as we have."

Aurelia laughed. "And whose fault is that?"

She took a breath, her vision clearing. Her parents wore similar expressions: anguish and confusion. When her father moved to speak again, Aurelia cut him off.

"I won't hear it. I am grateful that you never stopped searching for me." She swallowed, the lump in her throat threatening to burst into tears. "Truly I am. But my place is not with you right now." She paused, then turned to Jastyn, whose eyes lit with such ferocity Aurelia wanted to hold this moment in time forever. "My place is with her."

The clearing was quiet, stunned into silence by her proclamation. Aurelia felt dizzy, unsure if all of the words that had poured from her had in fact been spoken aloud. But the resolute gaze of her mother was undeniable.

Her mother's lips parted slowly. "I will not lose you, too."

Aurelia's eyes closed to block the barrage of tears forming. Brennus, the memory of him, was so close now she could hear his laughter, see his bright smile. She steeled herself before speaking. "You won't, Mother. But I will not go back. I cannot return. Not now."

It was quiet for a moment.

"Very well," her mother said finally, her voice even. Her gaze shifted to Jastyn. "Don't make Aurelia regret this decision."

Aurelia replied. "I won't, Mother. Trust me."

Slowly, the crowd shifted. Coran joined Aurelia and Jastyn on their side of the fire as the guardsmen readied their horses. The elf stood back while her parents mounted, pulling their reins toward the trees.

"Darling," her father said in a final effort, "you can play out this folly back in the village. Please, come home with us."

Tears threatened, but Aurelia bit her lip to keep them at bay. "I can't come home," she said, her voice shaking. "After everything." She shook her head, memories of Brennus resurfacing. She leaned into Jastyn, who wrapped her good arm around Aurelia's shoulders. "I can't."

Her father nodded solemnly. Her mother didn't look at her, only directed their party back into the Wood. When the final line of guardsmen vanished into the trees, Aurelia fell against Jastyn.

"I can't believe that just happened."

Jastyn turned so they stood face-to-face. The ferocity she'd seen in Jastyn's gaze shifted to a brightness that hadn't been there in weeks.

"What?"

Jastyn grinned. "You're coming with me?"

Aurelia rewound her mind, recalling what she'd said. Her own face lifted in a smile. "I am. I will help you find the cure for your sister."

Jastyn dropped her arm, holding her injured one like a baby. "You're sure? I won't be angry if you change your mind." She gestured to the elf. "He can take you back. Sneak you into the castle without your parents' knowledge."

Aurelia considered their motley foursome, standing alone in the depths of the Wood. "I'm a woman of my word, Jastyn. It would be an honor to accompany you. Besides," she added with a playful nudge of her hip, "you wouldn't make it a week without me."

Jastyn snorted. "I think you've got your roots crossed, Princess."

Aurelia couldn't hide the smile on her face. She turned to the elf. "I'm sorry, by the way, about the sleeping draught."

The fae laughed. "It was clever, for a human." He knelt beside his fallen companion.

Jastyn spoke. "I'm sorry. He's gone."

The elf nodded. "I know." He laid his hands over the fae's eyes. Suddenly, the blades of grass sprouted higher, lacing themselves over the fallen elf. The earth rumbled, and they watched as the grass pulled the body of the elf beneath the ground until nothing was left but the unbroken stretch of green.

Coran squeaked. "Where did he go?"

"The earth will return him to our queen. She will give him a proper burial."

"I never thought to ask your name," admitted Aurelia.

"I am Rigo. Leader of the seventh elven clan."

Coran looked impressed, and Jastyn stared.

"You're not going back, Rigo?"

He leaned against his large bow. "Like I said, I am at your service."

Jastyn stuck out her chest, making Aurelia laugh. "Very well. Coran?"

"You should go back," Jastyn said before he could answer. "Your mother is probably a mess. Plus, there's Roisin."

Coran puckered his lips, clapping his hands together. "Roisin." He sighed. "I will see her again. And my mum is stronger than half the women in the village. Not yours, o'course," he added at Jastyn's sharp glare. "The king and queen will tell her I'm fine. But honestly," he said, grinning, "I haven't had this much fun since we swiped those mares from the stable when Elisedd wasn't lookin'."

Jastyn laughed but stopped when she saw Aurelia's face. "We were ten," she muttered.

"Very well," Aurelia said, her voice cheerful. Dawn lit the trees, making golden rays fan out over the clearing. Morning jays sang from their nests. The sun scattered the clouds, bringing with it the warmth of a new day. Coran put out the fire, and Rigo grabbed their flask. Aurelia scooped up Jastyn's satchel, then placed her hands on her hips. When they looked at her expectantly, Aurelia turned to Jastyn, who smiled.

"Shall we?"

About the Author

Originally from Dallas-Fort Worth, Sam Ledel now resides in Southern California with her girlfriend and their Jack Russell terrier. She is currently working on her third novel.

Books Available From Bold Strokes Books

Daughter of No One by Sam Ledel. When their worlds are threatened, a princess and a village outcast must overcome their differences and embrace a budding attraction if they want to survive. (978-1-63555-427-4)

Fear of Falling by Georgia Beers. Singer Sophie James is ready to shake up her career, but her new manager, the gorgeous Dana Landon, has other ideas. (978-1-63555-443-4)

Playing with Fire by Lesley Davis. When Takira Lathan and Dante Groves meet at Takira's restaurant, love may find its way onto the menu. (978-1-63555-433-5)

Practice Makes Perfect by Carsen Taite. Meet law school friends Campbell, Abby, and Grace, law partners at Austin's premier boutique legal firm for young, hip entrepreneurs. Legal Affairs: one law firm, three best friends, three chances to fall in love. (978-1-63555-357-4)

The Last Seduction by Ronica Black. When you allow true love to elude you once and you desperately regret it, are you brave enough to grab it when it comes around again? (978-1-63555-211-9)

Wavering Convictions by Erin Dutton. After a traumatic event, Maggie has vowed to regain her strength and independence. So how can Ally be both the woman who makes her feel safe and a constant reminder of the person who took her security away? (978-1-63555-403-8)

A Bird of Sorrow by Shea Godfrey. As Darrius and her lover, Princess Jessa, gather their strength for the coming war, a mysterious spell will reveal the truth of an ancient love. (978-1-63555-009-2)

All the Worlds Between Us by Morgan Lee Miller. High school senior Quinn Hughes discovers that a broken friendship is actually a door propped open for an unexpected romance. (978-1-63555-457-1)

Falling by Kris Bryant. Falling in love isn't part of the plan, but will Shaylie Beck put her heart first and stick around, or tell the damaging truth? (978-1-63555-373-4)

An Intimate Deception by CJ Birch. Flynn County Sheriff Elle Ashley has spent her adult life atoning for her wild youth, but when she finds her ex, Jessie, murdered two weeks before the small town's biggest social event, she comes face-to-face with her past and all her well-kept secrets. (978-1-63555-417-5)

Cash and the Sorority Girl by Ashley Bartlett. Cash Braddock doesn't want to deal with morality, drugs, or people. Unfortunately, she's going to have to. (978-1-63555-310-9)

Secrets in a Small Town by Nicole Stiling. Deputy Chief Mackenzie Blake has one mission: find the person harassing Savannah Castillo and her daughter before they cause real harm. (978-1-63555-436-6)

Stormy Seas by Ali Vali. The high-octane follow-up to the best-selling action-romance *Blue Skies*. (978-1-63555-299-7)

The Road to Madison by Elle Spencer. Can two women who fell in love as girls overcome the hurt caused by the father who tore them apart? (978-1-63555-421-2)

Dangerous Curves by Larkin Rose. When love waits at the finish line, dangerous curves are a risk worth taking. (978-1-63555-353-6)

Love to the Rescue by Radclyffe. Can two people who share a past really be strangers? (978-1-62639-973-0)

Love's Portrait by Anna Larner. When museum curator Molly Goode and benefactor Georgina Wright uncover a portrait's secret, public and private truths are exposed, and their deepening love hangs in the balance. (978-1-63555-057-3)

Model Behavior by MJ Williamz. Can one woman's instability shatter a new couple's dreams of happiness? (978-1-63555-379-6)

Pretending in Paradise by M. Ullrich. When travelwisdom.com assigns PR specialist Caroline Beckett and travel blogger Emma Morgan to cover a hot new couples retreat, they're forced to fake a relationship to secure a reservation. (978-1-63555-399-4)